Eagle Court

Kind neighbours are not always nice

Sheena Billett

Honey in the mouth
Knives in the heart
(Ancient Chinese Proverb)

My thanks to Glen, Lorraine and Lindsey for their beta-reading skills and to Lyndsey for proofreading Eagle Court for me.
Also to Kostis, for another wonderful cover design.
I couldn't have written this book without the never ending patience and support of my wife Glen. Thank you.
And last, but not least, a huge thank you to everyone who has followed my Eagle Court writing journey on Facebook. Your encouragement and support has kept me going.

Chapter 1

I ris adjusted the new recliner to just the right angle for watching TV, leaving the settee with its back against the wall. She ran her hand along the smooth, empty mantelpiece, enjoying the sensation. The cluttered, gloomy place that had been her mother's house, where Iris had lived all her life, was a world away. She had brought nothing from her old life with her. No reminders of all those dark years. The last few days had been the best Iris could remember as she'd unpacked and arranged all her new things, making sure everything portable was out of sight in various cupboards and that all the surfaces were clear.

After the long-awaited death of her mother, Iris had wasted no time in selling the house and getting a clearance company to empty it of all the contents. She would be forever grateful to Margaret Thatcher for allowing her parents to buy their council house at a knock-down price back in the eighties, and although she'd had to wait until she was sixty-seven to realise her dream and reap the rewards of her parents' investment, the waiting made it even more special. Now she had her own money and her own place, Iris could do as she pleased and had splashed out on a top-of-the-range TV. She patted the unresponsive black rectangle with affection.

The small development of three bungalows in the newly created Eagle Court had caught her attention in the estate agent's window, and immediately, Iris had known this was the place for her. She savoured the name, saying it aloud under her breath – Eagle Court – it sounded posh and successful and she, Iris Walker, could live there. In her mind, she saw the neat group of bungalows, each with a patch of lawn at the front that was well-tended by friendly and cheerful neighbours who washed their cars on Sundays. In Iris's mind, they were all single – either by choice, or widowed – and content to live quiet lives uninterrupted by the outside world, maybe venturing out to local choirs or bridge clubs. Iris herself had never sung in a choir, played bridge, or any card games, but she would be willing to learn if necessary. Maybe she could go to classes.

There was only one problem. Now that she had a clean slate, a fresh start, Iris wasn't sure what to do with it. The freedom to choose was overwhelming. It was as if she had exhausted her energy in choosing where to live and in buying the bungalow. And now, wandering from room to room, the future loomed disconcertingly ahead like an endless white sheet stretching into the distance.

Pull yourself together, Iris. Still as spineless as ever! A spineless beanpole.

Some things had not been left behind, but Iris would not listen to the insidious worm in her head. She drew herself up to her considerable height and strode into the kitchen, where she put her new green kettle on to boil. The back garden was an equally empty canvas, although this time it came in the form of a green rectangle contained by a brown wooden fence marking out her territory. Pouring a coffee, Iris had a thought. Maybe she could make a beautiful garden like those makeover programmes on the telly. It couldn't be that hard, and she had plenty of time. She would go to the garden centre this afternoon and start right away by getting some plants. Bouncing on her toes in anticipation, Iris could already see banks of flowers edging the lawn, and maybe a water feature in the centre. When the autumn came, and the nights drew in, there would be plenty of time to contemplate bridge. Better to wait until she got to know her new neighbours, Iris reasoned, she didn't want to spend time and money learning it for nothing!

After an egg-sandwich lunch, Iris locked the front door, checking it twice. She studied the front of Number 1 and held her bag to her chest as she imagined where tubs of flowers could be arranged around the front step. Her thoughts were interrupted by a large 4x4 entering the Court. It came to a halt in front of Number 2 and deposited an unruly mob of children and a harassed young woman onto the drive. Iris hurriedly unlocked her car and got in, and under the pretence of searching for something in her bag, took in the young woman, dressed in a black-and-white striped top under a green body warmer, the look was completed with jeans encased in knee-length boots. Iris knew expensive boots when she saw them. The young woman's blonde hair was wound up and held in place by a large clip. She watched her open the front passenger door and help an older lady to her feet, whose arm, Iris noticed, was in plaster.

'For God's sake, Daisy. Eagle Court? Whoever thought *that* was a good idea? As if we're going to see eagles in rural Nottinghamshire!'

Iris stiffened at the strident tone.

'Come on, Mum. Never mind about the name. Think about how close you'll be to the shops and everything. Kids, come on, let's see Granny's new home!'

As the family disappeared inside Number 2, Iris remained motionless, her mind in a whirl at the sudden noise and commotion following her first peaceful few days in the Court.

3

A growing sense of unease was compounded when a large removal van appeared, blocking her in. She hit the steering wheel in frustration. She should have gone while she'd had the chance. Tutting, she got out of the car and strode toward the lorry, where two removal men were already opening the doors.

'Excuse me, I need to get out.' Iris held herself primly as she remembered the teachers used to do at the girl's grammar school she'd attended. They had been the best years of her life, albeit brief.

'We're here now, love. Sure you can't squeeze past?'

Iris didn't reply. She had no idea about spaces and widths of cars.

The silence lengthened.

'I'll move the wagon over and give you a bit more room,' he conceded. Iris noted from his ID that he was Aaron.

The gap didn't seem any bigger to Iris after Aaron had moved the removals lorry, but she inched forwards, waiting for the first crunch. The two men stood watching, hands on hips, and Iris felt herself go hot with embarrassment.

For goodness' sake, Iris. Making a fool of yourself, as usual.

She gritted her teeth and stopped, unable to go forwards or backwards. In the rear-view mirror, she saw Aaron beckoning for her to reverse, waving a hand towards his chest. He shouted instructions. 'Keep straight. Right hand down! Yup, that's it. Forward a bit! Left hand down.'

Sweat was forming on her back. Iris had no idea what he was talking about, but eventually managed to extricate the car from the gap.

She jumped as Aaron appeared from nowhere, knocking on the window. 'Tell you what, love. Hop out and I'll do it for you.' This was not how anyone would have spoken to her teachers at the grammar school.

Iris uncoiled herself from the car, noticing from the corner of her eye that the next-door family had appeared. She refused to look at them as they all stood and watched Aaron move her car to the front of the lorry with practised ease, compounding her humiliation.

'There you go! All sorted.' He gave her a patronising smile.

In a cloud of misery and anger, Iris got into the car, but not before she heard a child sniggering. 'That old lady can't even drive her own car...' She slammed the door shut.

Iris's afternoon was ruined. She went to the garden centre and sat in the cafe, her thoughts boiling and churning as she re-ran the events in her head. All-too-familiar sensations of anger and humiliation took hold as she pressed her feet into the floor until her ankles ached. She drank three cups of tea and devoured two pieces of cake without tasting them, staying until closing time and ignoring the pointed looks of the cafe staff waiting to close up. She made a point of holding her head high as she left. After all, she was the owner of a bungalow in Eagle Court.

Once in the car, Iris sat, chewing the corner of her thumbnail. Would it be safe to go back? What if the lorry was still there? She couldn't face a replay of this morning's fiasco. She would not allow Aaron to speak to her like that again. Could she park on the road and walk to Number 1? No, better to check first, and if it was there, she would drive on and maybe visit Zed at his usual haunt in the burger place on the ring-road. With a plan of action in place, she set off for home.

Nosing her way into the close, Iris heaved a sigh of relief. The lorry was gone. The car had also departed from next door, presumably along with its noisy occupants, and all looked peaceful. Just as it should do.

That evening, as she watched her programmes, Iris's mind continued to simmer with anger and humiliation, this time at the thought of her new neighbour. How dare that awful woman laugh at the name Eagle Court. It was obvious from the way she and the tribe she had brought with her spoke that she'd had a very different life. She'd married, had children and grandchildren, and Iris would bet that she had money. A life she took for granted, no doubt. Iris glared at the newsreader until a solution presented itself.

She, Iris Walker, would rise above it all. She would not allow Family Woman and her brood to ruin her new life. Unlike her, she was just the right sort to own a bungalow in Eagle Court. She would show Family Woman by setting an example. She would start with a second visit to the garden centre tomorrow to get everything she needed to have an eye-catching display of flowers on the front step. Maybe Family Woman would take note. But then Iris remembered that tomorrow was Homeless Day. She would go to the garden centre on Sunday. Congratulating herself on her patience and understanding, Iris turned her attention back to the ten o'clock news.

Chapter 2

The minute she saw the ridiculous name, Eagle Court, Celia had known she would hate the bungalow. She'd gone along with the purchase to keep Daisy happy. The suspicion, although she wouldn't admit it, even to herself, that Daisy and Luke had urged her to downsize after Alan's death because they wanted an advance on their inheritance, rankled in the back of her mind. Her daughter had never said it outright, only dropping hints.

'You don't need that big house now, Mum. Big houses are for families.' She'd gestured towards her three children as she spoke. Luke had made a brief visit for his father's funeral before heading back to San Francisco where he'd built a successful career as a university lecturer. She and Alan visited him a few times, and he had dutifully shown them the sights, but to Celia he was a stranger – she didn't really know her son anymore. She never voiced this thought aloud. As far as the outside world was concerned, she had the perfect life and the perfect family with clever, successful children. Except for Fred, of course, but she rarely mentioned him and hadn't seen him since Alan's funeral. It seemed that he wanted to have as little to do with the family as possible, and there was a tiny part of Celia that was relieved. She would tolerate her new home for the sake of her children and grandchildren – after all, it was only right that they should have the money when they needed it most, when they had growing families. It was the practical thing to do – she knew that. So although she'd not been able to suppress a comment as they arrived in Eagle Court earlier, she was now determined to set her face resolutely to the future.

'Look how light it is, Mum. I think you'll love it here. And look at the garden – you've always wanted to design something from scratch and now's your chance.'

Celia eyed the green rectangle and sniffed. 'You know they only put about a foot of topsoil in these new-builds. I doubt anything will grow.'

Ignoring her mother, Daisy plugged in the kettle they'd brought with them. 'Let's christen the house with a cup of tea.' The sight of the familiar, battered old kettle here in this alien environment almost brought tears to Celia's eyes, but before she could weaken the two younger children were shouting excitedly that the removal van had arrived. Seb remained unmoved, glued to his phone.

When they arrived she'd been vaguely aware of someone in the car on the next door drive but had taken no notice as her family swept her along into her new home. Celia had no intention of socialising with her neighbours. Alan had been the sociable one in their marriage. 'Let's invite the Cummings and the Dawkins over at the weekend. I'll do a barbecue.' Celia had enjoyed being part of the group, but somehow, without Alan, she knew things would be different. Those days were over. And anyway, how could she invite their old friends over to this...Eagle Court? She shuddered at the thought.

Following the younger children to the door Celia saw a tall woman talking to Aaron, gesturing towards her car and then the lorry. Daisy rolled her eyes as Aaron attempted to manoeuvre the lorry to allow her room to get past.

'She's got bags of room!'

If Alan had been there, he would have gallantly gone and fought her new neighbour's corner and insisted on Aaron removing the lorry back to the top of the drive. Alan had that kind of authority. But Alan wasn't here. Celia watched as her new neighbour, after a failed attempt, eventually allowed Aaron to drive her car past the lorry. Seb, who had abandoned his phone, apparently sensing some drama, echoed his mother in a much louder voice. 'That old lady can't even drive her own car. And what is she wearing?'

'Seb!' she admonished him curtly.

'What?' he answered, meeting her gaze.

'That was rude, Seb. That lady might have heard you.'

'So?'

Celia looked to Daisy for backup, but she was already in deep discussion with Aaron and his team. If Seb had been her son, she would have told him exactly what she thought of his insolence and sent him to his room for the rest of the day. But he was her grandson, and she had to tread carefully. Frustrated, she turned and strode into the bungalow.

Aaron and Jack made short work of unloading what remained of her old life. Everything else had been put into storage. Somehow, Celia couldn't get rid of anything. She needed to know that her old life was there, ready to be resurrected at any moment, almost as if she was expecting Alan to come back and that life might revert to normal.

But now, watching the furniture take its place in the bungalow, Celia wondered if she'd made a mistake. Her beloved kitchen table was too big for this kitchen and the settees the children had grown up on looked out of place in the lounge. They were simply a sad reminder of what she'd lost – not the comforting familiarity she'd imagined. The lump in her throat became too big to swallow, and she had to take several deep breaths before she could turn back to her family.

Celia knew that Daisy loved her work as a GP, but she was always rushing around, trying to fit everything in. Even today, when she had taken a rare day off work to help her mother move, Celia knew that now the lorry was unloaded, she would be itching to be off – all thoughts of tea forgotten. She had to get Seb to swimming class – or was it judo? Children had such a packed itinerary these days.

'Are you sure you're going to be alright, Mum? With this.' Daisy gestured at the plaster.

'Of course, darling. It's not as if I've broken my leg! You go. I'll get sorted and have an early night.'

'Such a shame that you've had to move in with a broken arm – I should have been there to help you sort out that attic,' Daisy said, turning the TV on and fiddling with the remote. 'Just checking that this is working,' she continued, without looking up.

'It'll be fine, and if it's not, I'm quite capable of sorting it. I haven't become old overnight just because I've moved into a bungalow, Daisy.' Seeing her daughter's shoulders tense, Celia softened her tone. 'Honestly, I'm fine. Come here.'

She gave her daughter a rare hug. 'Thanks for today, darling. Now be off with you all and leave me in peace.'

'Bye Granny.' Seb and Lucy went to give her brief, dutiful kisses, Seb apparently having forgotten their previous confrontation, as Daisy held 2-year-old Evie up for Celia to kiss goodbye.

'Go on! Off with you!'

When they had gone, Celia closed the door and leant against it for a few moments, taking a few steadying breaths and listening to the silence in her new home.

She made round of toast and sat at the kitchen table with a glass of wine. Was this her life now, just endless silence? Had all the bustle and business happened for her now? It seemed as if she had become old overnight. What would Alan be saying?

'Come on Ceel, you've never been a moper. Chin up and best foot forward.'

She felt his loss as a physical pain in her chest – his positive attitude to life, his ability to see the humour in anything. How would she manage without him?

Chapter 3

I ris hummed as she checked the urns had been switched on. She was happy back in this familiar environment – except for Tina. But Tina was nothing new.

'Boss incoming,' whispered Wendy, busying herself buttering a mound of bread slices.

'Don't put so much butter on, Wendy. And Iris, we need to get the potatoes dished up. Customers are arriving.'

Iris ignored her.

'Does she think she's on *Masterchef* or something?' Wendy grumbled, scraping some of the butter off the slices.

'I don't think she'd last five minutes on *Masterchef*,' Iris replied, roughly spooning mashed potato into the dishes. 'She thinks she's so high and mighty. I could tell you a thing or two about her.'

Wendy turned, eyes wide. 'What?'

'Not now.' Iris gestured over Wendy's shoulder as Tina threw up the shutters. 'Show time!'

After a few stealthy stalking expeditions, Iris knew all about Tina and had 'taken her down a peg' several times. From her car, Iris had seen Tina crying when she had received the latest letter. The woman she lived with trying to console her. 'We're just friends,' was the line she gave everybody, but Iris knew different. People like Tina, with such a seedy secret, deserved to be punished in Iris's view.

All thoughts of Tina were swept away by the flood of customers surging through the door, the vicar trying to create some sense of order. 'Come on, guys. One at a time. There's enough for everyone.' Iris smiled to herself as the tide surged past him, unheeding. Serving the dinners was the part Iris enjoyed most of all, even though her back ached by the end of the session. Church hall tables were not made to accommodate tall people.

'You're a saint,' muttered Maurice as she spooned the stew onto his plate. He always said the same thing, but it never failed to give Iris a warm glow. He was right, she was a saint giving up her time and missing lunch to dish up meals to these smelly, penniless characters. It was always nice when someone recognised it though.

'Watcha, Iris,' said another man whose name she didn't know, even though he apparently knew hers.

'Alright?'

'Mustn't grumble,' was the response.

Iris thought that if anyone had reason to grumble, it was men like this.

'Tinker.' He held out a grimy hand by way of introduction.

Iris kept a firm hold on the serving spoon and nodded with a smile.

'You know you're famous around here. Everyone talks about Iris. Apparently you give generous portions.' He winked and gave a salacious laugh, nodding at the others behind him in the queue.

Iris felt herself blushing, partly out of embarrassment and partly out of pleasure that they all thought she was wonderful, even if it was only for giving large portions. She covertly added an extra half spoon to his plate, making a great display of looking over her shoulder. 'Mustn't let the boss see, or else I'll be out on my ear.'

'Come on, mate. Some of us are hungry! Now's not the time to be chatting Iris up.' The man behind gave him a hard nudge and Tinker moved on to the sponge and custard, giving the man the finger behind his back.

Some took the food without comment, although most at least gave a nod.

'How are you, Iris?' A pair of unblinking blue eyes met hers.

Iris shifted her weight from one foot to the other. 'Fine thanks, George. All the better for seeing you.' She had become expert at banter over time, but it was always as if George could see right inside her.

Iris ignored his penetrating gaze.

'Shift up, mate!' George and his blue eyes were swept along in the queue, to Iris's relief.

Afterwards, it was expected that the 'helpers' would mix and chat with the 'customers.' Iris didn't mind this bit either as she sat with a sympathetic smile on her face listening, unmoved, to stories of betrayal, bankruptcy, and disaster, always astonished how most of them seemed to accept their lot with equanimity, uncomplaining. Maybe the alcohol and drugs helped.

She made a beeline for Mable, one of the few women. Seeing her approach, Mabel shifted several of her many bags onto the floor, creating a space for Iris to sit. 'Hiya Iris,' she mumbled and gave a toothless grin.

'Hiya, Mabel,' Iris mimicked the greeting. 'How's it going?'

'Me feet's playing up something terrible.' She had put both her feet up on the chair opposite.

'They'll get better now summer's coming, I reckon.' She sighed. 'Shame we can't have a fag in here. That would just be the icing on the cake.'

'There is a chiropodist you could see, you know. Want me to make an appointment?'

'No way!' Mabel shifted away from Iris in protest. 'I'm not letting one of those so-called professionals get anywhere near me!'

Iris stifled a sigh. Mabel's paranoid fear of 'professionals' had led her to this place in her life, a fear so ingrained that Iris doubted she would ever change. One morning she would be found dead in a shop doorway when someone came to unlock.

'Much luck outside Sainsbury's?'

'Not bad, a few apples and some sandwiches. One bugger even gave me a tin of baked beans, for God's sake! As if I had somewhere cosy to go and open them. I threw them right back at him. Bastard!'

Iris smiled at the thought.

'Right, better get on. The boss'll be after me if I'm not doing the washing-up.' Iris glanced over to where Tina was busy clearing dishes, a determined look on her face.

'I don't know how you put up with that bitch!'

'Ahh she's not so bad really.' Iris summoned up her best sympathetic smile. 'She's got her own issues, you know.' Iris leaned as close in to Mabel as she dared.

'Oh?' A gleam appeared in Mabel's eyes.

'Story for another time.' Iris tapped the side of her nose and winked as she stood.

Stan, resplendent in his brown working coat had already stacked up the few chairs that were unoccupied, and stood, poised with his broom, a thin smile barely covering his impatience to return the hall to its previously pristine state. Iris knew that by the end of the afternoon, the floor would be freshly waxed and polished, chairs and tables neatly laid out for the evening Bingo session – a much more sedate affair. It would be as if all trace of these undesirable members of society had been cleaned up and swept away.

Iris smiled to herself as she got stuck in to the washing up.

Chapter 4

'I can't believe we're actually doing this, Big Bear!' Trish bounced up and down on the campervan seat, her hands loose on the steering wheel.

'Yeah! Livin' the dream, baby.' Bob grinned, exaggerating the American accent.

Trish surveyed the interior of the RV in the rear-view mirror. 'Know what? We almost don't need the bungalow. We've got everything we need right here.' She paused. 'Maybe in time we'll sell that too! Who knows?'

'Watch out here. It's quite a turn for Dusty Roads to handle.' Bob pressed his foot to the floor as they approached the turning into Eagle Court. What he would have given to have had dual controls in Dusty Roads – the only thing he missed about his job as a driving instructor.

Trish laughed as she spun the wheel.

'Careful!' Bob pressed his body back into the seat and braced himself.

'Oh shit!' Trish slammed on the brakes as a groaning, creaking sound emanated from Dusty Roads.

Bob opened the door after a brief silence.

As they climbed down, Trish laughed. 'At least Eagle Court knows we've arrived!'

Bob leant to inspect the damage. Dusty Roads was well and truly wedged up against the brick post marking the entrance to Eagle Court.

'We'll have to back up and hope the post doesn't collapse,' he muttered.

'Oh come on, Bob. You've got to see the funny side.' Trish nudged him.

Ignoring her, he turned and climbed into the driver's seat. 'Stay here and watch the post.'

As he gingerly backed up, Trish stood, hands on hips, raising her eyes to the sky, before a crunching sound drew her gaze back to the post which had now crumbled into a pile of bricks.

'Oh shit, that's done it!' Trish lit a cigarette and took a long drag.

By the time Bob had piled the bricks on the side of the drive and had parked the RV outside their new home, it was past 8 o'clock. 'We should have got here earlier,' he said. 'And there's only just enough space.'

'Dusty Roads is a big girl.' Trish patted the dashboard lovingly. 'And does it matter about the time? God, you're obsessed with time, Bob. One day I'll take your watch away!' Trish chortled at the thought. 'This is only our temporary stop-gap between road trips, so who cares about the space?'

'I think our new neighbours might care,' said Bob as he climbed down.

'Come on, let's drink a toast to our new life. I've got beers in the cooler ready to celebrate.' Trish leaned over and retrieved two beer bottles, waving them in the air.

'We ought to tell the neighbours about the post.'

'Aww forget it! Live dangerously for once, Bob. What's the worst that can happen? We can sort it tomorrow.'

Trish opened every door in the bungalow and grimaced. 'I never thought I'd end up in suburbia. In a *bungalow*!'

'It was a good deal, and we can make it nice by—'

'*Nice?*' Trish cut in. 'I don't do *nice*.' She huffed.

'Anyway, we won't be here much. Let's get back in the van, crack open the beers and order a takeaway. That's one advantage of a place like this, there'll be a takeaway nearby. Not like that time when we were in a commune in Nepal. Did I tell you about that, babe? We walked bare-foot in the mountains to forage for food and made our own houses to connect with our ancestors...'

Bob didn't answer, busying himself with opening the beers and ordering the takeaway, zoning out Trish's chatter about the past. For all her claims of 'pushing the boundaries' she always ordered the same takeaway – Cantonese chicken and egg-fried rice.

Later, as Bob turned over – a tricky manoeuvre in a sleeping bag – he longed for his old bed, thankful that his neighbour's son, Sam, from Waterfield Close was arriving in the morning with the furniture they had packed earlier that day. The idea of becoming an old man, vegetating in the cul-de-sac that had been his home with Ann for the last fifteen years, had filled him with horror. And then Trish had come along, and downsizing and buying a RV seemed the only thing to do. He had felt slightly superior leaving the long-time residents of Waterfield Close to their small lives, boasting to them about travelling and seeing the world.

What was wrong with him? He was doing his best to adapt to the lifestyle he had always dreamt of, and Trish had seemed the ideal person to live this new life with. She was fun and impulsive. Everything was exactly as he wanted. So why did the old, anxious Bob keep intruding? He would have to try harder. But, however much he tried to focus on the deep-breathing

Trish had taught him, Bob couldn't stop thinking about the gatepost and the damage to Dusty Roads. He would have to get it fixed, otherwise what would his new neighbours think?

Not having met their new neighbours, Bob wondered if there would be children in Eagle Court, or more likely, grand-children. He smiled at the thought of children playing. He and Ann had not had children, and she had refused to investigate why. 'It's meant to be,' she'd said firmly, closing the subject. But Bob wondered what it would be like to hear his own grandchildren playing outside. Trish was dismissive about her own children, Ocean and Thor. 'They're adults and have to make their own way, just as the young in the natural world do. And anyway, who wants to be called "Granny"?' He found it strange that she had such little interest in where they were or what they were doing. Ocean, in particular, had become a taboo subject when Trish found out that she had changed her name to Sarah and was now a banker.

He remembered the neat semi in Waterfield close, a cul-de-sac just like this, and how all the couples had invited each other for drinks and nibbles each week. A time to discuss what was going on in the neighbourhood and whether they needed to do anything about it. Neighbours like himself and Trish would have been a cause for concern.

Bob wrapped the pillow around his head and tried counting backwards from a hundred.

Chapter 5

I ris watched Breakfast Television eating her usual slice of toast and jam. Because it was Sunday, everything seemed to be about cooking brunch. Iris huffed. Brunch was just an excuse to laze around as far as she could see. She switched channels and became engrossed in a real-crime show. She'd seen it before, but you could never rewatch these things too often as there were always details that escaped you the first time round. When the programme finished, it was 9.30. Iris calculated that by the time she had locked up and got in the car it would be twenty-to, and she could wait in the garden-centre car park if she was too early.

As soon as she stepped out of the front door, Iris knew that something was wrong, sensing a presence that hadn't been in the Court yesterday. And then she saw it, casting a shadow across the front of Family Woman's bungalow, in the morning sun. A huge campervan thing parked outside Number 3. Iris's heart lurched. Her vision of Eagle Court had included nothing larger than a 4x4 and even that would have been pushing it. Everything was all wrong. This wasn't how she'd imagined Eagle Court – and for a panicky moment she even thought about selling the bungalow and getting out of there. Maybe Eagle Court wasn't the place for her, after all.

Yes, that's you, Iris. Just run as soon as things get difficult. You've always been a coward.

Iris took a few moments to calm herself. She had to think clearly. No, this was her home and she would not let her neighbours spoil it. She would make them change. Iris Walker was not going to give up.

Before she could overthink anything, Iris marched up to the door of Number 3 and knocked briskly. When there was no answer, she knocked again. Tutting, she stepped back, scanning the front of the bungalow. Having watched many detective and police programmes, she knew exactly what to do next. She went up to the front bay window and, shielding her eyes by placing a hand on either side of her face, she peered in. The room was unfurnished except for an untidy pile of unpacked boxes. The bungalow seemed deserted, but Iris was sure the owners of the campervan were in there. She hovered, chewing her fingernail.

For goodness' sake, Iris. Just make a decision for once!

There was nothing she could do now, so she would make her way to the garden centre and lose herself in a restful world of flowers and plants, putting this out of her head for now. If the van was gone when she returned, the problem would have solved itself. Maybe it belonged to visitors who had helped the new people move in. Comforted by this thought, she put her mind at rest.

Iris went back to the car and drove up to the Court entrance, almost stalling when she saw what was left of the gatepost and the bricks piled anyhow on the pavement. How dare someone damage Eagle Court in this way! Leaving her car where it was, she strode back down to Number 3, and examining the campervan, her fingers traced the recent scrapes and dents along one side.

Feeling as if someone was suffocating her, Iris leant against the van, gasping for air. Everyone was out to get her, to spoil

22

her new life. Even here, in Eagle Court where everything should have been perfect.

Without warning, the van door was flung open, almost pinning Iris to the side of the van.

'You alright, love?' The husky voice belonged to a woman in a dressing gown, her thin face dominated by large, hoop earrings.

It was a few moments before Iris could speak. She hadn't expected her neighbours to be actually *in* the campervan. But once she had recovered, anger drove her on. 'Did you do that to the gatepost?'

'Oh yeah. Sorry about that, love. Dusty Roads here ain't built for tight corners.' She smirked.

Iris snapped her mouth shut before she could voice her thoughts. *Maybe you should have thought of that before buying Number 3!*

'I'm Trish, and this...' she turned as a man appeared behind her, also in a dressing gown, 'is Bob.'

Iris drew herself up to her full height, realising that Trish and Bob were quite short in spite of the height advantage of the campervan, and gave them her best glare.

'I live at Number 1.' Iris didn't feel the need to say more.

Bob broke the silence. 'Look, if it's about the gatepost. We'll get it fixed. Don't worry.'

Don't worry? Iris controlled her anger. She'd had years of practice. 'Well, that's good to hear. I'm Iris,' she said, holding out her hand. Trish ignored her, already turning back into the van, but Bob responded to the gesture.

'Sorry again.'

Iris forced a smile. 'Anything you need, just ask.' She inclined her head towards the campervan. 'Are you planning to be away quite a bit?'

'Yes, that's the idea. Reliving our youth and going where the spirit takes us and all that.' He gave a sheepish grin.

Iris nodded. 'If you ever need your bin putting out, just let me know. I'll always keep an eye on everything while you're away.'

'Thanks, that's very kind. Well, I'd better get dressed. Can't go out like this.' Pulling the dressing gown around his ample stomach he turned to go.

As if Family Woman and her brood wasn't enough! But Iris wasn't going to let her new neighbours spoil Eagle Court. Even now, after what they had done, and what they were, she would not let these people get to her. These were not the neighbours she imagined, but she would rise to the challenge in this new life and not let them destroy her dream. Giving herself a mental pat on the back, Iris congratulated herself once more on her patience and kindness. She was going to make everything look nice, with tubs and planters for the front of Number 1 to set an example that maybe the others would follow. Iris drove to the garden centre, willing herself to be calm and strong.

While she waited for opening time, her fingers tapping the steering wheel, an idea came into Iris's head – an idea that once it had taken root, wouldn't let go. Her fingers ceased their drumming, poised in the air. She could come back and get her plants later.

Iris examined her appearance in the rear-view mirror, her greying hair held back with a scrunchie, a style unchanged since her youth apart from on one memorable occasion. She studied her face, tracing wrinkles and blemishes with her fingers, noticing stray hairs here and there.

It was as if a magnet had drawn Iris, unresisting, to the shopping centre. And once there, she knew exactly where to go – a store where women with money and not a care in the world whiled away afternoons replenishing their already full wardrobes.

Over the years, Iris had spent many hours wondering these halls and galleries. It had been her weekly treat while her mother was at the daycare centre. Often only able to afford a coffee, she had passed the time watching shoppers glide in and out of shops, accumulating bags as they went, overhearing snippets of conversation.

Iris's wardrobe consisted of M&S jeans (the only shop to accommodate her height) matched with a rotating variety of long-sleeved tops, and cardigans, knitted by her mother. And now, as she entered the store, up until now only familiar from the outside, excitement fizzed in her stomach.

Running her fingers along various tops and dresses, enjoying the softness of the fabrics, Iris moved on to tailored trousers and cashmere jumpers, inhaling the scent of expensive clothes. Steeling herself to take garments off the racks, Iris took a deep breath and headed for the changing rooms. She hung her treasure trove on the rail provided and stood, biting her thumbnail. Could she do this? Could she, Iris Walker, put these clothes on, even though they were not meant for the likes of her? Rolling her shoulders back, she took a deep breath and took a pair of tailored trousers off the rack.

The length was just right. So it wasn't only M&S who had trousers for someone her height, after all. She matched them with a silky top and her breath caught in her throat at this new Iris. She moved back from the mirror to get the full effect.

'How is everything?'

The assistant, swiping the curtain back, stood hand on hip, admiring her. 'Goodness! Not many women have the legs to carry those trousers off. Hang on just a minute.'

Iris waited, frozen in the mirror until the woman reappeared. 'Here, put this on.' She slipped a tailored jacket along Iris's arms and adjusted it before standing back in admiration.

'Do you know? This job gives me such a buzz when I find just the right outfit for one of my ladies.'

One of her ladies? Iris made herself look at the wall-to-ceiling mirror, her heart beating in her throat. She watched herself turn and examine her reflection from every angle as a zip of excitement ripped through her body. She could be this, new, Iris.

'And if you wanted something a little less formal, what about this?' She handed Iris a green cashmere jumper. Iris froze as the woman looked at her expectantly. She had never undressed in front of anyone since she was a small child. After a few seconds, the woman got the hint saying, 'I'll leave you to it.'

Iris smoothed the soft jumper over her stomach and smiled. Yes, this was the new Iris. Newly confident, she stepped out of the cubicle. 'What do you think?'

'Oh my! Long legs *and* a flat stomach.' The woman walked around Iris, examining her from every angle. 'Do you know how many women would die for a figure like yours?'

Iris smiled and luxuriated in the warmth of this unaccus-tomed admiration of her body.

'Can you find me some other outfits? I need a whole new look.' Iris gestured at the shop, reckless in the exhilaration of freedom and approval.

Sometime later, Iris looked at her watch and then at the growing pile of garments on the rail. She needed to get on, but she couldn't remember when she had last enjoyed herself as much. 'I'm sorry, I have to go. I'll take all of these.' Then a thought struck her. 'Just one more thing. Do you have stripy tops and trousers that can be turned up – like a sailing look?'

'Let me see. And maybe a pair of deck shoes to complete the look?'

'Brilliant.'

Iris felt like one of those paper dolls that you could put new outfits on with tabs that folded around the back to keep things in place. She'd spent hours playing with these when she was a child. And now she was doing it for real. She bounced on her toes in anticipation of the final touch to her new wardrobe.

'Here you go.'

Iris retreated behind the curtain.

When the new Iris looked at her from the mirror, she gave a half-laugh, half-gasp. It was all about the clothes – and the money to buy them. In the end, it was all about wearing the right uniform.

Iris looked at her watch again. 'I'll take everything. Can I keep these on?'

'Everything?' The woman's impeccably shaped eyebrows shot up in surprise.

'I'm making up for a lifetime of not buying clothes.' Hearing herself laugh without a care, Iris was a little unsettled by this new version of herself.

'Certainly, madam. I'll take the tickets to the till for you.' And brandishing a shiny pair of scissors, she deftly cut off the labels. Iris flinched as the woman touched the back of her neck.

'Is everything alright?' The woman asked, scissors poised in the air.

'Yes. Sorry, I'm...I'm just a bit ticklish.' Iris willed herself to endure this unexperienced physical contact.

As she strode towards the hairdressers, Iris covertly glanced at her reflection in every shop window she passed, growing taller with each one.

'What can we do for you today?'

'Something shorter? Something stylish?' Iris hadn't thought about hairstyles in any detail.

'It would be a shame to cut that beautiful, straight hair you've got. And it's so thick.'

'Are you sure?'

'Absolutely. I'll give you a shampoo and tidy it up. Maybe you could come back for some colours next time.'

Iris was transfixed as her hair became a shining, silky frame around her face. She couldn't tear her gaze away from the mirror.

'All done. What do you think?'

Iris's mind went blank. A hesitant 'Thank you,' was all she could manage.

Iris floated to the cosmetic counter at the department store, smiling at strangers, tucking a strand of hair behind her ears as she went.

When her eyebrows had been shaped and her face made-up, the transformation was complete. Iris had completely forgotten about her Sunday lunch, and looking at her watch, she saw it was already past 2 o'clock. Taking a last glimpse of herself in a shop window, Iris returned to her car.

This new Iris even drove differently. She had more confidence and parked in the first space she saw at the garden centre without giving it a second thought.

Munching a scone with clotted cream and jam in the cafe, Iris leaned back in the chair and casually looked around her. She had been here so many times in the past but this was a new, defiant, Iris, blithely ignoring the voice in her head.

You'll clap the weight on if you eat that, Iris. Then you'll be a fat beanpole!

She didn't recognise the weekend staff in the cafe, so there was no one to comment on how different she looked. Iris felt a tug of disappointment. Never mind, she would come back in the week.

A helpful young man called Sean, gave her advice about compost and tubs, and suggested what plants to buy. She told him she wanted things with lots of flowers. She revelled in his polite and deferential manner. It was all so simple. You just had to wear the right uniform. Her purchases complete and deposited in her car by Sean – Iris hadn't thought twice about asking him – she was ready for home.

But as she drove, a voice curled its way into her head.

Mutton dressed as lamb. Who do you think you are?

As she approached Eagle Court the voice became louder and more insistent.

Mutton dressed as lamb. Who does she think she is?

A thought occurred to Iris. What if everyone had been secretly laughing at her? The assistant in the shop, the hairdresser, and the make-up woman. After all, they would have said anything to get her to spend, wouldn't they? She couldn't unsee the image of the three women sniggering behind their hands. The phrase started on a continuous loop in her head:

Mutton dressed as lamb. Mutton dressed as lamb.

By the time she got home, Iris's head was in a whirl. Leaving everything in the car, she rushed to the front door and let herself in. In the kitchen she clung to the edge of the worktop, gasping for breath.

Who do you think you are? Waltzing about like a slut! Mutton dressed as lamb. Mutton dressed as lamb!

Iris got herself out of her new clothes, all angles and ungainly movements and put on some old jeans and one of her usual tops. She scraped her hair back and, in the bathroom, scrubbed at her face until all trace of the makeup was gone. Only then could she breathe. What had she been thinking? The real Iris looked at her in the mirror and smiled. This was who she was – not some sort of fake Iris that people might be laughing at behind her back. There were other ways to make people respect her. And why would she want to become like Family Woman, anyway? Someone she despised. Even so, the thought that she could wear expensive clothes and become some other version of herself if she chose left a pleasant sensation in Iris's mind.

The new garments were hung with care in her wardrobe before she shut the door and turned her back on them.

Chapter 6

'I guess there was always going to be one nosy old bag wherever we moved. You know what "keeping an eye on things" means! She'll be organising a one-woman neighbourhood watch at this rate. She gives me the creeps.' Trish shuddered. 'I can't believe I've ended up in a place with neighbours like her and that middle-class snob next door. I saw her measuring up her front porch earlier. Can't stand tape-measures. I could tell by the way she's dressed and the way she looked Dusty Roads up and down, she's already disapproving of us and we haven't even met. What's she even doing here? Looks as if she belongs in a stately home.'

Bob had been relieved to see the white van reversing into Eagle Court just after Iris had departed. Sam wasn't known for his time-keeping but had surpassed himself this morning, especially as it was a Sunday.

'Watcha, Bob.'

'Hi Sam. You're almost early.'

Sam grinned. 'Got to get back for the match. United are playing today.'

'Right then. Let's get this stuff unloaded.'

He and Sam deposited all the furniture in the living room. Bob didn't want to ask Sam to do more – he was already in his debt for storing the van overnight and helping out today.

When they had finished, Bob slipped Sam a couple of twenties. 'Buy your mates a round on me.'

Sam looked at the notes. 'Not being funny, Bob, but this won't go far.'

Bob felt himself blush. He gave Sam another two notes.

'Thanks, mate.'

'Thank you, Sam, for giving up time on a Sunday.'

Sam glanced at Trish, sitting on the RV step, her eyes closed, a cigarette dangling from her lips as she swayed to some kind of inner music.

'Are you taking the van back now?' Bob could sense Sam comparing Trish and Ann with some perplexity.

'Yep, then off to the pub.'

Bob clapped Sam's back. 'Thanks again.'

Sam turned to Bob as he was getting into the van. 'You won't forget to pop back and see Mum and Dad, will you? I know Dad's going to miss you.'

Bob nodded. 'Of course not. Tell them I'll be around soon.' He pushed the nightmare thought of visiting Waterfield Close with Trish to the back of his mind, focussing on more immediate issues.

'Come on, Trish. Let's get these things sorted.'

To his surprise, Trish extinguished her cigarette and followed him into the house without comment.

Inside, she moved past the furniture, positioning herself by the window. 'First, I need to feel the space.' She closed her eyes, spread her arms and swayed from side to side as she turned, emitting a low groaning sound. Bob made a move to start on the bed.

'Don't move, Bob! You're disturbing my karma.'

Bob stopped, one foot in front of the other, as if frozen in a game of musical statues.

Ten minutes later, having left Trish to it, Bob was awoken from a pleasant doze as she shook his shoulder.

'Come on, Bob. I'm ready. It needs to be done now!'

After they had repositioned the furniture to Trish's liking, following the rules of Feng Shui, Bob heaved a sigh of relief and made them both a cup of tea, grateful for her sudden burst of energy.

'See? It isn't so bad.' Bob felt more settled now with familiar furniture around, although he was aware that none of this was familiar to Trish. She didn't seem to care. Physical belongings meant little to her. When he'd met her, all her belongings had fitted into one bag. 'I travel light, Bob.' At the time, he had found this an attractive quality and had almost envied Trish. But now, more comfortable with his things around him, he was beginning to sense that he and Trish were very different.

Bob felt a tremor as Trish carelessly placed her mug on the coffee table, imagining the ring already forming on the oak. It had been one of the first things he and Ann had bought together, and she had lovingly polished it for the forty years of their marriage. Bob reminded himself once more that this was the life he had always dreamed of – RV road trips with no routine. There would always be time to return to homely things – as long as he knew they were still there, waiting for him.

'I'll take a look at the post later and see if I can sort it.' But even as he uttered the words, Bob knew it was beyond fixing with his limited DIY skills and that a builder would need paying.

There was no response from Trish who was busy painting her toenails.

'I could probably get the bloke who built these bungalows to come and sort it. If not, he'll know who built the posts. Yes, that's what I'll do.' Happier now that a plan had been formed,

Bob picked up the mugs. 'I'll wash these and then maybe we could do some unpacking.'

Trish slammed the nail-polish bottle down on the table. 'For God's sake! Stop wittering like an old woman, Bob. All this can wait.' She gestured around at the piles of boxes. 'Today we're going to have some fun and take Dusty Roads on an adventure. I can't wait to get away from this place. It's suffocating me already! This'll all still be here when we get back.'

Trish's interest in their new home had evaporated as suddenly as it had arrived. Bob smiled. 'You're right. Old habits, I guess. Let's get out there and have some fun. We'll see where Dusty Roads leads us.'

Trish tittered. 'That's the Bob I fell in love with. Come here, Big Bear.'

Bob allowed himself to be soothed by Trish's affection, and went to get dressed, carefully blocking Ann's disapproving frown from his mind. Ann would have hated Trish.

'Where shall we go?' Bob had planted himself firmly in the driver's seat before Trish had time to object, but she didn't complain.

'Okay, when we get to the road. Right or left?' She bounced on the seat in excitement, Bob feeling her infectious love of life.

Getting into the mood, Bob said, 'Let's flip a coin. Heads right. Tails left.' Digging a pound coin out of his wallet, he flipped it in the air and it landed under the seat. He got out of Dusty Roads and felt around until he found it.

'Well? Heads or tails?' demanded Trish.

'Heads.' Bob had no idea. But at this point he just wanted to get past the starting post.

'Okay, left it is, Big Bear.'

'No, we said that heads would be right.'

Trish leaned her head back and closed her eyes. 'Okay. Let's go right, then.'

After a few hours of driving along increasingly narrow lanes where, mercifully, they met very few oncoming vehicles, Dusty Roads deposited them outside a small pub. Some of the tension left Bob's body as they headed in for a welcome cold drink.

'That was fun, wasn't it?' Trish leaned back in the chair and sighed. 'I wonder where we'll end up this afternoon?' She took a sip of lager. 'I know it's nothing like trekking in Peru and just coming upon Machu Pichu, but it's a start.'

Bob felt a moment of panic. If this was the start, he wasn't sure he would stay the course. One step at a time, he reminded himself. Don't think too far ahead. This was what Trish had said to him when they met at a Bob Dylan tribute gig. He had literally cried into his beer as he told her about Ann and the pain of his loss. Trish had been comforting and helped him face the future, and her advice had brought him here. But what if one step at a time led you to the wrong place – gradually, without you realising it? Was he in the wrong place? Bob didn't know, but maybe a bit of strategic planning was important in taking one day at a time.

He looked up to see Trish gazing at him. 'Everything okay, Big Bear? Those sad thoughts getting to you again? Remember. One minute, one hour, one day at a time.'

Bob echoed the last part of the sentence with her and tried to believe it.

'Come on! We need more adventure. I'm driving this time.'

Bob forced a smile. 'That's an adventure in itself!'

Trish manoeuvred Dusty Roads out of the carpark and turned right. 'It's a day for turning right,' she said, turning to him.

'Watch out!'

Trish slammed on the brakes and a motor bike screamed past, narrowly avoiding them. Unfazed, she said in a breathy voice, 'Wow! Wouldn't you just love one of those? You ever been into motor bikes, Bob?'

'In my teens I had a bike for a while – and the leather jacket to go with it.' He indicated the leather jacket he was wearing. 'Not this one, though. I had to get a new one after about twenty years. Ann insisted, and in the end I had no choice as she threw the old one out when I was at work one day.'

Under her breath, Trish muttered, 'Bitch!'

'She meant well.' Somehow Bob couldn't help defending her.

'When are you going to grow a pair, Bob?' You still wear the leather jacket and the jeans. You're still into Bob Dylan, but you haven't got a bike to complete the look. Trish speeded up as they turned right onto a main road. 'Just think back. Can't you remember the thrill of riding your bike? Speeding along? It's the nearest thing to flying!'

Bob thought back and remembered the exhilaration his younger self had experienced skimming along on his Suzuki and how the girls had flocked to him. But somehow, he knew that his older sixty-something self would be terrified, seeing an accident around every corner, maybe the result of thirty years as a driving instructor. It was scary enough travelling in Dusty Roads, whose bulk would keep them safe in most circumstances. A motorway sign brought Bob back to the present.

'Hang on Trish. We said no motorways.'

'Shit!' hissed Trish as they sped down the slip road.

Bob held onto the seat with both hands, foot pressed firmly to the floor as Dusty Roads zig-zagged in and out of the traffic without signalling. Trish threw her head back and laughed.

'Hell! Isn't this fun?'

Angry horns beeped behind them as they left a trail of angry drivers in their wake and hogged the fast lane at 55 miles per hour.

'I think you should move in.' Bob summoned up his best driver-instructor voice.

'Okay, Big Bear, whatever you say.' Trish went to move to the left without looking in the mirror or indicating.

'No! Not yet.' Bob could barely speak as a huge truck appeared in his wing mirror, the fog-horn hoots of the angry driver ringing in his ears. 'Okay. Indicate now and he'll let you in.'

'What? Where's the indicator? And maybe I'm having too much fun, anyway!'

Bob leaned over and turned the indicator on, and grabbing the steering wheel, he guided Dusty Roads into the middle lane, waving thanks to the truck driver as Trish gave him the finger.

'This is fun, both of us driving at once,' Trish giggled.

'We need to pull over. Dusty Roads can't manage this speed for any length of time.' Bob indicated once more and steered into the inside lane.

'Right. Slow her down a bit, she needs a breather.'

'Aye, aye, cap'n.' Trish gave a mock-salute.

Bob watched the temperature gauge inch towards critical. 'Pull over, Trish. She's overheating.'

As they eased to a halt on the hard shoulder, Dusty Roads released great plumes of smoke from under her bonnet. 'That was fun! I just fancied a bit of speed when I saw that motorbike, and when we ended up on the motorway, well...' She patted the dashboard. 'Sorry Dusty.'

Bob wasn't surprised when a police car pulled in behind them, lights flashing.

Chapter 7

As it was still warm and sunny after tea, Iris set to work. Noticing with relief that the campervan had gone, she unloaded the four pale-green planters from her car, along with bags of compost that Sean, the nice young man at the garden centre, had recommended. Finally, she placed the trays of flowers on the front step. Looking at the labels she could see they were called begonias, geraniums, and petunias. They looked very small, but Sean had assured her they would soon grow.

Forking the soil angrily, Iris's head was still full of voices. *Fancy wasting all that money! What makes you think you can ever be like the women who shop there? Maybe I could be...one day.* She jumped when a familiar voice interrupted her inner dialogue. 'I hope you don't mind me saying, but you're planting those far too close together. And I would have thought that May is too early for bedding plants.'

Iris did mind...very much. She leant back on her heels, shielding her eyes from the sun with a gloved hand, and looked up at Family Woman. She had no idea what 'bedding plants' were, but Sean had said these were what she needed for a splash of colour that would last all summer.

'I'm Celia.'

Iris struggled to her feet. 'Iris,' she replied, unsure whether a handshake was appropriate. It had seemed natural with Bob, but with Family Woman, she wasn't sure. Instead, she rubbed her gloved hands together, scattering soil all over the paving. Celia was dressed in almost the same middle-class uniform as Iris had hanging in her wardrobe, striped shirt with the collar turned up under a padded quilt jacket. Linen trousers and deck shoes completed the look. Her left hand sported a thick wedding ring and engagement ring with a generous sized diamond. Iris hated this woman and her patronising attitude.

'Have you seen what they' – she gestured towards Number 3 – 'have done to the gatepost?' She said the first thing that came into her head. 'They've knocked down the whole thing!' Iris reiterated when Celia didn't respond.

'So they'll have to sort it out then.' Celia said brusquely, seemingly more concerned about the plants. 'If you space them out, they'll have more room to grow.'

'Okay, thank you for your advice. I'll maybe get some more pots. I'm hoping they'll make a nice show for the summer.' Iris was determined to be positive. 'Or I could give you some if you'd like. Maybe brighten up your place a bit.' She gave a meaningful glance at the bare entrance to Number 2.

'Thank you for the offer. I am planning to have some shrubs at the front – they're already on order from a specialist nursery.'

Iris's gloved hands clenched at her sides.

'Nice to meet you.'

And before Iris could respond, Celia strode away.

She looked back down at her planters and kicked the nearest one in frustration. Why had she been stupid enough to start at the front in full view of everybody? She huffed in frustration. Today was turning into a nightmare. That's what happened when you tried something new. She should have stuck to her usual routine. However, it was done now and she might as well finish, but the pleasure had gone out of the task.

As Iris was tidying up and washing her hands she wondered if she should get a book about gardening. She should have done that before she started instead of rushing in like an idiot.

You always rush into things, Iris. No wonder you get everything wrong.

Iris couldn't remember when she first started hating her mother. When she passed the eleven-plus to get into grammar school, Iris had rushed home in excitement. Her father had given her a hug, saying, 'Well done, Iris. We've got some brains in the family at last!' But what she remembered most was her mother sniffing and saying, 'They've obviously lowered the standards, then.' Was that when the first seeds of hate had germinated?

Iris had enjoyed the routine of the all-girls grammar school and did her best to please the teachers. She revelled in any praise, however slight. She even made a few friends, although she never invited them home. They all lived in much posher areas, and even though she didn't want to admit it, Iris was ashamed of the area she lived in – and her parents. When, all too soon, the regimented years of school were over, Iris had got a job in the local council offices. Although she gave most of her earnings to her mother, who controlled the finances in the Walker family, Iris had enough to buy clothes and had her hair cut in a trendy page-boy style. She had dreaded going home, knowing that there would be some acid comment from her mother. And she was proved right.

'I don't know why you bother spending your money, Iris. No lad's ever going to look at you, not unless he's 6 foot 6.' She'd tittered at her own joke.

Yes, that was when the hatred had grown branches and become rooted in her mind. And the thing was, a boy *had* looked at her, and done more than look at her. Iris had been swept away by the shallow flattery and become pregnant.

40

Once her mother noticed the inevitable bump, it was too late for an abortion, and Iris was sent away to an aunt until the baby was born.

After just a few hours, her little boy had been taken away and the whole business had never been spoken of again. Iris did not want to think about those times. She never thought of him as her son, who would now be a man, only as 'the baby' or 'it'. But anger towards those who had everything she'd been denied festered over the years, along with hatred of her mother, who had been the architect of her loss, grew into something with very deep roots.

After this humiliation, Iris had to give up her job, and her mother made it clear she expected her to stay home and look after her ailing father after his stroke. 'You're not fit to be out in the real world, Iris. You'll stay here where I can keep an eye on you.'

When he died, Iris, in her mid-forties, found it impossible to get back into the world of work. And as her mother's health declined it was generally expected that Iris would look after her. So that was it. Her brief chance at normal life had been cut short, and she had spent the last forty years at home living a small, angry, life with her mother. Even the adulation from her mother's friends and neighbours was not enough to compensate for what she had lost.

'You're a saint, Iris. Not many girls would give up their lives like you.'

'She's the perfect daughter, isn't she?'

During long evenings in front of the TV, Iris spent many impotent hours imagining how she might pay her mother back for her lost life. Powerless in her own home, Iris took some pleasure in venting her anger elsewhere. But the real cause of her rage was always sitting there, right in front of her.

One day, getting the shopping, she overheard the girl at the till talking to the vicar.

'Maybe come along to our lunches for the homeless on a Saturday, Lisa. We open the church hall for a few hours and invite those less fortunate than ourselves in for a good, square meal. We'd love to have you. Just turn up.'

Lisa hadn't looked convinced, replying, 'That'll be sixty-six pounds and seventy-three pence please.'

When the vicar produced his card to pay, she added, 'Got a loyalty card?' and then watched impassively as the vicar dug around in his pockets.

'I'm sure I've got one somewhere...'

'Never mind, you can always add the points on next time,' Lisa added mechanically.

Iris was glad that women always had handbags to keep such things at the ready. She always had her loyalty card ready before she reached the till.

When it was her turn, she gave it to Lisa to scan and packed her groceries, just remembering the obligatory, 'Thanks Lisa. Have a nice day,' which Iris always doubted she would.

Her mind was caught up with thoughts of the homeless lunch. This was something she imagined herself doing. And the more she thought about it, the more determined Iris became. This time, she would stand up to her mother. She could prepare her mother something for Saturday lunch. She would be firm about going out. Even her mother couldn't prevent her, a sixty-year-old woman, from helping in such a worthy cause.

In the end her mother had just muttered something under her breath, apparently resigned to the inevitable. 'I bet they're not going to pay you.'

'Well, no, Mum, that's the whole point. It's voluntary.'

She wrinkled her nose. 'Rather you than me. All those disgusting old men. You be careful, Iris. Don't let them touch you.' She winced as she shifted her position in the chair. 'You know what you're like. You keep yourself to yourself.'

Iris couldn't help blushing at this reference to the past. But she was not going to be deterred. 'I'll ask Norma from next door to sit with you. You can watch one of those old films together.'

Her mother turned to the window, as if expecting Norma to appear immediately. Without looking back at Iris, she said, 'Haven't you got the tea on yet? Get a move on, otherwise we'll miss the news.'

Iris had loved the Homeless Dinners from the start and revelled in the praise and grateful comments she received from all and sundry for getting down and dirty with those who most people shunned. Iris never minded dirt and smells – in her experience, the more disgusting the job, the greater the praise.

Chapter 8

Celia looked at *Mansfield Park,* but the words on the page refused to organise themselves into anything meaningful. She put the book on the table and sipped her wine. Maybe she'd been a bit abrupt with that woman – what was she called? Iris. The way Iris looked at her with pale, slate-grey eyes had been unsettling. She'd been pleasant enough, though.

Celia hadn't wanted her to spoil all those plants and had gone out and spoken without thinking. Waste was something she couldn't tolerate, but more than that, she hated incompetence, especially where gardening was concerned. And where it was right on her doorstep, Celia couldn't let it go. The woman obviously knew nothing.

Celia was astonished at the ignorance of some people. She had seen them in garden centres, buying plants because they were in flower and looked nice, with no idea about where they should go and what to do with them when they finished flowering. Overhearing conversations, she had had to bite her tongue on several occasions to stop herself from putting them right. She suspected that some dug them up and threw them away, only to replace them with the latest flowering variety when they'd gone over. Anyway, Iris had seemed more bothered about the campervan and the gatepost. Celia was sure that both of those issues would be resolved in one way or another – they were nothing to do with her.

Taking another sip, she leant back in the chair, and sighing, closed her eyes. If she kept them shut, Celia could almost imagine she was back at home – because she knew this place would never be home – and in her mind looked around the familiar kitchen, warmed by the Aga in winter, taking in the two worn settees, battered by her children and their friends over the years. She looked through the French doors to the patio with its numerous pots, their seasonal contents creating a riot of colour. Further on, she saw the lawn and herbaceous borders, carefully tended and nurtured by herself over many years, and at the bottom of the garden the familiar group of apple trees, joking known as 'The orchard'. Enjoying the sun on her face, Celia could hear the shouts of her children as they played on the swing Alan had made for them – attached to a branch of the sturdiest tree. She saw them playing on the lawn with their friends or playing cricket with their father on a summer's evening, herself laughing as she brought out a tray of glasses filled with homemade lemonade, placing it on the large outdoor table.

Those days were gone. Celia opened her eyes to face the sterile, oblong room she now found herself in. Granted, there were patio doors and some paving, but beyond that there was only a rectangle of newly laid turf. She felt stifled and closed in by the small outdoor space.

Impatient, Celia stood and took the empty glass into the kitchen. She wouldn't be able to drive for another few weeks. Daisy had ordered several internet shops, but it wasn't the same somehow, and anyway, she didn't want Daisy knowing everything she bought.

She had to stop feeling sorry for herself. This was a time for back-bone, to show that she was made of stern stuff, to make the best of a bad job. Alan would have known how to make her laugh, how to make everything bearable. But now she was on her own and was going to have to make her own sense of positivity.

She would make the best of the garden when her arm was fully functional again. And in the meantime, she could plan, even though now was prime time for planting things. She gritted her teeth and forced back the tears. Maybe she could re-read all the Jane Austens. She'd already started on *Mansfield Park* when other activities had been limited because of her broken arm. Maybe it was time to get back to her book club. When she could drive, it would be the first thing to do. Something from her old life that would still be there. And there was always *The Times* crossword to challenge her every day. Thank goodness it was her left arm in plaster and she could still write. Yes, some things would still be the same.

She picked up *Mansfield Park*, determined to read, but her eyes wouldn't obey. Instead they began to deposit drops on the page. Celia brushed them away with an abrupt sweep of her hand.

'Stop feeling sorry for yourself, Cee. This isn't you.'

'I know, Alan. But everything's such a challenge.'

'Things'll get better, you'll see.'

'It's so hard without you. We've always faced everything together, even...'

No, she would not go there. Not tonight.

Outside, Iris had tidied up and gone in. The small plants looked forlorn in their planters, already drooping. The stupid woman hadn't even watered them in. Celia fetched a watering can from the pile of boxes. Levering it out with her good arm, she filled it and opened the front door. She looked over to check that Iris wasn't around. It was ridiculous having to act so furtively outside one's own home, but she couldn't let the plants die. Avoiding the front window, Celia stooped and gave the planters a good water.

Back indoors, she put the watering can away and went back to the front window. The plants were perking up already and Celia congratulated herself for saving their lives. She felt much better. Tomorrow she would stop moping around and message Eleanor and Wanda, her book-club friends, tackle the crossword (thank goodness she had arranged delivery with the paper shop), and maybe start thinking about the green-rectangle challenge outside.

Celia was pleased to hear Daisy's 4x4 pull up on the drive. She needed a distraction from sad thoughts.

'Hi, Mum.' Daisy pulled her hair back from her face. 'Just a flying visit before I get Lucy from ballet. Ignore Seb. He's in a mood.' Celia's heart sank when she saw the angry face and folded arms as Seb trailed behind her into the bungalow.

'Oh my! You've not done much unpacking, Mum. We'll get more done when I've got a bit of time. I'll have a cuppa now, though.'

'Remember the woman from next door?' said Celia as she filled the kettle. 'I met her when she was putting in some bedding plants at the front. She was planting them far too close together.'

'Oh Mum! I hope you didn't offend her.'

'Not at all. She seemed grateful for the advice.'

'That old woman who couldn't drive her car? I thought all old people knew about gardening!' Seb sniggered.

'Seb. You shouldn't generalise people into categories like that,' Daisy said, sipping her tea.

Celia inwardly raised her eyes to the ceiling.

Seb, returning to his phone, didn't make any further comment, ignoring Celia as she placed a glass of fruit juice beside him.

'That's teenagers for you,' said Daisy with a wry smile, seemingly unconcerned about her son's lack of manners.

'I'm not a teenager yet!' Seb scowled.

'Well, you will be in a few weeks, so that's near enough.' She turned to Celia. 'When are you having your plaster off? I could try and come with you.'

'Still several weeks yet. You don't need to worry, Daisy. I'll get a taxi and be in and out in no time.' Celia looked out of the window. 'And then I'll start on the garden.'

'You need to be careful not to overdo it in the first few weeks, you know, Mum.'

'I know, I know.' Celia changed the subject. 'How's Mark doing? Any news about the consultant's post?'

She listened as Daisy gave a detailed account of hospital politics and how Mark was working to get everyone on his side for the upcoming board interviews.

'Actually, Mum, we were wondering whether you could help us out a bit now you've got the money from the house.'

She took Celia by the arm and led her into the hall. 'We'd like to send Seb to Milford College. He'll get a much better education there – a much better start in life. The school he's at...well he's getting in with the wrong crowd. Private school will get him back on track again. We all want the best for him, don't we? Do you think you could do that for us?'

Celia had expected requests for money from time to time, but nothing on this scale and level of commitment. After all, she had given each of her children £10,000 when the sale of the house had gone though. 'What about the money I gave you?'

'That's going towards the new extension. I told you about that.'

'How much are these school fees?'

48

Daisy ignored her mother's stern tone. 'It's about £10,000 a term I think,' said Daisy waving her hand impatiently, as if the amount was irrelevant. Her phone beeped. 'Sorry Mum, got to go. Lucy's waiting to be picked up. Come on Seb. You can choose what you want for tea on the way home,' she cajoled.

Celia watched as, once they were outside, Daisy answered a call, walking up and down the Court as Seb waited, shuffling his feet. She took a sharp breath as she saw him pick one of Iris's plants and throw it in the air. It landed on the bonnet of Iris's car. He was just about to wrench another from its bed as she strode forward.

'Put that down. Now!'

Seb stood and ran his fingers through blond, wavy hair. 'What!'

'I'll give you, "What!" Take that plant off the lady's car now and put it back.'

Daisy finished her phone call. 'What's going on?' she glared at Celia.

'Gran's going mad, just because I got a plant and threw it in the air. I was bored.'

'Get it off that car and put it back.' For once, after a hesitation, Seb did as his mother told him, roughly shoving the plant into the soil. 'Get in. We're already late.' Daisy glared at Celia as she turned the car to leave.

Celia stood on the step, her head whirling. Did Daisy really expect her to fund her children's education? Because it wouldn't be just Seb. There would be Lucy and Evie, too. But did she have any choice if she wanted a peaceful life? Reflecting on the unpleasant boy Seb was becoming, she wondered if maybe it might be the best thing. It had not escaped her notice, however, that Daisy had left it until right before she left before she broached the subject, giving Celia no time to give an immediate response.

Celia sighed and turned to go indoors. As she did so, she caught sight of a curtain twitching at Number 1 and wondered how much of the drama Iris had seen and heard. She hesitated. Should she go over and say something? No. If Iris mentioned it, then she would apologise. Otherwise, just let things be, she reasoned. She needed a glass of wine.

Chapter 9

I ris noticed a movement from the corner of her eye while she was watching the news and went to the window, taking cover behind the curtain. She held her breath and clutched the curtain hard as she watched Celia crouch to water her plants. Was Family Woman mad? Did she not realise that Iris Walker missed nothing?

When Celia had disappeared inside Number 2, Iris clenched her hands and teeth. How dare that woman sneak onto her property? How dare she do that? Iris staggered to the chair, willing her breathing to settle so that she could think, still wanting to keep the anger burning, not wanting to lose the adrenaline that came with it.

She willed herself to focus on the news, and then *Country-file*, which was covering an interesting storyline about identity theft, but before she could get settled with her second mug of coffee, Iris heard a commotion outside. Huffing, she went back to her position behind the curtain. She saw Family Woman's daughter on her phone, ignoring the boy. She saw the boy wrench one of her plants out of the soil and throw it. All the air was sucked from her body. Unable to move, she saw it land on the bonnet of her car. Iris watched as Family Woman took a step forwards and shouted at the boy, who, as his mother approached, took the plant and roughly replaced it in the trough before getting into the car. When they had gone, Iris watched Family Woman standing on the doorstep, lost in thought. She waited for her to come over and apologise, and just for a moment it seemed as if she might. But then, apparently changing her mind, she headed back indoors.

Iris found a way to move and made her way to the chair, grabbing hold of the settee and mantlepiece on the way. It was some time before she stopped shaking. She couldn't think about what had happened. She just counted breaths in and out.

Before she knew it, *Countryfile* had finished and *Antiques Roadshow* was on. Iris chewed her thumbnail. Had she been wrong to think that now she had money, and could buy a bungalow somewhere like Eagle Court that people would respect her? That she would somehow, effortlessly, become one of them? Her dreams for the future had crumbled within a few days. She thought about the new outfits, waiting in the wardrobe. That Iris wouldn't have allowed herself to be treated like this. But she couldn't become the fake Iris. The time wasn't right. Not yet. For now, she had to be herself.

Iris leaned back in the chair and looked at the ceiling, hating this weaker version of herself. A few minutes passed before she realised that a new drama had followed *Antiques Road Show*. Normally, Iris would have been glued. She loved a good accident or disaster. But tuning out the TV, Iris turned her thoughts to Eagle Court. Maybe there was another way to show her strength – to prove that she wasn't weak. She'd never thought that Eagle Court would be full of snobs, of vandal brats and hippy types with campervans. This wasn't right. She'd been patient enough, and, her chest tightening, Iris decided it was time for action.

She recalled Celia's broken arm. She would start there, having learnt from many TV dramas about criminals and psychopaths to always strike when you have your target at their weakest. Not that she, Iris, was any of those types of people, of course, she only wanted to make the world a better place for people like herself. But it didn't do any harm to borrow some of their tactics. From the limited conversation she'd had with Family Woman and what she had noticed – because Iris had learnt to be observant over the years – you never knew when snippets of knowledge might come in handy – Iris judged that her neighbour was a woman who liked being in control, someone who had very little sympathy for weakness. A broken arm would make her vulnerable and also – Iris just had a sense of this – Family Woman was not happy to be living here. Her anger simmered pleasantly as she remembered the disparaging comments about Eagle Court.

Iris continued planning as the drama morphed into the ten o'clock news, thankful that she could remember and plan in her head; a skill that had been honed over the years, as Iris could never risk writing anything down. She had learnt from an early age that you could live in your head, and if you were clever enough, no one would know what you were thinking. You could say all the things you wanted to, things that you could never say aloud. Iris had got great pleasure from this internal freedom over the years.

She went into the kitchen and stared at the orange sky, bouncing on her toes like a sprinter ready for take-off. Iris was alive again. How had she thought things could be any different? How had she thought anything could change? This was who she was. This was what brought her to life – the intoxicating pleasure of getting her own back. It had only been a week, trying to fit in, trying to ignore the way her neighbours treated her as if she was nothing, but now she felt good, back to her old self. Didn't all those self-help books always say, 'Be Yourself.'? And Iris had to agree. Being herself was where she was happiest. She would make them sorry. Make them notice her.

◆━━━━━━━◆

Iris found Zed at his usual haunt, in Burgers for U on the ring-road.

'Hiya, Iris. Watcha doin? Not seen you for a while.' Zed continued typing without looking up, hunched over his laptop.

'Hello, Zed.'

She leaned across the table. 'I'm going to need your help again.'

'It's been quiet, man, without you.' He looked around the Monday afternoon, half-full seating area. Burgers for U was never empty and Zed could make a donut and coffee last for a few hours while absorbed on his lap-top.

'I need a can of spray paint.'

Zed's eyes lit up. 'Cool. What colour?'

'Something to stand out on a beige campervan.'

Zed's fingers tapped for a few seconds before he turned the laptop to face Iris. 'What about this fluorescent pink? Pink and beige are on opposite sides of the colour spectrum, you know, so the pink will really pop!' His fingers tapped the table. 'Could I...? Could I do it for you? I know you're good, Iris, but I would love a job out in the field. Are you thinking after dark, or in broad daylight?'

Most of Zed's creative work was done at night. Under railway bridges, on derelict buildings or anywhere that was deserted and enabled a quick getaway. Iris had met him one night as he'd been spraying graffiti on the end wall of the street where she lived. When he turned to run, she'd called out, 'Stop. Tell me how you do that.' She'd long been fascinated with the possibilities of spray paint. So public and much more sophisticated than anonymous letters, although they still had their place. They were both art forms in their own right,

Over the last few years, she'd dabbled with graffiti here and there – with her mother's carer, Jasmine, and the manager at the charity shop where she'd volunteered for a bit. Iris loved that no one would suspect an elderly, frumpy old lady.

'You're not in MI5, Zed!' Iris said, returning to Zed's suggestion. 'No, this one is something for me. It needs to be personal.'

'Okay, I get it.' Zed turned back to the laptop.

'But there *is* something else. Something only you can do, Zed.'

'Just say it and I'm your man!' Zed leant back in his chair, giving Iris his full attention. A bit of morale boosting always did the trick.

'I need you to get into someone's phone. Can you do that? Without having the actual phone, I mean.'

'Easy. Just get me the number and I'll be in. What about social media? You know that's my real speciality, right?'

Iris hesitated. She didn't know if Celia or Trish was on Facebook or that Insta thing. She guessed probably not. But Daisy would be, and maybe the oldest of her brats.

'Hold fire on that, Zed. I need to do a bit of detective work first.'

Zed hammered on the keyboard with renewed enthusiasm. 'Okay. Pink paint ordered. It'll be here next week.'

Hearing Iris's frustrated sigh, Zed hastily added, 'It's from a specialist supplier. You can't just use any old spray paint on vehicles. You want it to be permanent, right? Nothing but the best for you, Iris.' He shuffled in the chair. 'And speaking of which, could you give me the twenty up front in payment?'

'Twenty pounds?' Iris, conscious of her raised voice, leant forward once more, and whispered, 'Show me!'

'Sorry it's gone now.' Zed gave her his best angelic smile. Iris knew from experience that she was not going to get past that.

She opened her purse and slipped out a twenty-pound note.

'Under the table. We don't want to be seen!'

Iris sighed once again, passing the money under the table. She had forgotten about Zed's obsession with spies and intelligence services. He used the name Zed, he had told her once, so that he couldn't be tracked – either in real life or online. Iris had no idea what his real name was.

'Let me know when you've got the phone number and I'll get cracking on some stuff.'

Iris got up and edged her way around the table, squeezing her way past an excited group of small children that had materialised at the next table, complete with balloons and presents. They would all be sick from too much junk food and excitement by the end of the day, Iris thought grimly.

She left Burgers for U without turning back. Zed always insisted on her not acknowledging him as she was leaving, which suited Iris just fine.

Chapter 10

Iris kept a close eye on Eagle Court. Although it was only 7 am, she didn't want to miss anything. Smoothing the page of her notebook, she was ready to document everything that happened. Although she knew she could remember, something about writing everything down made it real. And she didn't have to hide anything now, did she? Not now that she was free.

An anonymous white van trundled into the Court. Iris frowned as the driver did a rapid U-turn outside her house, almost demolishing one of her planters. On the way out, a newspaper was flung onto the paving outside Family Woman's door. Making a note, Iris strode to her own front door, opened it and glanced around the Court. No sign of movement. Hurrying the short distance, she picked up the paper. *The Times*. 'Snob!' muttered Iris under her breath before folding it neatly and laying it on the step.

Family Woman gets Times delivered everyday just after 7.

She resumed her post and poured a tea from her flask and unwrapped a jam sandwich. This operation had been planned down to the smallest detail.

The next hour passed slowly and Iris made a quick visit to the bathroom, as scheduled. Just as she was getting settled, Bob emerged from Number 3, stretching his arms up into the air. Enjoying the space and freedom from that awful woman, no doubt. Noting the time as 8.25, she watched as he circled the campervan and disappeared from sight for several minutes. Iris huffed in annoyance. When he reappeared, he was running his hand along the body work. Something about the movement and the way he touched the van reminded Iris of the way riders stroked their horses. That damned campervan obviously meant a lot to him. She might have her work cut out to get rid of that eyesore from Eagle Court.

Bob loves campervan. Glad to get away from Hippy Woman.

Soon after Bob disappeared indoors, at 8.30, Celia appeared in pyjamas and a dressing gown. She picked up the paper, looked at it and then glanced around the Court. Iris held her breath – folding it and putting it on the step had been an error. But Iris liked things tidy and just hadn't thought. She clenched the pencil in frustration until it broke. She poured another cup of tea to soothe her nerves. Detectives on TV did surveillance like this all the time, but Iris had to admit it was hard work. She got up and walked around the room to ease her aching back.

Hearing the campervan start up, Iris hurried back to her post. Bob had driven forwards and then with practised ease, reversed and headed up the drive. She caught sight of Hippy Woman in the doorway in tatty old jogging bottoms and a T-shirt. Iris couldn't read the slogan on it, but opening the window a crack she heard her call, 'Don't be long, Big Bear!' before replacing a cigarette back between her lips. Iris narrowed her eyes. How had she ended up with these people? It was as if fate was conspiring against her, just as it always did. But she would show them, she, Iris Walker, would not be beaten.

For a few hours, all was quiet. Iris did several laps of the living room. All this watching wasn't good for tall people like her. Her back was aching and she thought of calling it a day. Maybe another half hour. Iris was rewarded by the sight of a van nosing uncertainly down the drive. It came to a gentle stop outside Number 2 and two uniformed, men appeared. One knocked on Family Woman's door while the other operated a hydraulic lift at the back. Iris craned her neck for a better view.

The two men began unloading a number of large plants and small trees, placing them in a group on the drive. Family Woman appeared, now dressed in the all-too-familiar cropped trousers and stripy top. Noting the time, 11.20, Iris opened the window a crack to listen as Celia issued orders in a bossy know-it-all-voice. 'No, those two need to go at the back. Be careful! I don't want any of the smaller branches damaged.'

'Right you are.' The taller of the two men ignored her and carried the small tree to the back gate, dragging the branches along the wall. Iris smiled.

'I'll want my money back, if these are damaged!' Celia stood legs apart, gesturing at the tree.

The man disappeared into the back garden, apparently unconcerned.

'These go here, either side of the front door.' Hampered by her plastered arm, Family Woman tried to position them as she wanted them. 'This one needs to turn ninety degrees to the right.'

The second man turned the shrub, but the position was not to Family Woman's liking. Trying to adjust the shrub with her foot, she huffed in frustration. 'Never mind. Leave it! I'll get my daughter to move it when she comes. At least she understands what ninety degrees is!'

Iris was enjoying herself.

Family Woman used to giving orders. Bossy like Tina.

And to make her day, when Celia went out of sight into the back garden, the second man spat into the shrub.

Just as the van was ready to leave, Bob appeared in the campervan, leaving no room for the large van to get out. Hippy Woman appeared on the doorstep of Number 3, wearing the same clothes as earlier. There was some discussion between the men, interrupted by Trish shouting, 'For God's sake, Bob. Where've you been? I've been on my own for ages!' Bob waved a placatory hand in Trish's direction and eventually the situation was resolved as Bob reversed back up the drive to let the van out. When Dusty Roads was eventually parked in place, a red-faced Bob climbed out. 'We can't keep this here, Trish. Dusty is too big. I'll look into parking her somewhere else.' Hippy Woman shrugged and went indoors, impeded by a fit of coughing.

Hippy Woman possessive and needy.

Iris had plenty to go on. It had been a profitable morning. She put some eggs on for lunch.

The afternoon passed quietly and Iris closed her eyes a few times. She was woken by a great deal of shouting as Daisy and her brood piled out of their 4x4. Daisy was admiring the shrubs by the front door as Family Woman came out to greet them. The girl ran towards her, clutching a large piece of paper in her hand. 'Look what I did, Granny!'

Celia bent to look, putting her glasses on. 'Oh, that's wonderful, Lucy. Is that Mummy, you and Granny, with Seb and Luke?'

'Yup! And Mrs Wallace says it needs to go on the wall at home. But our walls are a bit full. So I'd thought you'd like it, Granny, as you don't have much on your walls.'

Iris saw Celia fumble for a tissue from her pocket.

Family Woman soft where grandchildren are concerned. Esp the girl.

'That's lovely, Lucy. Thank you. When I've unpacked, I'll have plenty of pictures to put up and things will look more like Granny's old house.'

'These are nice,' Daisy inclined her head towards the tubs.

'Wait until you see around the back. I've made a start.'

Iris was aware of general chatter from the back garden. She peered through the kitchen window but couldn't see anything. She frowned and pressed her lips together.

As expected, Daisy and her brood didn't stay long, and Iris was poised for their departure. 'We'll see you at the weekend, Mum and we'll make a start on that unpacking, won't we kids?'

Seb shrugged without speaking, glued to his phone as he got into the car.

Seb little bastard. Needs a good hiding.

'Lucy?'

'Yes! We'll help make everything lovely for you, Granny.'

Once Evie had been held up for the obligatory kiss, the car and its accompanying noise disappeared up the drive. Iris heaved a sigh of relief.

She made a cup of tea and settled down to watch *The Chase*, her mind racing with ideas.

Chapter 11

Celia threw the scissors in frustration as the box slid off the pile of other boxes onto the floor. Kicking it out of the way with her foot, she put the kettle on for a coffee.

Putting her elbows on the table, she held her head in her hands. Damn that loft ladder. She'd been up and down it in the past with no trouble, and now this! Just when she needed to be at her fittest. 'Pull yourself together, Celia.' She pulled the paper towards her and made a start on the crossword. At least some things hadn't changed.

The doorbell made Celia jump. Sighing, she went to the door, prepared with a brusque 'No thank you.' expecting those awful door-to-door sales people. She had to bite back the comment when she saw Iris looming over her on the doorstep.

'Oh, hello, Iris.'

It was the first time she had seen her neighbour smile.

'I'm off to the shops and was wondering if you needed anything, you know, with your arm.' Iris glanced towards the bright pink plaster, chosen by Lucy.

'My daughter has ordered an internet shop for me, but...' She didn't want Daisy to know about everything she bought.

Iris waited, head cocked to one side, smiling, as Celia deliberated. The least she could do was take Iris up on her offer, especially after what Seb had done the other day. Celia decided not to mention it. Later that evening, she had gone out and repositioned the plant, clearing up any evidence of Seb's vandalism. She hoped Iris hadn't noticed.

'Actually, I could do with a couple of bottles of wine and could you get some chocolate biscuits for when the children come round? I forgot to add those to the order.'

'Of course. Any wine in particular?'

'Pinot grigio – or any kind of white, really.'

'These look very smart.' Iris indicated the shrubs. 'Are these the ones you told me about?'

'Yes. They'll look better once they've grown a bit.'

Iris stepped back, eyeing them. 'I hope you don't mind me saying, but do you think this one could do with turning a little bit? Maybe ninety degrees to the right?'

Celia took a breath. 'You must be telepathic. That's exactly what I thought. I meant to ask Daisy, but she was here and gone before I thought about it.' Maybe she had underestimated her neighbour.

'Let me.' Iris turned the pot. 'There. What do you think?'

Celia came onto the drive and looked, head on one side. 'Thanks Iris, that's perfect. Maybe when you get back you could come in for a coffee and we could crack open the biscuits.'

When Iris had left, beaming, Celia immediately regretted the invitation. She knew nothing about this woman. She had invited her in because of Seb and because it was only good manners since she was doing the shopping.

Celia banged the wall with the flat of her hand in frustration. She wouldn't have had second thoughts on Broom Hill, at her old house, inviting a neighbour in. This Iris wasn't the sort of person Celia would want to make friends with. And there was something unsettling about those pale, grey eyes. It was as if they were curtained windows, and Celia had a sense that she didn't know what was going on behind them. But, she reasoned, Iris had been kind enough to think of her, so maybe this was part of a new start. She would just invite her this once, to be neighbourly.

Returning to the crossword, Celia tapped the table with her pen. She hated allowing other people to do things for her — unless they were paid, of course. Looking at the calendar on her phone, she counted the days until she could have the plaster off. Not long now. Only a few more weeks.

19 down was proving to be especially tricky. Looking up possible answers in her thesaurus, Celia huffed as she was interrupted once more, this time by the phone on the table beside her. Daisy.

Celia got her best cheerful voice ready. 'Hello, darling. Everything alright?'

'Yes, Mum. Just checking in on you. I've got a minute between appointments.'

'I'm fine. Actually the woman from next door popped round to see if I needed anything. We're going to have a coffee when she gets back.' Celia didn't mention the wine.

'I wouldn't have thought she was your type, Mum.'

Before Celia could reply, Daisy said, 'Got to go. Next patient's here. Glad you're okay.'

And that was that. Celia knew she should be grateful that at least one of her children cared enough to check up on her. But it was like checking up – a dutiful daughter checking up on an aged parent.

'Put those thoughts right out of your head, Ceel. Daisy is a good girl and you should be thankful. Haven't you solved 19 down yet? I would have thought you'd have got that in an instant.'

It took Celia another ten minutes to work out the answer. By the time she'd succeeded, Alan was gone.

64

Celia had completed the crossword by the time Iris reappeared. Putting the shopping away, she stifled a sigh at the cheap brand of pinot grigio. The temptation to retract the offer of coffee and biscuits with some kind of excuse was almost overwhelming. 'I'm so sorry, Iris, I've just remembered I've got a dentist appointment. Another time?' No, scrub that last sentence. But in the end, she heard herself saying, 'Take a seat, Iris. I'll make us a coffee.'

No mention was made of Seb's rudeness, to Celia's relief. Iris seemed more bothered by the people who'd moved into Number 3.

'You know, they've done nothing about the gatepost. Thank goodness they go out most days in that awful campervan. Dusty Roads – for God's sake.' She snorted.

'I know. It's a bit much isn't it?' Celia was so relieved that Iris hadn't mentioned Seb's behaviour, that she uncharacteristically went along with the conversation, even though the people at Number 3 were the least of her worries. 'Let's hope they sell it now they've moved in. Have you spoken to them about the gatepost?'

'Yes. The woman, Trish, I think she's called, obviously couldn't care less. But the man, Bob, seemed concerned and said he would get it fixed.'

'There you are, then. I'm sure it'll all be fine.'

Iris sniffed and took another biscuit. 'Is your daughter coming back to help you unpack?' She looked around at all the boxes.

'Yes, she will when she has time. She has a busy life. She's a GP, you know.' Celia couldn't resist adding the last sentence. 'And in the meantime, I can do quite a bit myself. I'm not an invalid!'

'I'm happy to help. You don't want to have all this around you.' Iris finished her coffee. 'How about we make a start tomorrow? Your daughter will be thrilled to see everything done when she comes.'

Before Celia could object, Iris continued. 'That's settled then. See you in the morning.'

Horrified, her heart beating in her head, Celia could only manage a faint, 'No, it's alright. I really don't think...'

'We need a sharp knife or some scissors.' Iris shook her head. 'This'll do the job,' she said, seizing Celia's keys from the table and briskly cutting through the brown parcel tape.

Folding back the flaps of the box, she took out a pile of newspaper-wrapped items. Celia bit back a stern reprimand at Iris's forward behaviour, reminding herself that her new neighbour meant well.

'What lovely plates. Where shall we put them?'

Swallowing, Celia made herself speak. 'In that cupboard.' She indicated down to the cupboards next to the hob.

'Hmm.' Iris paused. 'But maybe they would be better higher up so that you don't need to stoop. What about up here?' She gestured to the cupboards above the worktop.

Celia had to admit that Iris had a point. She was just assuming they would go where they had always been – in the cupboard next to the cooker. 'Pass me the smaller plates. I can manage those.' Celia was not going to just sit and watch Iris unpack all her things.

They moved on to the next box. Celia sat, her body rigid, as Iris lifted out framed photos.

'Oh, this must be your lovely family. Is this your husband?' There was a gentleness in Iris's voice.

Celia was determined not to weaken. 'Yes. Alan.' She paused. 'He died six months ago.'

'I'm so sorry.' Iris's eyes filled with tears. 'I'm so clumsy, barging about in your private life.'

Celia looked out of the window, focussing on a blackbird expelling alarm calls on the fence.

'You must be lost – without your husband and your home.'

Iris delved back into the box and retrieved several other framed photos. 'Oh look, this must be your wedding.'

'Yes.' Celia could think of nothing to say. If she had been paying this woman, she could have told her in no uncertain terms to put those personal things back in the box, but as Iris was her neighbour and helping her out of kindness, Celia was at a loss – in uncharted territory.

'What year would that have been? 1970s by the look of the clothes.'

'1978.'

Iris rubbed her sleeve over the photo, as if cleaning off imaginary dust before placing it carefully on the table. 'Alan looks so handsome! You can tell he worships you.'

Iris delved back into the box. 'Oh look, these must be your children when they were small. Aren't they sweet? What are their names? I love this little baby. What beautiful blonde hair.' Iris gazed at the picture, head on one side. 'What—'

Celia could take no more. 'I think we've done enough for now.' She stood abruptly, the chair screeching on the floor.

Iris took no notice of her tone. 'Oh. Well, we've made a start at least.' She eyed the rest of the boxes.

'Thank you so much, Iris. It's been kind of you to give up your time.'

'You're welcome, Celia.' Iris gave her a warm smile. 'Moving is so stressful isn't it? Bad enough without having one arm in plaster.'

Iris picked up her bag, but just as she reached the front door, she turned. 'By the way, it might be a good idea to give me your mobile number – in case you ever think of anything extra you might need with any shopping or anything. I'm always popping to the shops, and we neighbours need to help each other out. Don't we?'

'I don't think—'

'Let me ring you and then you'll have my number.' Iris rummaged in her bag and fished out a notebook. 'I'll write it down because I'll never remember it. Call it old age.' She laughed, pen poised.

Feeling she had no choice, Celia recited her mobile number.

Iris rang the number and the phone obediently rang on Celia's worktop.

'There. Now we can ring each other any time.'

'We can do some more tomorrow.' Iris stood, and before Celia could protest, she said, 'I'll let myself out. Don't worry. See you tomorrow. Oh, and I'll take these newspapers and put them in the recycling for you.'

She gave a little wave and was gone.

Celia gave a shaky sigh. She told herself that Iris was being kind, and it would be good if all the unpacking was done before Daisy came back in a few days. But somehow she felt...violated. Was that too strong a word? It was as if Iris had barged in and taken away her privacy, handling personal things that Celia would have liked to unpack herself, privately.

She couldn't think of a reason to put Iris off the following day, so earmarked boxes that she knew didn't contain personal things. But in a way, everything was personal. This was her life – packed up in cardboard boxes. A year ago she could never have imagined such a thing.

As if things couldn't get any worse, that afternoon, there was another ring on the doorbell.

Celia took a step back. 'We thought as you can't drive, we'd come to you,' trilled Eleanor. 'We've brought cake, so you don't need to do anything, and we'll make the drinks. You just sit down.'

Celia sensed she was losing control of her life. Everyone was telling her what to do. Her old self would have been the one making all the decisions.

'Right,' said Wanda, once they were all seated. 'Who's for carrot cake?' As she cut slices and passed them round, she added, 'Shop bought, I'm afraid. Just didn't have time to bake today. Just had to fit you in between Pilates and a gardening job this afternoon.' She laughed, turning to Celia.

Celia despised herself for laughing and pretending that Wanda's put-down was a joke.

'How are you managing in this little bungalow after your lovely old house?' asked Anna, skewering a piece of cake with her fork.

'It must be hard, especially so soon after losing Alan,' added Joanne.

Celia swallowed. 'I'm fine.'

'You know we're all here for you if you need anything, don't you?' said Anna, looking around the functional kitchen. 'This'll be a lot less work than managing the upkeep of the other house, and you'll have time for other things,' she added.

'How awful for you to have had to move so quickly like that, though. We all feel for you.'

There was a chorus of agreement with Eleanor's statement. 'You know you can always come to ours, Celia, if you need to get away for a few hours.'

Once more, there were echoes of 'Same here,' and 'Absolutely,' around the table.

'I don't expect you've had a chance to even look at *Mansfield Park*,' said Eleanor, 'so we'll save that for next time.'

'Well, actually—'

'Good idea,' said Wanda. 'We'll wait until you're up to it. By the way, have you all heard about Grizelda? She's been having an affair with her dentist!'

'No!'

'Really? I never would have thought it. She's such a quiet little thing!'

'And her dentist is a woman!' Wanda swelled with importance as she delivered this punchline.

'Goodness me,' said Anna. 'Although sometimes I can't help thinking it wouldn't be such a bad idea.'

This comment was greeted by several sharp intakes of breath. 'Sometimes husbands can be so...difficult, can't they? To be honest, I don't blame her.'

Celia didn't know how she got through the next half-hour without breaking down and screaming at them all to go. But she had reminded herself that she was made of stern stuff, and that these women were her friends and their comments were kindly meant. She willed the tears away and joined in the gossip as best she could, knowing full well that she herself would have been the subject of much book-club chatter.

'Come on Ceel. You've got to change and adapt, you know.'

'I know, Alan. But we could never have imagined this!' she gestured around the kitchen. 'This...bungalow!'

'No, because we lived for the present. We didn't spend our time worrying about the future, but it had to come one day. And now it's here.'

Celia wiped her eyes with her sleeve.

'They came this afternoon, the book club.'

Alan was leaning casually against the mantlepiece.

'Eleanor even said, "How awful for you to have had to move to that bungalow. You know you can always come to ours, Celia, if you need to get away for a few hours. We're always here for you." They just don't see me in the same way anymore, and I was the one that founded the group!'

'You've got to find a way to be more positive about things. Not everything hinges on where you live, you know. Hold your head high and they'll soon forget about where you live. Remind them who you really are. The old Celia hasn't changed just because she's moved. Remind them of the positives of not having an old house to maintain, things like that. If that doesn't work, maybe it's time to find some new friends.'

'I think I'm a bit past that stage.' Celia sniffed. 'We've known them for years. All our children went to school together.'

'It's never too late to make new friends. This could be a new start in lots of ways. Come on, Ceel. This isn't like you. I've never known you to be defeated by anything. Not even...'

'Don't. Don't go there, Alan.'

Celia stood and blew her nose. 'I'm going to walk to the little shop along the road and clear my head. Do you want me to get you anything?'

Alan disappeared, but she could hear his laugh ringing in her ears. What a stupid thing to say. Sometimes Alan seemed so real she forgot he was dead.

Chapter 12

I ris tapped her foot, glancing out of the window towards Dusty Roads. She wondered why Trish and Bob didn't just move in to the bloody thing and be done with it. She'd had her mid-morning coffee and was eager to get on. Iris disliked sitting around and wasting time. She liked to fill every minute of her day with something useful. But sometimes, taking people down a peg or two required patience and waiting, so Iris could do it if she had to. Her plan had to be carried out in a public place, somewhere that neither Bob nor Trish would connect with her.

At last! Bob climbed into Dusty Roads and started the motor. Iris sprang into action, snatching up her bag, and hurrying to the car. She waited at the corner of the drive until she saw the campervan indicate left, and once they had pulled away, she followed. Fortunately, there was only one car between her and Dusty Roads.

Iris relaxed, enjoying the drive. Things were going well with Family Woman, and she had provided her with several bottles of the posh, middle class wine she liked – even though it was much more expensive than the ones Iris had originally chosen. Celia seemed happy for Iris to do her shopping and they had now unpacked most of the boxes and Iris had a comprehensive inventory of Celia's belongings. She had made sure to linger over photos and other items which might be sentimental, and even though she herself had produced tears, Family Woman continued to maintain a granite exterior. She would break her eventually, but Iris needed to work fast, because in a few weeks Celia would be having her plaster off and able to drive again. In the meantime, she had learnt a lot about Family Woman. Maybe now was the time to step things up a gear.

Iris was dragged back to the present as Bob and Trish turned into a pub car park. She followed, parking in the far corner. She watched them climb out of Dusty Roads and head for the entrance, hand in hand. Iris snorted. *For God's sake!*

Giving it five minutes just to make sure, Iris retrieved the can of spray paint from the glove compartment, and, checking that the carpark was empty of customers, scurried over to Dusty Roads. She crept behind the van, out of sight from the pub. There were no cameras – she had already checked.

Shaking the can vigorously, Iris felt a familiar sparkle of adrenaline rush through her body, a sensation that came with the intoxicating sense of destructive power. She knew she was good, having been trained by the best, or at least Zed seemed like the best to her. He didn't just do odd letters under railway bridges, she'd watched him do pictures and illustrations on the sides of buildings and had been amazed at his skill. 'You could be like that Banksy,' she'd whispered to him in awe.

Zed had just expelled a cynical laugh in response. 'Oh yeah? So middle-class!'

He'd shown her how to spray in long, confident sweeps, creating swirls and letters. Iris had been thrilled. So far, she'd only had a few forays on her own, spraying BITCH on Jasmine's front door, and some swirls and shapes on a wall not far from her home. She'd been very proud of her work and was furious when she passed a few days later to find the council scrubbing off her masterpiece.

She'd already decided what to spray and without pausing, she created the words GOLDDIGGER on the side of the van. In a rare moment of impulse, she added a swirl at the end before standing back and admiring her handiwork for a moment. Zed was right, fluorescent pink really popped, and the letters had been joined just as he'd taught her. Zed would be proud of her. She wished she knew how to use the camera on her phone. She could take a photo to show him. Maybe Zed could teach her.

Iris was tempted to stay and watch the effect of her handiwork on Trish and Bob, but resisted. Zed had taught her that the first thing people did on discovering graffiti was to look around for the culprit. And she guessed that, although they seemed self-obsessed, they might recognise her car – especially Bob. So, regretfully, she headed home via Sainsburys to get a little treat for Celia before tackling her next challenge.

'Bob! Oh my God!'

Bob climbed down from the driver's seat and rushed around the front of the RV. Trish stood, hand over her mouth. He followed her gaze and gasped at the message defacing Dusty Roads. GOLDDIGGER. Had someone mistaken their RV for another vehicle? Realising the unlikely existence of another Dusty Roads, tingles of alarm spread thorough his body.

'Why would anyone do this?' Trish wailed. 'It's not even true,' she added as an afterthought. When Bob didn't reply, she took his arms and shook him. 'Bob! You don't believe this, do you?'

'No, of course not!' Bob tried to keep his voice firm.

'I know who did this!' Trish hissed between clenched teeth. 'It's that cow—' Before she could say anymore she was seized with a coughing fit. Bob helped her into the van and waited for her breathing to settle.

'Are you alright?'

'Yes, stop fussing. I didn't have my usual herbal tea this morning, that's all.'

It seemed to Bob that Trish's coughing fits were getting worse, but she angrily refused to go to the doctors believing that they were agents of the state, trying to control the people. Trish's tendency to believe in conspiracy theories had coalesced during Covid, and she had thrown herself into the anti-vaxxer movement with evangelical enthusiasm. When they met, Bob had seen this as a loveable characteristic that made Trish eccentric and different, but now he was becoming increasingly concerned about her intransigence and refusal to get help. At least he didn't have to worry about Trish's erratic driving, though. There had been no discussion about who would drive since the motorway incident, when her licence had been suspended.

'It's that Iris, from Eagle Court. I just know it!' Trish brought Bob back to the immediate issue.

'Oh, come on, Trish. Can you imagine someone like Iris wielding a spray can? This looks like it's been done by someone who knows what they're doing! No, I don't believe it.'

'Don't you get it, Bob? It's someone who knows us. It's aimed at me.' Trish's laid-back attitude had disappeared.

The silence was heavy on the drive home. Bob now had two things to sort out. The gatepost and restoring Dusty Roads to her former glory. As they drew up to the traffic lights before Eagle Court, he glanced over and was alarmed to see that Trish, her head back against the headrest, eyes closed, was deathly pale.

'Trish? Are you okay?'

She came to with a start. 'It's just been a shock, that's all. I'm fine, honest.'

She leant on his arm as they made their way into the bungalow. 'Just make me some of that herbal tea, and I'll be ready for anything.' She gave him a lascivious wink.

Chapter 13

Iris was struggling to replicate Celia's large and loopy writing. Fortunately she only needed to master the art of capital letters as Celia always did her crosswords in capitals, but they were still scrawly. Iris imagined that someone with her level of education would have had better handwriting. She was proud of her own, neat and round script. The teachers at school had often complimented her on it. Studying the crosswords in Celia's old newspapers, Iris spent several hours between *Cooking with the Stars* and *The Chase*, practising. She worked hard and now she had something that could pass as Celia's scrawl. Massaging her aching wrists as she sipped her tea, Iris was pleased with her efforts, although something still didn't look quite right. One trick, she discovered, was to write quickly and confidently like Celia did, much like the graffiti technique. Cutting letters from magazines and newspapers was much easier, and so much more fun, but it wouldn't work for this plan.

Iris looked at her watch. 5.30. she would have to forego the rest of *The Chase*. She needed Zed's opinion before she hijacked Family Woman's paper tomorrow morning.

As they sipped their Burgers for U coffees, Zed compared Iris's imitation with Celia's own crossword entries. 'I'm not really into handwriting. It's a bit old-school,' he muttered.

'Everyone should be able to write properly,' Iris said, primly. 'Maybe one day, we'll all have to get back to it, if all this,' she indicated the laptop, 'crashes.'

'That won't ever happen,' mumbled Zed, tapping away. 'Everything will always be backed up somewhere. We'll never go back to the dark ages.' He paused. 'Right. I've scanned in both sets of handwriting and downloaded some software to compare them.' He looked furtively around the restaurant before turning the laptop for Iris to see. 'The Os aren't quite as narrow as Celia's, and the Ms aren't quite tall enough.'

'Let me have another go.' Iris wrote rapidly in her notebook. 'Try this.'

'Better.' Zed nodded in approval. 'Just the B to sort. Make it thinner.'

Iris dutifully tried again, this time writing several letters in rapid succession.

As she passed the notebook to Zed, Iris saw him stiffen as one of the 'team members' came up to the table. 'Hiya, Zed. Watcha doin'? Looks like you're a couple of spies trading secrets.' *Clare – your server today*, flicked her long blonde plait over her shoulder and giggled at her own joke.

Zed stood, rapidly gathering his things, and, without speaking, left the restaurant. Clare looked at Iris, eyes raised, a smirk hovering.

Iris stood and summoned her best grammar-school teacher voice. 'I hardly think we would have been so obvious if we were really spies, do you? I'm Zed's aunt, and he was just helping me write a letter.'

'Ri-ight.' Clare sniggered.

As she strode to the car, Iris huffed in annoyance. She hadn't been able to give Zed Family Woman's phone number. Now she would have to find him again, at another Burgers for U branch.

The next morning, Iris was ready for the paper delivery van as it drew up at Celia's door. Gone were the days of paper boys. She wondered what children did now to earn their pocket money. Steal phones and deal drugs, she guessed.

Once the paper was opened at the crossword page, Iris sat, pencil poised. Celia always did the crossword in pencil, rubbing out answers that were wrong. There might be quite a bit of rubbing out today. She looked at 1 across. *Bird seen in a museum*. 3 letters. Iris looked at her green kettle and before she could overthink it, wrote DOG. Next, she looked for something longer and more challenging. Running her finger over the clues she stopped on *Country singer performs album, including nice introductions*. 5 letters. Without giving it a second thought, Iris wrote DOLLY. Maybe this was even the correct answer. After all, Dolly Parton had to be one of the most famous country singers. Time to look at something down. This time Iris's finger came to a halt on *Cancel my order for plant*. 8 letters. Iris frowned for a few moments before taking a deep breath and writing SENDBACK. This crossword lark was a piece of cake! Okay, one more. Iris's finger continued to follow the list of clues until she came to 15 down. *Raise the lid off stew*. 5 letters. Iris used to love a good stew, and she hadn't had one in years. She thought back to school dinners and her mouth watered at the thought. There was only one possible answer. MMMMM. Iris sat back, pleased with her work. She got one of Celia's completed crosswords and compared the two. She could see no difference. Maybe just one more. She scanned the page and noticed *How to leave these squares*. 5 letters. There was only one answer, and she confidently wrote BLANK. Iris chuckled to herself. She had not had as much fun in ages. She could get quite good at this.

It was already 8 o'clock. She needed to get a move on if she was to deliver the paper before Celia got up. She knew that Family Woman never did the crossword until after coffee, but even so, she wanted it to be in place on time.

She padded over to Celia's and quietly placed the folded newspaper on her doorstep. Hesitating, she retrieved it and, standing a few feet away, hurled it at the door. Iris wasn't going to make that mistake again. She froze and waited for a few seconds, holding her breath. When there was no movement, she hurried back to Number 1.

It was Saturday, and she had a busy day ahead. First she needed to pop into Number 3 and commiserate about poor Dusty Roads, and then off to the Homeless Dinners. She rinsed her breakfast things and got ready to go out. When had she last felt this good? Weak, powerless, Iris had been banished and strong Iris was in control. As she passed the wardrobe, it occurred to her that she didn't need different clothes to be strong, she could simply be her real self.

Chapter 14

B ob moved to answer the door.

'Leave it, babe.' Trish cuddled him tight on the settee. But Bob couldn't leave it.

'I've just seen your campervan. What a terrible thing.' Iris's voice was breathy, as if she had been rushing.

'I know. Just some vandals. I'm having it dealt with tomorrow – it'll need sanding back and a complete respray on that side, though.'

'How awful. And what a shocking thing to put!' Iris's eyes welled with tears. 'Who do you think might have done it? Maybe someone who knows you...or Trish?'

'I can't think of anyone who could do something like that.'

'Some kids, I'll bet! Don't you wish you could give them a good hiding, like our parents would have done?'

Before Bob could agree or disagree, Trish's voice interrupted. 'Who is it?'

Bob looked at Iris, willowy but solid on the doorstep. 'Come in. I'm sorry we got off on the wrong foot the other day. Come in and have a drink.'

As they entered the lounge, he saw Trish, arms folded, glaring out of the window. But it was too late to take back the invitation now.

Iris sat down and smiled at Trish. 'I just had to say, how awful for you, that word on your campervan.'

Bob hovered. 'Coffee?'

'Oh for God's sake, Bob. Let's have something stronger than coffee!'

'Coffee would be lovely, thanks, Bob.'

Trish huffed and tightened her arms across her chest.

In the kitchen, Bob could hear Trish coughing. He made her one of her herbal teas. Maybe that would put her in a better mood.

Iris was leaning forward, sitting on the edge of the chair. 'Are you alright, Trish? That sounds bad. I can hear it on your chest. My mother used to cough just like that until eventually I got her to the doctors.' She nodded her thanks as Bob placed a mug of coffee on the table. 'I won't say any more. You don't want to hear about my problems.'

Trish leant back in the chair without answering as Bob handed her the tea.

'So how are you settling in?'

Bob was forced to fill the silence. 'It's still early days.'

'We won't be here much, it's just a base really. We'll be travelling most of the time – going wherever the spirits take us. We're ready for adventure, isn't that right, Big Bear?'

Bob nodded.

'This is our time and we're not ready to vegetate in boring suburbia yet.'

Bob noticed that Iris's lips were pressed into a thin line.

Trish seemed to have perked up since she had drunk her tea. 'Don't you ever want to see what's beyond the horizon? Explore the unknown? Have new experiences, Iris?'

'I can't say I do. I feel very fortunate to have moved into Eagle Court.' Bob noticed the clipped tone and was anxious to change the subject.

'What brought you here, I mean to this development?'

'I looked after my mother for many years until she died. I can't say it was easy, but I always tried to do my best for her. Last year she died, and...I just couldn't stay in that house, with so many special memories.' Iris's voice quivered, and she looked down at her lap for a few moments before taking a breath and lifting her head. 'So I decided to make a new start. And here I am.'

Bob admired her courage. 'Goodness, Iris. That must have been tough. I know a little bit of what you've been through from looking after my first wife.' He felt a shared connection with his new neighbour.

Iris managed a weak smile.

Trish shifted about on the settee, huffing and puffing. 'That's enough of morbid talk. Life is for the living, and when our times up...poof!' she made a releasing gesture with her hands. 'I don't want anyone fussing over me when it's my turn. I'll just hide away and die, like the animals do.'

She turned to Iris. 'Come on, Iris. Haven't you ever wanted to let your hair down and live a bit? You look as if you could do with it!' This was followed by a fit of coughing that made any other conversation impossible.

Bob felt a tinge of sympathy for Iris and admired her restraint in not responding. Instead she turned to Trish. 'You know, I really don't like the sound of that cough. Haven't you been to the doctor?'

'Don't believe in all that state interference.' Trish leaned back on the settee, spreading herself out and getting comfortable. 'My body is my own.' She took another sip of tea. 'Maybe you should take a leaf out of my book and then you wouldn't be so uptight, Iris. Loosen up. Maybe make her some of my tea, Bob.'

Iris drained her mug.

'Actually, I'm off to serve lunch to the homeless. And that's not for the faint-hearted, I can tell you!' Trish turned back to her tea with a snort of disdain. Bob could just make out a muttered, 'Do-gooder!' as Iris stood and turned to him, placing her hand on his arm. 'I hope you get the van sorted, and it doesn't cost too much.'

'I said we should just leave it. It would be fun to see the reactions we get!'

Ignoring Trish once more, Iris stood.

On the doorstep, Bob felt he had to apologise for Trish's rudeness. 'I'm so—'

'Not to worry, Bob. I understand.' Iris gave him a sympathetic and knowing smile.

Bob came to the uncomfortable realisation that Iris actually felt sorry for him. She seemed a nice woman. Ann would definitely have liked her.

He returned to the lounge to find that Trish had fallen asleep. They had been planning their first big trip and part of him was looking forward to it. The idea was to do the North Coast 500 route around northern Scotland. Bob had never been there before. He got the road map out and started planning, jotting down road numbers on a pad. He would memorise it and pretend it was spontaneous once they were on the road. Thankfully, he would be doing all the driving.

He was packing for their departure when Trish appeared in the bedroom.

'Packing so soon, Big Bear? We're not going until tomorrow,' she crooned.

Bob knew he would have to finish the packing later.

Chapter 15

Iris was glad to be back in the church hall, and it took the peeling of many potatoes before her pulse stopped racing and she could think clearly after her visit to Number 3.

There were a few hippy types that came in to lunch, and Iris would bet that if Trish hadn't met Bob that might have been her fate too. She'd have been glad enough of a hot meal if she was on the streets. She wouldn't have the luxury of calling Iris a do-gooder. Iris smiled as the phrase 'bite the hand that feeds you,' came to mind.

'You're quiet today, lovey.' Wendy nudged her arm as she put the finishing touches to the Lancashire hotpots. Wendy had spent years as a school cook and knew how to make a good stew. 'I enjoy having people to cook for,' she'd say. 'Now that there's only me at home. And I'm used to feeding the five thousand.'

'Everything alright?'

Iris realised she needed to come up with an answer. 'Oh, it's nothing, Wendy. Nothing that won't sort itself out.'

'Well, you know what they say about a problem shared.'

Iris couldn't imagine what Wendy would say about the way she was solving her problem. Wendy was the meek sort that would just learn to live with the likes of Celia, Trish, and Tina. Not like herself. She was made of stronger stuff, and no one got to push Iris Walker around – not these days.

While waiting for the familiar faces to appear, Iris noticed a gallery of children's pictures mounted on the hall walls. 'The children have been thinking about families and how important they are,' said the vicar, appearing beside her. 'Of course, families can come in many forms these days,' he added with a magnanimous gesture. Iris wondered about the poor little sods who were stuck with a family like hers. A family they couldn't wait to escape.

'Time to let the hordes in!' said Stan, looking at his watch. 'I told the school not to use Blu-Tack on my walls! I'll be doing a complete repaint to get rid of those grease marks!' he muttered.

'Maybe some of the children could come and give you a hand. Life skills and all that...' The vicar turned away to open the doors before Stan could vent his thoughts on such an idea.

The street produced the usual characters, and Iris was soon in the swing of constant motion and banter.

'How's my best girl today?'

Iris felt herself blush as Maurice winked at her.

'Here you go, Maurice. Have some of Wendy's best.' She put a generous portion on his plate.

'Thank you, doll.' Maurice winked again before moving on.

George's blue eyes didn't leave her face as she served him. 'Alright, George?'

'Are *you* alright, Iris? That's more to the question.'

Iris looked down, scooping up the next portion, and was relieved when he had moved on. He gave her the jitters.

Once they had finished serving, Iris headed to sit beside Mabel, but was deftly intercepted by George.

'Come and have a chat with me, Iris.'

As they sat, she noticed his eyes were like deep, blue pools. Pools that could suck you in and where you could lose yourself. Iris hurriedly shifted her gaze to the floor.

'So, what's your story, George?' This was one of Iris's opening gambits in any of her conversations with the homeless. Usually accompanied by a tilt of the head and a sympathetic smile. This time, she kept her gaze firmly fixed at a point beyond George's left shoulder.

He sighed. 'The usual, I guess. Good job. Divorce. Revengeful ex-wife, blah-blah. But you know all about revenge, don't you, Iris?'

The question was slipped in so casually that it took Iris's breath away.

She turned to him. 'What?'

'You know all about revenge. Wanting to get your own back on people,' he clarified.

'I don't know what you—'

'Come on. Don't get all holier-than-thou with me. I can see the truth. I can see it in the way you stand, in your eyes, and in the way you hate Tina behind all that false compliance. Not that I blame you for that,' he added.

Iris felt as if she had fallen from a great height. The breath had been knocked out of her. She put her hands on her knees as if to support her body before turning to George. 'So why haven't you...?'

'Taken revenge on those who've reduced me to this?' he indicated himself with a sweep of his arm. 'Good question. For a start I can't do much with no resources.' He gave a wry smile. 'But that's no excuse. There's always something you can do. But I've chosen to take responsibility for the things I've done, and I've done some bad things. I've chosen this life. I let a lot of people down, people who deserved better. Most of all, I let my family – my children – down. I lost my job. And now I'm paying the price.'

'But...'

He glanced at the pictures on the wall, moving to look at one of them. 'See this?' Iris glanced reluctantly at an arrangement of several children, with one adult in the middle. Underneath was written in a childish hand, *My class is my family.* 'This brings tears to my eyes. It's not how things should be. I wonder what my children would draw. I'm guessing I wouldn't figure in the picture at all.' George wiped his eyes with the back of his hand. 'I have a friend who lets me use his house every other weekend to see the kids. They and their mother don't know about all this.' He gestured around the room. 'And I'm lucky. I get to have a shower and a comfy bed for a few nights.'

'But...' Iris, irritated by the distraction of the picture and talk of George's children, was anxious to get back to the subject of revenge.

As if reading her mind, George continued. 'I've gone off the point. Let me tell you about revenge. My father was a bully. He was violent to us and to my mother. I hated him. I plotted various ways to kill him. To make him suffer...'

Iris was gripped. She could understand this.

'So one day I killed him. We were out on the farm, and I set the bull on him. I watched him suffer, just as I'd imagined all those years.'

Iris leaned forward, her attention fixed on George. 'And?'

'I thought I'd feel wonderful. It was what I'd always dreamed of. The thing is, though, the euphoria wore off very quickly. And all these years, no matter how much I hated him, all I've been left with is guilt.' He covered his eyes with his hand, spreading his finger and thumb across his forehead. 'That's why I'm living this life. It's a kind of penance, I guess.'

He turned to Iris. 'So I know it gets you nowhere in the end, even though it makes you feel great for a while. I did spiteful little things to other people, but when the high wears off, you have to do more things. Maybe more extreme.' He took a sip of his cold tea. 'Know what I think? I think it's like a drug, an addiction that eats you from the inside.'

The spell was broken.

Iris started collecting plates and cutlery, avoiding his gaze. 'Very interesting, George, but I need to get on. Nice chatting to you.'

Clenching her fists under the soapy water, Iris was annoyed that she had allowed herself to be sucked in by George. He wasn't her. He was too weak. Iris knew that guilt was something she'd never experience. She knew it with an absolute certainty. Her mood brightened at the thought of Family Woman and the thought that she would have already opened her newspaper to the crossword page.

Chapter 16

I ris searched all three Burgers for U in and around the town before she found Zed.

'Wassup, bro,' he said without looking up from his game.

'I'm not your bro.' Iris sat beside him, leaning over to see what he was doing. 'In fact, I'm your aunty.'

She smiled. That got his attention.

'You what?'

'That's what I told – Clare – was it? You know from the other place? Thought it would sound plausible,' she added.

'Yeah, well, I suppose.' Zed didn't seem enamoured by the idea.

Iris slid the piece of paper on which she had written Celia's phone number along the table. Zed placed his hand over it and slipped it into his pocket. 'Under the table would have been better,' he whispered, glancing around the restaurant, now busy with weekend families.

Iris frowned. They would all be too busy eating to notice a tall, older woman, and an equally tall youth sporting a faded T-shirt, hunched over a lap-top. No one took any notice of anybody in places like this. They were all too busy storing up problems for the future with all that processed food.

'So what did you have in mind?'

Iris brought her attention back to Zed. 'What?'

'About the phone!' There was a hint of impatience in his tone. 'I can't wait to get started. This is going to be great fun!'

Iris leant forward, speaking in a half whisper. 'I need you to send some fake messages – texts.'

Zed's face fell. '*Texts?* Who does those these days?'

'I do – and people like me,' Iris replied in a stern voice.

'Okay, sorry – sorry.' Zed drummed his fingers on the table. 'Can you send some texts from somebody called Alan?'

'No problem. Who's this Alan?'

'Her dead husband.'

Zed leant back in his chair and looked at Iris in admiration. 'Wow Iris! This is in another league. Just...Wow.'

'Can you do it or not?' Iris was enjoying Zed's admiration, although she was careful not to let it show.

'Yeah. I can find him in her Contacts, assuming she's not deleted him.'

'No, she won't have,' Iris said with conviction.

'So what should I say? *Hi from graveland?*' He sniggered.

'No, just message as if he was still alive. Say things like...' Iris thought for a moment. '*Don't forget we're...*' what would people like Celia and Alan be doing? '*Don't forget we're having Sunday lunch with Daisy and family on Sunday.* And maybe another a few days later – *Staying at the golf club for lunch.*' Iris had noticed a set of golf clubs at Celia's and had seen a photo of Alan on the golf course.

'What about emojis?'

'Emojis?'

Zed sighed. 'You know, those little pictures...faces and things. Wait.' He opened his phone and showed Iris a page of something called WhatsApp. 'See? Like this.'

Iris had seen them before on TV. Lots of dramas showed phone messages now. She hadn't known they had a name. Somehow, it didn't seem the kind of thing that Family Woman would use, so likely not her husband, either. She would have to take a gamble.

'No. No emojis. I don't think they're those kind of people.'

Zed rolled his eyes.

'Can you do it or not?' Iris could feel her patience wearing thin.

'Consider it done. Give me a day or two to hack in, and then it's all systems go.'

The table vibrated as Zed's leg bounced in excitement. He tapped frantically on the keyboard.

Glancing idly around, Iris froze as she saw Daisy and her brood come in. She hated it when things didn't go to plan, and this scenario had certainly not been planned for.

Iris looked on helplessly, tamping down her panic, as Daisy ordered in a brisk voice; a voice that was used to being obeying by everyone except her children it seemed, who shouted over her with conflicting orders.

'Are you sure you want to have donuts, Lucy? You know they make you hyperactive.'

The server leant on one hip, studying her nails.

When Lucy indicated with a glare that yes, she was sure, Daisy sighed and said, 'Well on your head be it.'

Lucy, grinning, obviously didn't care.

Eventually, their complex order completed, the family collected their trays and headed to the other side of the restaurant.

Iris for once, thankful for Zed's paranoid tendencies, was glad they were tucked away in a corner, and was relieved that the noisy family had retreated to the far side of the restaurant. Even so, Iris moved her chair so that she was at right-angles to Zed and turned her collar up.

'What? What you doin'?'

Zed shrank away from her, moving the laptop and pressing himself against the wall.

Iris leaned over and whispered, 'See that family over there?'

'Yeah.'

'That's Daisy, Famil—Celia's daughter and her awful children.'

Zed gave a covert glance. 'You know she'll be on Facebook don't you? She's just the type. Or Insta. Perfect family and all that. Want me to check her out?'

'No, not yet. Just stick to Celia for now.'

'Here.' Iris slipped a number of ten-pound notes across the table. 'I'm going to try and slip out through the back door.'

'I don't think they'd notice if you walked right past them.' Zed gave a rare grin.

Iris could hear the row without turning her head. Seb shouting at his mother, her shouting back and the youngest one bawling its head off. But, halfway to the door, Iris's worst fears were realised.

'Hey, it's that weird woman from next door to Gran. The one who can't drive properly.' Seb's still unbroken voice carried clearly across the crowded restaurant.

Iris stood, feeling the eyes of everyone piercing into her back like countless small arrows as a hush fell. A hush she remembered from school when someone did something bad or was in trouble, and the class like a crowd of vultures, waited to enjoy the humiliation of the victim, whether girl or teacher. But now, in this moment, she was the victim. There was no one else.

As the weaker voice of Daisy was heard mildly chiding Seb for his rudeness, Iris recovered the power of movement, and resisting the almost overpowering urge to run to her car, stood tall and rolled her shoulders back. Making herself amble casually over to Daisy and her brood, she plastered a wide grin on her face. 'Hello Daisy. Fancy seeing all of you here!'

The children fell silent in Iris's towering presence.

'Hello, Iris.' Daisy gave an uncertain smile.

'I'm just here with my nephew. He's helping me fill in some online forms.' Iris glanced over her shoulder to the empty space where Zed had been seated. 'He had to get back to work. I'm hopeless at all that online stuff,' she added. Looking at Seb, she said, 'I'm sure you're completely at home, what with Facebook, Instagram and all this social media.'

Seb replied with a scornful hissing sound and returned to his phone.

Iris waited a second, but as no one else spoke she judged she could safely leave. 'Right, I must be off. Have fun!'

Iris walked to the door, refusing to give in to the urge to start running.

Fortunately, her car was parked out of sight of the diners and she sat, willing herself to take deep breaths. She replayed the conversation, knowing that her nerves had let her say far too much. All the wrong things.

You're pathetic, Iris. D'you know that? You'll always be a failure. Look at you. No wonder everyone laughs at you.

She brushed the gathering tears away with her sleeve. This was what happened when things didn't go to plan, when she wasn't in control. She wished she could wring that little sod's neck. But Iris reminded herself that she needed to keep Daisy on side, at least until Family Woman had been dealt with. She leaned back as far as she could in the seat, bracing her feet against the pedals, making her body as stiff as she could. It was the only way to control the boiling anger and humiliation that surged and coiled itself in the very pit of her being.

Time passed, and eventually Iris was able to let her body relax, but her legs remained stiff and cramped. She daren't get

95

out of the car, so she rubbed them until the blood began to flow again and she could drive home.

Chapter 17

'Iris? Have you seen the coffee jar?'

Iris ignored Celia and carried on folding the last of the boxes. She couldn't resist a small smirk. Things were going well and Family Woman was rattled. Maybe it was because of the crossword. Whatever the reason, she had lost some of that unbearable I-know-best attitude. Iris went into the kitchen, where Celia already had their mugs ready. 'Maybe it's slipped behind something.'

As Celia continued to root around in the cupboards, Iris waited a few seconds before going to the fridge to get the milk out. She cried out in surprise. 'What's this doing in here?'

'You need to take more water with it, Celia.' Iris chuckled, handing Celia the milk along with the jar of coffee.

Celia frowned. 'I didn't put it in there. Why would I?'

'Well, never mind. At least we can have our coffee now.'

Morning coffee had become part of their day, but even though she had established a routine, Iris still had to think about keeping it going now that all the boxes were unpacked.

'Are you alright, Celia? That's the second time you've...mislaid something. The other day, you found your keys in the oven. Remember?'

'One of the children will have put them in there as a joke.' Celia munched determinedly on a custard cream.

Iris persisted. 'And what about the other day? You completely forgot you asked me to get those things from Sainsburys.' Iris was pleased with her plan to use a previous shopping list that Family Woman had given her, and had taken care not to crease it, making it look as if it had just been written.

'You don't remember asking me to get those things, do you?' She gazed at Celia with a gentle smile, head on one side.

Celia placed her hands, palms down, on the table and took a deep breath before standing. 'I've got a lot on my mind at the moment. And, yes, as a matter of fact, I *do* remember giving you the list now. And if you don't mind, Iris, I'm meeting some friends for lunch.'

Iris remained seated. In spite of her anger at the patronising tone, she was pleased that Family Woman was riled. 'That's the last of the boxes unpacked. I'll bet you're feeling a bit more at home now, with all your things around you.'

'You make it sound as if I've moved into an old people's home!' Celia snapped. When Iris didn't reply, she sat down on the edge of the chair and took another sip of coffee, replacing the mug on the table.

'I don't think I'll ever be at home here. Not without Alan.'

Iris was taken aback at this sudden moment of weakness and reached over to put her hand on Family Woman's arm. The granite exterior had cracked at last. 'You must miss him so much.'

Uncharacteristic tears welled in Celia's eyes. 'You've no idea,' she said, dabbing her cheeks with a tissue.

Iris resisted the urge to slam her hand down on the table and shout. 'How dare you patronise me, just because I've never been married!' Instead, she took Family Woman's hand. 'I'm so sorry, Celia. I'm always here for you, you know that, don't you?'

'I know, and thank you, Iris. You've been a godsend these last few weeks. It's hard keeping up appearances all the time, pretending that I'm alright in front of the family. But I don't have to bother with you. I can be myself.'

Iris steeled herself to remain calm. She could enjoy her anger at this statement when she got home. For now, it made her all the more determined to make Family Woman pay. She listened, eyes brimming with matching, sympathetic tears, as Celia continued.

'Daisy does her best, but she's so busy. It's almost like I've become a burden to her.'

'What about your other children?'

'Luke's in Australia. He's a professor, you know. And then there's Fred. He's...in between jobs at the moment.'

'It's a shame he hasn't come to give you a hand.'

Celia sat up straight and smoothed her hair. 'His health isn't good. And anyway, once this wretched thing is off, I'll be back to normal.' The iron-clad Family Woman had returned. It was as if the fleeting moment of weakness hadn't happened. She took her hand away and stood up for a second time.

Iris hid her disappointment. The glimpse of vulnerability had been brief, but she knew now that there would be others. 'Of course you will. Right. I'll be off then and leave you to your crossword.' Iris noticed Family Woman stiffen. She stood and put on her coat. 'Got your list ready for this afternoon?'

'This afternoon?'

'It's Monday, Celia. Shopping day.'

Iris strode back to her bungalow, a spring in her step. Sod the fake Iris, locked away in the wardrobe. She didn't need her.

Celia's heart thumped in her chest as she closed the door. What on earth had possessed her to share all that with Iris? She hardly knew the woman! She leaned against the door, trying to forget Iris's blank, slate-grey eyes.

After a few minutes, when she felt calm enough, Celia picked up the phone to message Eleanor about going to the next book-club meeting. Noting the call from Iris from a few days ago, she put the number in her Contacts. It would never hurt to have each other's numbers, she supposed. What she saw when she came back to her home page made her breath catch in her throat and Celia threw the phone down onto the settee as if it had burnt her. Although Alan came to visit her sometimes, he wouldn't be sending texts. She clasped her trembling hands together, willing them to be still. She was imagining things. All these happenings were in her head. When she picked the phone up again, the message would have disappeared. She was sure of it.

Making another, stronger, coffee and swallowing a large mouthful, she activated the screen and slowly turned it towards her. The words were still there, blaring out at her, demanding her attention as everything else fell away. *Alan*. Once more, she hurled the phone away from her and this time it landed on the floor with a dull thud. For the first time in many years Celia didn't know what to do. Strong, capable, dependable, Celia, unflappable in a crisis had disappeared to be replaced by this fearful shell who looked the same but was seeing things, imagining things and generally falling apart. The old Celia – and Alan – would have castigated her. 'Come on, Celia. What's all this nonsense? Get a grip and stop being ridiculous. You're spending too much time moping about. Get out and see Eleanor and the gang. They're your friends in spite of what you imagine, so stop overthinking things.'

Several hours later, after unsuccessfully trying to distract herself with the crossword and lunch, Celia summoned up the courage to look at the message.

Don't forget lunch with Daisy and the gang on Sunday x

She deleted it with shaking hands and poured herself a glass of wine, and when she had finished that she poured another. Fortified by the alcohol, she gingerly picked up the phone again. There was no message. It had all been an illusion.

But, still, the old Celia wouldn't come back, and had deserted her in her hour of need. The new Celia put a cushion over her eyes and wept.

'I'm worried, Alan. Something's happening to me.'

When Alan, leaning casually against the door-frame, didn't reply, Celia continued, 'I'm forgetting where I put things. This morning the coffee was in the fridge and the other day the keys were in the oven. I was so confused in front of Iris. Am I getting dementia or something?'

She continued into the silence. 'Iris is so good, getting the shopping and helping out, but it makes me feel sort of...useless. Talking of which, the other day she bought things that I was sure I hadn't ordered. But then she showed me the list and apparently I'd written it all down. I know they're only little things, but...'

'Come on, Ceel. Don't fret. You've had a lot on your plate. You know what they say about life-changing events and you've had a bereavement and moved house, all within six months. You'll be fine. Have you spoken to Daisy?'

'God, no. She already thinks I'm past it because I'm living in a bungalow. Comes to something when you're patronised by your own children!'

'Come on, Cee. Buck up. Get out and see people. You'll be able to drive soon. Get back to your book club. You'll be fine.'

'Do you know the worst thing? The thing that has frightened me most?'

'Go on. Whatever it is, it can't be that bad.'

Celia had forgotten Alan's dismissive laugh. The way he could make anything into a joke with his endless positivity.

'It's nothing.' Suddenly she wanted him to go but didn't know how to get rid of him. Finishing the wine, she closed her eyes.

Following a restless night when she was constantly haunted by Alan reminding her that she should get back to her old self and where, Celia, back in her old home, searched high and low for her old self before waking breathless and in a sweat, she made a decision.

After many unsuccessful attempts to get a doctor's appointment, she resorted to mentioning her inability to sleep to Daisy.

'It's not surprising, Mum, after what you've been through. I'll get you in this afternoon with Louise. She's brilliant.'

And so Celia found herself talking to Louise. She exuded just the right mixture of professional empathy and competence, and for the first time in weeks Celia felt some of the tension leave her body. She didn't mention any of her memory lapses and hallucinations, though. Especially not the text from Alan.

'I'm going to give you some sleeping tablets, Celia. I think you'll find that if you are sleeping, everything will be easier to manage,' Louise said, glancing at Celia as she typed the prescription.

'Thank you so much.' Celia wondered if Louise had heard the tremor in her voice.

'If you're still struggling, come back. There are plenty of other things we can try.' Louise smiled and stood, indicating the session was at an end.

Heading to the chemist to collect her pills, Celia was convinced that now that she was guaranteed a good night's sleep, everything would resolve itself.

For the first time, she entered Eagle Court with a smile. A good thing the surgery was within walking distance. And another good thing, only a week until this damned plaster came off. Things were looking better already.

Chapter 18

If he was honest with himself, Bob was relieved when they turned Dusty Roads into Eagle Court. The trip had been something of a disaster – from breaking down in the middle of the North York moors where there was no signal, to becoming wedged up against a stone wall in the too-narrow road Trish had insisted they take. Unfazed, she had assured him that this was how adventures should be. Although they had agreed to avoid motorways, sometimes Bob had yearned for the familiarity of the M1. They never made it to Scotland, Trish insisting on many diversions down roads that looked 'interesting'. 'Let's see what's down there.' Then there was that unpleasant confrontation with the farmer in whose field they had camped in for the night. Trish had insisted that they had a right to own the countryside and to camp where they liked. Bob had secretly felt sorry for the farmer.

He had been firm about calling a halt to the trip when Trish had suggested at last that they head for the north of Scotland. She hadn't argued with his decision. The main reason he insisted on returning home was the increasing severity of Trish's alarming coughing fits. Also, there had been days where she had lain in Dusty Roads and had not seemed able to get out of bed.

Today he was enjoying a brief respite at home as Trish had, uncharacteristically, decided to visit her daughter,

Ocean/Sarah. Although Bob found this strange, he didn't question her about it. Her family was Trish's business. It had been made clear early on that her children would not be part of their joint lives. He finished the long-overdue unpacking and was enjoying a quiet drink.

Glancing out of the window, he was surprised to see that Trish had already returned and seemed to be having some sort of animated conversation with Iris. He opened the window a crack, wanting to know what they were talking about without having to get involved. He didn't want a repeat of Iris's last visit.

'I know what you've been up to, you cow. Think you can turn Bob against me? Think you can intimidate us? Well, you've chosen the wrong one there, lady.' Trish had her hand on Dusty Roads' bonnet and was coughing.

'I only came over to see if you'd had a good time!' Bob could hear the annoyance in Iris's voice.

'You should mind your own business!'

'And how long do you think you can keep this from Bob?' Iris pointed at Trish's chest.

'You're bonkers, you interfering old bat!'

'And don't think I don't know about your "tea" – much good it does you.'

Bob's breath caught in his throat at Iris's tone. This was a far cry from the sympathetic, caring Iris he had encountered so far. He sensed an unsettling venom in the way she spoke to Trish.

'What the hell do you know about weed?' Trish muttered, leaning over the bonnet.

'I know more than you think! And maybe I'm not what I seem. You shouldn't judge by appearances.' Iris drew herself up to her full height, towering over Trish, now in the throes of a violent coughing fit.

Bob resisted the urge to run out and bring Trish indoors.

'You nosy old cow. I could report you for stalking! I know it was you who did that.' Trish could hardly breathe now, and doubled over, pointed to the side of Dusty Roads. 'And don't think I haven't noticed what you're doing to that woman next door, pretending to befriend her—'

Iris cut in before Trish could continue. 'It sounds like cancer to me. Think you can heal yourself with your potions? Think again!'

Bob gasped and put his hand on the wall to support himself. Head bowed, he listened.

'Nature has to take its course. I'm not taking any poisons into my body. Anyway, if it's what you say, it's too late now. Things have to take their natural course.'

Bob couldn't stand by any longer. He rushed out of the bungalow. 'Trish! Is this true? Why didn't you tell me?'

Suddenly Trish's knees buckled, and it was all Bob and Iris could do to get her indoors where she collapsed onto the bed.

'Is she okay do you think?' Bob looked at Iris in panic, all unsettling thoughts about his neighbour evaporating.

'She's okay. She's just asleep. I think all that manic ranting and raving has exhausted her,' said Iris.

'I noticed this more and more while we were away. She goes into this kind of sleep state. Often it lasts for several hours.'

'We'll leave her to rest.' Iris steered Bob out of the room, quietly closing the door behind her.

Without comment, Iris made two mugs of tea.

They sat in silence, Bob on the settee and Iris in the armchair.

After a few minutes, Iris leaned over and took his hand. 'I'm here, Bob, if there's anything I can do...'

Bob didn't reply. If Iris was right about Trish's illness, he was about to lose a second wife.

'I can't believe she kept this from you and let things get to this stage!'

Bob turned to Iris, gently removing his hand from hers to pick up the mug of tea. 'I guess she thought she was protecting me. In some ways, I think she didn't want to believe it herself.'

'What are you going to do? Can you get a doctor in?'

'No, she won't want that. I'll just look after her, and as she says, let nature take its course.'

'Bob. You do realise that she will be in a lot of pain – more than she is now. Can you put her through that? Can you cope with that?'

Bob shook his head. 'I don't know. I can't think now. As Trish always says, I'll take one day at a time.'

A sudden wish for Iris to go came from nowhere, and he stood, an unspoken signal for Iris to do the same. 'Thank you Iris. I know Trish wasn't very nice to you. Thank you for being so...gracious with her.'

'Well, you know where I am.' Iris's eyes brimmed with tears as she turned to go.

Iris returned home in an animated state. She knew all about caring for sick people. This was her second time round.

She smirked as she prepared an omelette for her tea. Trish hadn't expected her to know about cannabis. But the time Iris had spent with Zed over the last year or so, it was surprising she hadn't got high herself, the smell of weed that accompanied him everywhere. That had certainly taken the wind out of Trish's sails – and her lungs.

Iris slid the omelette on to a plate and wondered what had made a nice man like Bob marry that awful woman. But, as Iris knew only too well, people did strange things when they were vulnerable after a bereavement. Look at Family Woman. Iris pressed her lips into a thin line as she cut up her food.

Emmerdale seemed to be going through a dull patch and Iris's mind kept flitting away to other places, planning in her head as she'd always done. A new project was exciting. A visit to Zed would be in order to get cannabis for Trish. Maybe ask for something stronger. Iris would get him to find out online whether or how it interacted with other drugs – assuming Trish allowed any. But Iris knew that eventually things would get to a point where Trish wouldn't be strong enough to have a say in anything, and she imagined it might be quite soon.

Iris rang Zed, something she rarely did, knowing he hated talking on the phone. 'Why talk when you can type?' But Iris was not about to go out to a fast-food restaurant at 8 o'clock in the evening. Who knew what undesirables might be hanging around?

'Yo!' Zed sounded uncharacteristically upbeat.

'It's Iris.'

'I know that, Iris. Wassup? You know you're the only person who ever actually rings me to talk, right?'

'It's the texts for the number I gave you.'

'Yep. I sent one.'

'Good.' Iris waited. When no more information was forthcoming, she huffed. 'Well? What did it say?'

'Just something about Daisy and the family coming for lunch...'

Iris could hear frantic tip-tapping. 'Are you in the middle of something?'

'Just about to get to the next level on *Baldur's Gate*. I've been working on this for days.'

Iris made a sound, half tut, half sigh. How could playing a game be considered work in anyone's book?

'Anything else?'

Zed's voice drifted away amid more frantic typing.

Iris sniffed. 'I'll leave you to it. You're obviously *busy*. But I need to meet to talk to you about getting some...' she hesitated. 'I'll see you soon and fill you in on the details.'

'Later.'

Iris needed to calm the adrenalin rushing through her body. She made a soothing hot chocolate, and as a special treat, she added a shot of brandy. Cradling the mug in her hands, she remembered making this for her mother when she was still well enough to hold a mug. She could see her now, a discontented frown on her face. 'This is far too strong, Iris.'

'I'll make you another, Mum.'

'No, it's alright. You've made it now. I'll make do.' She pictured her mother wrinkling her nose in disgust as she drank.

Later, Iris would double her tablets in a small revenge.

Eventually, Iris had been in total control as her mother lost the power of speech and nearly all movement. Thinking about it now, she could have done more. Not to make her life better – she didn't deserve that – but to make things worse. She'd only had a few months to make her mother pay for a lifetime of misery. It hadn't felt enough. Whatever small things she did, it was never enough to satisfy the insatiable hunger of the anger and hatred that had grown inside her. Maybe if she'd been less of a coward and made her mother suffer more, she wouldn't be doing this now. But her mother had still held a strange power over Iris, even when she was incapacitated. It was almost as if when she tried anything, her real mother would burst out of the shell in the bed and catch her in the act, punishing her for months by stopping her allowance, even though she was a grown woman, or locking the doors and hiding the keys so that Iris couldn't leave the house. Maybe if she'd had more courage to make her mother really pay – to enjoy the suffering in her eyes, it would have been enough and Iris could have got it out of her system. Maybe she could have got on with life. It hadn't worked for George though, had it? Iris came back to the same thought as she always did when she thought about George – he was different – hampered by guilt, a weakness that Iris knew she would never have. But whatever the reason, and regardless of what or what hadn't happened in the past, Iris couldn't ignore the growing anger she felt towards Family Woman, Daisy, and Trish.

On the front step, the following morning, Celia saw Iris getting out of her car.

'Hello Celia, how are you doing? Not long 'til that thing comes off, hey?'

Iris locked her car and came over to Celia. 'When is it?'

'Next Thursday. I can't wait to get back to driving again and normality.'

Iris made a fuss of looking for her door key in the large canvas bag she always used. 'So how are you getting there? I expect Daisy's taking you.'

Celia was tempted to lie and say that Daisy was taking her, but the deception would be too complicated as Iris missed nothing. She resigned herself to the inevitable. 'No I'm getting a taxi. I'll be fine,' she added hurriedly.

'You'll do no such thing! What time's the appointment?'

'10.30.'

'Lovely. We can have a coffee after or maybe lunch in the hospital canteen.' Iris was animated. 'Make a day of it.'

Celia shuddered, but was comforted by the thought that once her plaster was off, Iris would no longer have an excuse to do things for her. Even though she appreciated her kindness, Celia was looking forward to having her home back to herself. Not being reliant on someone she still didn't feel she knew, even after all the hours she and Iris had spent together. But there was still that underlying unease that in some way she was in Iris's debt, which was why she accepted her lift to the hospital. Celia hoped that was the last time she would require any help from her neighbour. Although, when she thought about it, when had she ever asked for Iris's help...with anything? From now on. A short but polite 'No thank you.' would be in order.

As Iris loped away, Celia went back indoors. She sat and pondered on the truly terrifying incident that had happened a few days ago. The thing that she'd been about to share with Alan. The thing she hadn't shared with Louise. Thinking about it rationally, Celia could see now that it must have been some kind of hallucination or memory lapse brought on by lack of sleep. All that would stop now. But when she remembered it, Celia still felt prickles of fear run up her back as she relived the moment she'd opened the paper to do the crossword and saw she had already filled in some of the clues. She'd folded the paper shut and then opened it again, but there was no doubt that the clues had been filled in with her handwriting. But what made things worse was that the answers were all complete nonsense, except for one, which might have been right. She'd remembered standing and staring out of the window, willing normality to reassure her, but all she saw was the sterile green rectangle reminding her that everything that anchored her to reality was gone. Was she going mad? What was happening? Returning to the paper, she had rubbed out the incorrect clues, leaving just one – BLANK. Forcing herself to remain calm, she completed most of the puzzle by lunchtime and had almost convinced herself by then that the whole thing had been some sort of dream.

Even so, every morning since, Celia had scooped the paper up, heart pounding as she fumbled her way to the crossword page, heaving a sigh of relief when she saw the crossword, pristine and untouched.

Chapter 19

I ris was enjoying her tuna sandwich. She loved the hospital cafe and had often visited over the years to watch the comings and goings. Tearful families sobbing into tea and biscuits waiting for news of loved ones. The faces of those waiting for appointments that they knew would bring bad news. Most were at some crisis in their lives. Many times she had sat at this very table with her mother, after or before endless appointments. But even then, she'd enjoyed a chance to be out of the house and glad to have a reason to be there.

Over the last few years of her life, her mother had become increasingly reluctant to go anywhere. Eventually, apart from her sessions at the day care centre and hospital appointments, she stopped leaving the house. And when the daycare manager had said that she didn't think it was a suitable option for her mother any longer, they had both been at home, their days timetabled by meals and TV programmes. Her stand about The Homeless Dinners on a Saturday had been one small victory for Iris, and apart from hospital appointments became her only time away from the toxic environment at home.

Today was so different and Iris was enjoying Family Woman's discomfort. Her covert glances around the reception area told Iris that Celia was embarrassed to be seen in the hospital cafe with her. Iris guessed she was dreading seeing anyone she knew and despised her for it. So she would spin things out as long as possible, relishing the control and savouring the hospital shortbread. Celia couldn't leave until Iris was ready, even though she'd refused the shortbread.

'Fancy seeing you here!' Stella appeared, leaning heavily on her walking frame.

Iris raised a laugh at the familiar joke. Stella had said that every time she had met Iris and her mother at the hospital. For a moment, it seemed as if she had fallen back into her old life again.

'So sorry about your mum, Iris. It was a happy release in the end, I suppose.'

Iris's eyes glistened with tears.

Stella turned to Celia. 'She is such a saint, this one.' She nodded her head towards Iris. 'What I wouldn't give for a daughter like her.'

'Stella, this is my friend, Celia. She lives next door to me in Eagle Court.'

'Well, you got a good one there.' Stella patted Celia's shoulder with a large, heavy hand. Iris had to smother a smile at Celia's glassy eyed attempt not to flinch.

'So glad you're making new friends. It's time you got out and about a bit, Iris.'

Iris nudged Stella's arm and gestured across the cafe. 'Looks like you're needed, Stella.'

Stella turned and waved at a small man seated at a tabled loaded with cakes and sandwiches. 'That'll be us done for the day when we've polished that lot off. Save cooking tonight.' She looked at Celia. 'I'll love you and leave you. Take care, Iris.'

Iris and Celia watched in silence as Stella made her way across the cafe, scattering chairs and knocking into people on her way. 'Disabled person coming through!'

114

Iris wished she could bottle the look on Family Woman's face and the rigid way she held her body as if it might shatter at the smallest movement. However, much as she was enjoying herself, she knew she couldn't push things too far, and she didn't want to do anything to damage their 'friendship'. Iris had wondered whether Celia would say anything about the crossword or the text from Alan and was disappointed when neither subject came up. She was obviously still not enough of a confidante for Celia to share her worries. But looking on the bright side, Family Woman obviously didn't suspect her, otherwise she would have said something. And she would always have the last fifteen minutes to re-live and savour.

Iris brushed the crumbs from the table into her cupped hand and tipped them on to the plate. 'I suppose we'd better get you home. There'll be no stopping you now!'

Celia was already heading for the door.

Iris timed her watering of the tubs to chat to Daisy as she arrived for a late-afternoon visit to her mother. Iris had gleaned information about Daisy's visit from Celia that morning. She felt very proud of herself for managing her anger over the Burgers for U incident and focussing on the present. She reminded herself that there was plenty of time for Daisy and her evil offspring, but for now, she had to play the long game.

'Sorry to bother you.' Iris put down the watering can and walked over as Daisy was locking the car, relieved to see that she was on her own and not accompanied by her dreadful children, especially the older boy, Seb. That would have made her next move very difficult.

'Hello Iris. Mum has told me how you've been helping her with the unpacking. Thank you so much. And for taking her to the hospital today. It's hard for me to find time, what with work, children...and everything.'

Even though she conjured up an understanding expression. Iris began to despise Daisy even more than Celia. This was Family Woman times ten. She had given up everything to look after her parents, especially her mother. She had sacrificed everything this Daisy blithely took for granted. Career, family, love, independence – the list was endless. And now Daisy was glad that somebody like her, like Iris, was there so she didn't have to be. Somebody who didn't have the life she had. Hiding all of this in her head, Iris smiled. 'It costs nothing to be a good neighbour, does it?'

She stepped closer to Daisy. 'While I've got you on your own, between you and me, I'm a bit worried about your mum. I hope you don't mind me saying, but have you noticed she's getting a bit forgetful?' At Daisy's concerned face, Iris hastily added. 'Nothing major, just little things like forgetting what she's asked me to get her at the shops, and, if I'm honest, getting a bit tetchy until I show her the note she wrote. I always make sure I keep a note of everything now. And...I really didn't want to mention this, but the other day she got upset about the crossword. The answers were all nonsense, apparently. I wouldn't know. They were definitely in her handwriting, though. And if I didn't know better, I would almost think she was accusing me of writing them in. I feel a bit...you know, as if I have to be careful and make a note of everything.'

Daisy gasped, pulling her hands through her hair. 'I had no idea. Oh, Iris, I'm so sorry.'

Iris waited as Daisy got her head around this news. 'Look, I know it's a big ask, but could you do me a favour? Just keep an eye on her?'

'Of course. I usually pop in for coffee, anyway.'

'If you could make a note of these "incidents" that would be great.'

'Yes, I could do that.' Iris hesitated. 'What would your mother think?'

'I think it would be best to keep it between us for now, don't you?'

Before Iris could answer, Celia appeared in the doorway. 'What are you two chatting about?'

'Nothing, Mum,' Daisy answered with false cheer. 'Just admiring Iris's tubs. She says you've been a great help in getting them looking like this.'

Celia gave Iris a puzzled glance.

Iris inwardly skipped for joy at this unexpected cue from Daisy. 'Yes, they wouldn't be looking like this without your help, Celia. All the watering you've done and making sure they look ship-shape.'

As far as Iris knew, Celia had never repeated the initial watering foray, but she was never one to miss an opportunity.

Celia's mouth formed a puzzled 'o' before she uttered, 'But I...'

'Come on, Mum. Let's get the kettle on.' Daisy put her arm around her mother and ushered her into the bungalow, giving Iris a knowing glance over her shoulder as they went.

Iris noted that Celia seemed distracted as if her mind was elsewhere. She hugged herself in glee as she returned to the containers.

Celia went to put the kettle on and noticed, with alarm, a tremor in her hand and felt a now familiar tingle of fear run up her spine.

'Let me do that, Mum,' Daisy said and gently led Celia to a chair.

'What is it? What's the matter?'

Celia couldn't think. She was paralysed by panic. Somehow, she couldn't get her mind to work. It was all too much. She didn't want to tell Daisy what had been happening, she just couldn't. She wondered what Iris and Daisy had been talking about outside and was worried about the false brightness they turned on when she'd gone out. It was the way you acted in front of a child, or an elderly, infirm person. Someone who wasn't in control of their own life. She felt as if she was in some kind of nightmare and could only pray she'd wake up soon.

When she got back from hospital, Celia had never been so glad to be in her new home. She had shaken off her jacket, enjoying the use of both arms. Iris was trying to help, but somehow, her presence was becoming oppressive. It was hard to put her finger on exactly why or how. And that dreadful Stella person had just about been the last straw. But things would change now that she was independent. Everything would be different. The pills had done their stuff, and she was no longer tormented by Alan or anyone else. Feeling a bit groggy in the mornings was a small price to pay. Celia sensed something still wasn't right. What had Iris and Daisy been talking about that they couldn't say in front of her?

'Mum?'

Daisy was waiting for an answer. A note of irritation tinged with fear in her voice.

Celia thought hard for something convincing to say. 'I think the move and everything... Maybe it's all been a bit much,' she finished lamely.

'Oh Mum. I should have taken more time off and helped you.' Daisy pulled her fingers through her hair in a single, rapid movement. 'What about the sleeping pills Louise prescribed? Are they helping?'

'Yes...yes they are.' Celia sipped her tea, her mind empty of any more words to say.

'I know!' Daisy leaned forward and took Celia's hands. 'We're off on holiday to Corfu next week, and you're coming with us. A break will do you good. The schools break up for the summer on Friday and we're flying on Saturday.'

Before Celia could object, Daisy said, 'Right, that's that settled then. And now your arm's out of plaster, you'll be able to join in with everything. There'll be plenty of sailing. Remember how you and Dad used to love sailing in Salcombe and Dartmouth when we went on holiday as kids?'

Celia felt her face crease into a smile at those memories, thrilled that Daisy hadn't forgotten.

Daisy gulped down her tea. 'Right. Things to do, places to be. You look after yourself, Mum. And if you need anything, ring me. Or you've always got Iris next door. She's a godsend.'

Celia wasn't sure whether Daisy saw Iris as a godsend for Celia or for herself. The latter, she suspected.

When Daisy had left, already busy on her phone rearranging travel arrangements, Celia sat at the kitchen table and looked at her familiar old mug. *Best Mum!* – a Mother's Day present from the children when they were small – thoughtfully purchased by Alan. She rested her chin on her hand, elbows on the table. When had she lost control? When had others started making decisions for her? When had she lost the ability to say no?

Since she had moved into Eagle Court.

The answer was as clear as day. Sighing, she reflected that, although the idea of a holiday with Daisy and the family made her heart sink, it might do her good to get away. To regroup and come back and pick up her life. Lots of new things started in September and she could throw herself into them. She was sure things would improve then. In a more positive frame of mind, she set about packing and planned a trip to the shops for some new summer clothes.

Just as she had finished sorting things to take, looking forward to sun and the sea in spite of her misgivings, Celia's phone pinged with a text. Her heart beating, she told herself not to be ridiculous; it was probably Eleanor who had become quite solicitous lately. She was looking forward to telling her about the holiday. A look-what-my-lovey-family-are-doing-for-me phone call.

She pressed the text icon and once more, the world stopped. But this time, she didn't throw the phone away in horror. Hand over her mouth, she read:

Won't be home for lunch, staying at the golf club x

Her first reaction was to delete Alan from her Contacts. This was all too much. One text – she could imagine that hadn't really happened. But two?

Something stopped her. She couldn't delete Alan, it wouldn't seem right. Was someone else pretending to be him? Why would anyone do that? As her mind tried to make sense of it all, Celia couldn't string any coherent thoughts together.

She was losing her mind, in spite of the pills. The move and losing Alan had triggered some sort of dementia – there was no other explanation.

No holiday, however kindly meant, could change the fact that a bleak future lay ahead.

Chapter 20

I ris had never been abroad. She'd never even really had a holiday – not as an adult. When she was a child, there had been trips to the seaside where they had stayed in a military style B&B. She remembered many a rainy day cowering in seaside shelters eating soggy fish and chips, her mother berating her father as if the rain was his fault. They were always back at the B&B on the dot of six, the time they were allowed to return. Iris was always glad when they got home. She couldn't imagine a holiday where the sun always shone and where you knew the next day would be hot. It occurred to her that she had enough money to go to those places if she wanted.

Family Woman's holiday had been an unexpected interruption to Iris's plan, just when everything had been going so well! Although she would probably have her hands full looking after Trish and becoming indispensable at Number 3.

She imagined Celia and Daisy on their idyllic holiday in Corfu – her mother had always called it 'Corphew' – where everything was picture-perfect. However, Iris knew enough to imagine the tensions – that awful boy, Seb, would be enough to spoil any holiday. She made a note in her head to get Zed to look Daisy up on Facebook – she would bet anything the pictures wouldn't tell the full story. Maybe she should tell him not to send any more texts while Celia was on holiday, just in case she showed them to Daisy as they would be together a lot of the time, and in a different environment they might grow closer. Apparently these things happened on holiday. Maybe let Family Woman go for now.

That night Iris had dreamed of lying on a golden beach in the sun and being jumped on by a crowd of rowdy children who threw sand at her. Maybe none of these things were all they were cracked up to be. She put all thoughts of a foreign holiday to the back of her mind. She had more important things to attend to.

Retrieving the pile of magazines she had bought from a charity shop, Iris spread them out on the table, alongside glue and scissors. She thought for a few minutes about the recipient of her art work. What would they appreciate? Grabbing a copy of *Country Life*, she tore out a few pages consisting of countryside and horses. Yes, a rural theme would do it.

It took an hour or so to draw out all the letters, before Iris, back aching from stooping over the table, got up, stretched, and put the kettle on for coffee.

Settling herself in front of the TV she enjoyed the rest of *Homes Under the Hammer*, tutting at some of the rash purchases people made.

As the titles came up, Iris was ready to continue. She'd already bought a pair of sharp nail scissors which she knew would be perfect. Each letter was cut out with care and then placed on the sheet of white paper, ready for pasting. Cutting and pasting was so restful. Iris thought it should be recommended as therapy for all those people who complained of depression – even though most of the time it was all made up. Just an excuse not to work.

By lunchtime, all the letters had been glued into place and Iris stood back to admire her handiwork. She wondered if all artists were always as pleased with their work.

Leaving the letter to dry, she made lunch. Pouring half a tin of tomato soup into a bowl, she put the rest in the fridge for tomorrow. Taking a slice of bread, she waited for the soup to heat in the microwave while turning on for *Loose Women*. Iris loathed those women with their know-all attitudes, platitudes, and perfect makeup. The fake Iris had been based on a combination of these women and look where that had got her! She gave an angry thought towards fake Iris, hanging in the wardrobe. Although she enjoyed hating them, Iris never missed an episode if she could help it.

Once the lunch things had been washed and dried, Iris carefully folded the letter and placed it in a brown envelope. From the front window she saw that Dusty Roads was missing. Iris doubted whether Trish would be going out for many more lunches. No time like the present. Family Woman was away, so it was the perfect opportunity.

Striding across to Number 3, Iris slid the brown envelope through the letterbox before heading back to Number 1 to water her planters at the front.

Likely as not, they would be back soon and Iris was tempted to stay and listen for the drama to unfold. However, with Zed's warning ringing in her ears, she set off for a few hours at the garden centre. She deserved a large slice of cake after her morning's work.

Iris stretched the time out until 4 o'clock before she gave into the urge to get home and see what was happening. Dusty Roads was in its place and all was quiet at Number 3. Iris went indoors and opened the front window a crack, hoping to hear something. Wails, sobs, or maybe a row. But all she could hear was the muffled sound of the traffic on the road. Maybe they hadn't noticed the brown envelope on the mat.

This thought tormented Iris all night as she tossed and turned. What if all her work had been in vain? The brown envelope trodden on and unnoticed.

The next morning, Iris saw Bob getting ready to climb into Dusty Roads and walked over as casually as she could. She had to know.

'Morning Bob. Everything okay? How's Trish?'

Bob's faced clouded with a worried frown as he moved closer. 'To be honest, Iris, not good.'

'Oh?' After a pause, she prompted him. 'You can tell me, Bob.'

'Remember the graffiti on Dusty?'

Iris nodded. 'Terrible, I know. So upsetting!'

Bob swallowed before looking up at Iris. 'An anonymous letter came through the door while we were out yesterday. You didn't see anybody in the Court, did you?'

'I'm so sorry, Bob. I was out most of the day myself.' Iris paused. 'What did it say, if you don't mind me asking?'

'Nasty stuff. Very nasty. I won't repeat it to you. Trish is very upset. In the end, I crushed one of my sleeping tablets in her tea to get her to rest. I didn't know what else to do! I'm just popping out now to get a few things before she wakes.'

Iris filled her eyes with tears. 'Oh Bob! I'm so sorry. You don't need this, what with Trish's health like it is...' She trailed off. 'Look, why don't you let me get the shopping? I'm going out, anyway. You stay with Trish.'

Bob looked uncertain for a moment before relief flooded his face. 'That's kind of you, Iris. Would you mind? Here's the list.'

'Not a problem. I'm off now so I'll see you soon.' Iris gave a wave and returned to Number 3, where she did a little lop-sided jig in the hall. All her worries had been for nothing. The arrow had struck home.

Bob returned indoors to find Trish leaning against the bed-room door post.

'Whatever you put in my tea, it was something else, Big Bear. I loved it. Clean out for hours with no dreams.' She yawned lazily.

'I'm glad you're feeling better. And it's a secret.' Bob tapped the side of his nose and winked. 'Fancy some toast?' He wondered if she'd forgotten all about the letter and dreaded her remembering.

She sat at the kitchen table, chin in her hand. 'I know who it was.'

Bob turned from the toaster. 'Who what was?'

'It was that woman from Number 1.'

'Oh, come on Trish! Iris wouldn't do a thing like that. And she certainly couldn't have done the graffiti.'

'Maybe she got somebody to do it for her. And anonymous letters? It's such an old woman thing to do!' Trish studied the letter carefully. 'Someone went to a lot of trouble with this.'

'She pushed it across to Bob. Look how carefully the letters are cut out. Do you think grass and trees was a deliberate choice?' She blew out her cheeks. 'Someone must really have it in for me.'

Bob pushed a cup of tea and a slice of buttered toast towards Trish. 'Well, it certainly wasn't Iris. At this very moment she's out getting some shopping for us.'

'What?' Trish slammed the cup down onto the counter, spilling some of the tea. 'Are you mad?'

'She offered, and I didn't want to leave you. I wanted to make sure you were okay.' Bob reached for a cloth to mop up the spill.

'Oh Yeah! I was a bit psycho last night, wasn't I? She chuckled. 'We'd better make sure none of the seals have been tampered with on whatever she buys.'

'Trish!' Bob admonished half-heartedly.

Studying the letter again, Trish looked up. 'You know I've never been a benefit scrounger, don't you, Bob? I've been an activist. And I can tell you, it's not a career for the faint-hearted!'

Sensing Trish was becoming upset again, Bob reassured her. 'Of course not, Trish. That's what I love about you. You're one of a kind.'

Trish hugged Bob. 'I know, Big Bear, I know.'

'How about I run you a bath and you get dressed and we go out on an adventure?'

Trish studied the floor. 'To be honest, I don't think I'm up for an adventure today. Let's just have a quiet day in and watch some films.'

Trish had just reappeared after her bath when the doorbell rang.

'That'll be Iris with the shopping.' Bob went to let her in.

'Oh my God!' Trish put a dramatic hand to her forehead. 'The Eagle Court predator.'

Bob couldn't help a smile as he opened the door.

'Right. Everything on the list!' Iris jiggled two carrier bags. 'Shall I pop them in the kitchen?'

Before Bob could reply, she had brushed past and was already unpacking.

She looked at Trish. 'I'm so sorry, Trish, about what happened.'

'No worries. Didn't bother me. I've had worse.' Bob suspected that Trish's nonchalant tone didn't fool Iris after what he'd told her earlier.

Iris sat on the settee next to Trish and looked at her earnestly. 'Can you think of anyone who would want to hurt you? Anyone who has a grudge?'

'This isn't some TV crime drama! So don't make it something it isn't,' Trish snapped. She leaned forward and spoke in an undertone. 'Anyway, I think the culprit is close at hand.'

Bob saw Iris recoil as if she'd been slapped and intervened to prevent the situation spiralling out of control.

'Thanks, Iris. That was so kind of you. I think Trish is still a bit tired.'

'Of course.' Iris put her hand on Trish's wrist. 'You rest up.'

Trish snapped her arm away, glaring at Iris.

Bob ushered her to the door. 'Thank you again, Iris. You're a life-saver.'

Swallowing her left-over soup, Iris thumped the table in frustration. She sensed Trish could see straight through her, and on reflection, she was right. Anonymous letters were a bit old-womanish – a bit Agatha Christie. But it was what she was good at, and she enjoyed doing it.

Washing up the lunch things, Iris suddenly realised there was a perfect solution to her problem and wasted no time getting started.

After another pleasant afternoon of cutting and sticking, Iris observed her work, head on one side. It wasn't up to her usual standard and slightly shorter, but it would have to do. The rainbow letters were particularly fetching. She scrubbed her face in the bathroom until it was red and angry, ruffled her hair, and grabbed a handful of tissues. Crumpling her own brown envelope she set off for Number 3.

Bob opened the door with a weary expression on his face.

Before he could speak, Iris cut in. 'Oh Bob. Would you believe it? She stifled a sob. 'It's happened to me, too. I just didn't see the envelope until this afternoon. It had caught behind a curtain I have over the door.' Thrusting the letter at him, she entered the hall and wailed. 'I can't believe it! It's so awful.'

Bob read the letter. 'Oh Iris, I'm so sorry.'

He gave her an awkward one-armed hug.

Sniffing, Iris said, 'Could I have a look at Trish's? I think they look the same.'

Trish appeared in the doorway. 'What's going on?'

'Iris has had one of the letters, too.'

'No!' The sarcasm in Trish's voice made Iris want to hit her. But she kept her anger hidden. 'Do you think...?'

'What?' responded Trish, sitting down and lighting a cigarette.

'Do you think we've all had one? What about Celia? She's on holiday, so we don't know. She won't be back for quite a few weeks.' Iris paused. 'She might not say anything anyway. Very secretive, that one.'

'So Bob's been spared?' Trish gave him a suggestive wink.

'Maybe it's someone with a grudge against women.' Iris wiped her eyes with a tissue. 'I think we should all keep an eye out for any strangers in the Court.'

'Absolutely, Iris. We don't want any more of this. Maybe we should go to the police.' Trish's laugh was sarcastic.

'I don't think it's worth going to the police—' Iris's voice was lost in Trish's coughing fit.

Once it had subsided, she repeated, 'I don't think we need to involve the police. Not unless something else happens.'

'Oh, no. We wouldn't want to involve the police, would we?'

The malevolence in her tone was not lost on Iris. 'Well, I've taken up enough of your time. Sorry to burst in like that, but I didn't know who else to turn to.' Iris got up to go. 'We Eagle Courters need to stick together.'

Trish's eyes were closed and Iris sensed she had fallen asleep.

'I'm only over there if you need anything, Bob.'

'Thanks Iris. And thanks for today. We are grateful even if Trish is a bit...spiky sometimes.'

'Think nothing of it.'

Chapter 21

When the doorbell rang a few days later, Iris nodded to The Governess on the TV and said, 'I knew it wouldn't be long.' She knew who would be waiting on the doorstep.

Bob's dishevelled hair and the bags under his eyes told Iris everything she needed to know.

'Iris, I'm sorry to bother you, but could you...?' He looked down and swallowed noisily. 'Could you come and help? I don't know what I'm doing.'

'Oh Bob,' Iris closed the door behind her and locked it. 'Is it Trish?'

'It's awful, Iris, and she won't allow me to call anyone.'

Anger towards Trish for putting Bob though this passed through Iris's body like a knife as she closed the front door. 'Right, let's get her sorted, shall we?'

'I know she'll be furious that I've even spoken to you.' Iris could hear the tremor of desperation in Bob's voice.

As it turned out, Trish wasn't capable of being angry with anyone. Iris frowned as she saw her semi- conscious form curled up on the settee, various untouched drinks and plates of food littering the coffee table.

'Can you carry her, Bob? We need to get her into bed.'

Once Bob had lain her on the bed, Iris said, 'Right, leave everything to me. You go and wash up those dishes.' She nodded her head in the direction of the lounge.

'Thank you so much, Iris.' His eyes glittered with tears.

Iris hummed as she stripped Trish of all her stained and smelly clothes, noticing how thin she had already become. Rummaging around in various cupboards, she found an old pair of pyjama bottoms and a T-shirt that looked and smelled reasonably clean. She thrust Trish into the clothes and pulled the quilt up over her body. Iris tried to run her fingers through Trish's matted hair without success. Sighing, she made a mental note to cut it short when she had a moment.

Carrying Trish's clothes through to the kitchen, she flung them into a washing machine which she found after trying numerous cupboard doors. Bob, in a trance-like state, seemed oblivious.

Shaking him by the arm, Iris tried to bring him back to the present. 'Bob... Bob!' When he at last looked at her, she said, 'Look at me. Bob! How many sleeping pills have you given her?'

Bob ran a hand over his face. 'A couple last night... and one this morning. I just couldn't stand her wailing and crying, Iris. Honestly, it was terrible!'

'I know, Bob. I'm here now, so leave everything to me.' Iris scanned the kitchen. 'Has Trish got any more of those tea-bags she likes?'

'In the cupboard.' Bob pointed.

'Right, get the kettle on, and we'll make her a nice cup of tea. That might pick her up a bit.'

'She's dying, isn't she?' The tears ran down Bob's cheeks.

'We won't know for certain until she's been examined.' Iris sighed. 'You know that will have to happen, Bob, don't you? Whether she likes it or not.'

Trish continued to refuse any outside help, but after a few days, Bob, unable to stand the suffering she was in, called 999. The resulting visit to the hospital and various scans confirmed Trish's diagnosis. Bob and Trish were told by grim-faced doctors that there was nothing they could do except make her comfortable. Trish had been offered a place in a hospice, however, they both agreed that she would be happier at home.

Once Trish was settled, a nurse appeared several times a day to give support.

'It's such a shame,' said Iris, as Jenny changed the bag for Trish's morphine drip. 'You know she refused any medical help because of all these ridiculous conspiracy theories.' Tears came to Iris's eyes. 'She could have been looking at a longer life by now.'

'Everyone is entitled to their beliefs.' Jenny spoke briskly as she peeled off her latex gloves. 'Right. I'll go and check with Bob to see if there's anything else before I go,' she said.

'I'm sure we'll be fine,' said Iris, making her voice as frosty as possible.

Iris had made several attempts to befriend Jenny and get her on side, all to no avail. Jenny seemed to regard her as some kind of intruder, always deferring to Bob about any decisions. Why she should think this, Iris had no idea. After all she was giving up her own time – day and night – to look after Trish, even missing the Homeless Dinners. How many other people would do that? But what annoyed Iris more than anything was the way Jenny fussed over Trish, holding her hand and addressing her in a soft, soothing voice that Trish seemed to respond to. Iris had to grit her teeth, seething inside.

However, at other times, she was able to make Trish pay in various subtle and not-so-subtle ways. Nothing that Bob would notice. Iris wasn't going to repeat the weakness she had shown with her mother, now she had another chance. In many ways this was easier; she didn't have the same history with Trish, a narrowing path leading right back to the powerlessness of childhood. Maybe it was easier to vent her anger on someone she didn't really know. Iris put the thought that this was the coward's way out to the back of her mind. This was now – and this time, she would do a good job.

Iris started with small things she knew Trish hated, such as putting on the TV where she was subjected to endless game shows all day as she slept and dozed. When Bob said, uneasily, that maybe this wasn't a good idea, Iris replied patiently that sick people liked to have a sense of company and normality around them, regardless of their previous preferences. Iris knew he wouldn't argue. He needed her too much. Feeding Trish food that contained traces of meat, even though she was staunchly vegan, also gave Iris much pleasure.

Discussions with Zed had revealed that cannabis, when mixed with morphine, could result in some pretty nasty reactions. He had also supplied her with a quantity of newer, stronger weed, passed surreptitiously under the table in a Tupperware container. Iris had never imagined Zed possessing such a thing as Tupperware.

Bob spent many hours sitting with Trish, talking to her as she drifted in and out of consciousness, recalling stories she had told about her hippie past, about how they'd met.

Sometimes he read to her – poetry by Bob Dylan and other things that Iris had never heard of.

One evening, when Bob was asleep, Iris made tea for Trish with the stronger leaves Zed had given her. Trish sipped the beverage gratefully as Iris supported her head and held the cup. 'There, doesn't that feel better? Some of your special tea.'

Trish only managed to whisper. 'That's good stuff!' before drifting back into semi-consciousness.

By the next morning, Trish's breathing had become laboured. 'I don't like the sound of this,' said Jenny, listening through her stethoscope.

Once Trish was on oxygen, things improved, and Jenny left, happy that her patient was stable.

The second and subsequent cups of tea, over the next few days, as well as affecting Trish's breathing, caused her blood-pressure to rocket, and she was in a semi-conscious state for most of the time. Jenny seemed to accept this as a normal deterioration and didn't question anything.

But Iris had to be extra careful when Trish's daughter, Ocean, came to visit, and dialled back on the tea. She had been surprised to find out that Trish had children. Bob had explained with some discomfort that Trish had very little con-tact with her offspring. 'Oh what a shame Bob.' Tears flooded into Iris's eyes. 'Think of all the lovely times you could have had with your step-grandchildren.' Bob had looked out of the window and Iris sensed his sadness.

'What kind of woman has children, gives them ridiculous names and then ignores them? Selfish bitch!' she muttered, to Trish, later, turning up the TV before leaving the room and carefully closing the door behind her.

'I can't believe Ocean is actually coming to see me. It was good of Bob to contact her.' Trish had rallied after lunch at the thought of seeing her daughter.

'She calls herself Sarah, now apparently, and is something in finance.' Trish winced as she shifted to get more comfortable. 'I can't imagine how a child of mine could have become so...establishment.'

Ocean arrived in a BMW. Iris watched her get out of the car and noted the expensive business suit.

She entered the house in a flurry of importance and, ignoring Bob's offer of a coffee, went straight in to see her mother. She leant over Trish and gave her a peck on the cheek.

'Hello, Mum.'

Trish responded with a weak smile and held out a hand which Ocean took after some hesitation, Iris noticed.

When Trish only responded to questions with a squeeze of the hand, the conversation ground to a halt. Only after a few minutes did Ocean turn to Iris. And you are...?'

'I'm Iris Walker, a neighbour. I live at Number 1.' She waited in vain for some acknowledgement of her kindness.

'Mum should be having professional care 24-hour care, not some neighbour. No offence,' she added hastily.

Offence had been taken. 'Trish...your mum didn't want any professional care. A nurse visits every day, but if it wasn't for me...'

'You mean Bob would have been left to deal with everything?' Ocean paced around the room. 'How could this happen? Why wasn't something done sooner? Bob should never have let things get to this stage!' The anger in her voice struck Iris as uncalled for.

'You can't expect a man to be dealing with that sort of thing.' Iris, ignoring this last comment, gestured vaguely at the bed. 'It's not easy looking after someone when they're near the end. I went through this with my mother.' Iris's eyes filled with tears. 'Someone needs to make sure Trish...your mother, is comfortable.'

'I suppose I should thank you then. I wouldn't be any good at this sort of thing, and my brother, he's got issues of his own at the moment.'

Iris managed a sympathetic smile.

'You know, she was never there for us when we were growing up. We were always palmed off on anyone who happened to be around. We just moved from squat to commune and only went to school once we'd been taken into care. I was ten and Thor was eight.' Ocean picked up her bag. 'But in spite of her neglect, we've done alright,' she added, looking at the sleeping form of her mother.

'Even so. It'll have meant a lot to her that you came.' Iris patted Ocean's arm.

As the BMW disappeared up the drive, Iris muttered. 'Gold digger. Like mother, like daughter.' She hadn't missed Ocean's appraising glances around the bungalow and the campervan.

She returned to Trish, and turning up the pain meds, she smoothed her hair away from her forehead. 'Wasn't that nice of Ocean to come?'

It turned out later that Trish had no recollection of the visit.

Bob felt as if his life had been rewound and the same terrible months and weeks were happening all over again. First Ann and now Trish. This helplessness – the inability to do anything except watch his wife die. What had he done to deserve this? Trish had been so vital, so full of life and energy when they

137

met, planning all sorts of trips and adventures and making him feel he could do anything. He'd been envious of her carefree approach to life. But it had all slipped away. His inability to adjust to Trish's lifestyle haunted him. Why couldn't he have enjoyed those short months more? Would he have been able to if he had known time was limited? Would he have become more like Trish if they'd had longer together? Would he have been able to shake off Ann's disapproval, always hovering at the back of his mind?

Ann's death, although distressing and traumatic had been tidy and organised. Her final weeks were lived out in a hospice where all the terrible things about dying from cancer were hidden from Bob. Or most of them. He would never forget the pain etched on her face as she struggled to hide it from him towards the end. So unlike Trish, who never hid anything, pain or otherwise.

Bob heard Iris in the kitchen as he sat beside Trish, helplessly holding her hand. What would he have done without her? She had been there, solid as a rock over the last few weeks. How would he have cooked? How would he have done the laundry? He guessed Jenny would have known the right people to organise something, although the thought of having strangers in the house was unsettling. As was the visit from Ocean, whom he had never met before. Disapproval and blame oozed from her, acid-like, and he had overheard her comments to Iris. Should he have done more? Should he have ignored Trish's wishes? The eventual trip to the hospital had been bad enough. Surely it was right to allow Trish control over her life as long as she was capable of making her wishes known. Bob knew there was a son, Thor. But he never made an appearance, for which Bob was secretly grateful.

This last week, Iris had taken to staying over, insisting on sleeping on the sofa as Trish's needs became more frequent.

He wondered what made Iris so strong and resilient. So capable. Although, if he was honest, deep down, he was a little bit scared of her. There was something...he couldn't put a finger on it...it was almost as if she was too good to be true.

'I'm sorry, Big Bear.' Bob's attention was drawn back to Trish. He noticed the paper-thin skin on her arm as she stretched it out.

'Don't. Don't,' Bob murmured.

'But we were going to do so much. I wanted to take you to so many places...' Trish's voice fell to a whisper.

'You did take me to places, babe.' Shifting his chair nearer, Bob stroked her cheek. 'Rest now.' Trish closed her eyes as Iris appeared in the doorway with a bowl of soup on a tray.

'I'll see if I can get her to try some of this.' She spoke in the low voice that always seemed to accompany the process of dying. 'I've left you a cottage pie in the lounge, Bob. Take a break for a while. I'll sit with her.'

Bob got up, carefully stretching his stiff legs. He was reluctant to leave Trish, even for a moment, but took comfort in the knowledge she was in safe hands. What good could he be to her when she needed him, if he didn't look after himself? Iris was right about that.

From the next room, as he sat at the table, he could hear Iris. 'Come on now, Trish. Let's just try a mouthful. Just one.'

There was a moment's silence before a groan from Trish made him wince. He went over and closed the door, taking his cottage pie into the kitchen.

Chapter 22

C elia turned into Eagle Court to see Dusty Roads, like a shabby, elderly relative, squashed in beside a shiny black hearse. Her mind tried to make sense of it. Unable to get past, she left the car on the side of the road and walked down to Number 3, feeling disrespectful in her holiday cropped chinos and T-shirt. As she got to the door, Bob appeared, followed by Iris, a tissue to her nose. Seeing Celia, Iris came over.

'What's going on?' When Iris answered only with a shake of her head, Celia repeated the question with a growing sense of unease. 'What's going on, Iris?'

'Trish. The cancer got her in the end.' Iris's voice quavered, as she answered from behind the tissue.

'Cancer? But I've only been gone a few weeks!'

Iris glanced over to where Bob was talking to the undertakers. 'Sorry. Got to go. Bob needs me. I'll fill you in later.' Iris turned back, as if a thought had just struck her. 'You're welcome to come to the funeral, you know. I'm sure Bob would appreciate it. There won't be many other mourners there.' She dabbed her eyes again.

'Of course. Yes. I'll just get changed,' Celia murmured, unsure of what to say.

Once the hearse had gone, Celia had made her way into the bungalow and got changed into the outfit she had worn at Alan's funeral. This was not the way she wanted to come home after her holiday. She'd imagined easing back into her new life and making a fresh start, as if the terrible events of the previous months in Eagle Court hadn't happened. But how could she refuse to go to this funeral? Celia hadn't really known the couple at Number 3 – Bob and Trish – she'd been too busy dealing with her own issues. The RV had vaguely annoyed her, but that was it. She hadn't really noticed them. How could someone die of cancer within a month?

Shaken, Celia had got back into the car and drove to the crematorium, her holiday luggage still in the boot. What was it about Eagle Court? She hadn't been back five minutes and already things were going awry.

The funeral was a quiet affair. Most of those who'd known Trish were either uncontactable or dead. Iris sat at the front with Bob, a protective arm around him. She saw some mourners about the same age as Daisy and imagined they must be Trish's children, although she had never seen them before.

Memories of Emma's little coffin crept, unwanted, into Celia's mind. She pushed them away, instead, forcing herself to focus on a dappled rainbow, shimmering on the whitewashed wall as it was reflected through the single stained-glass window. She took her mind back to the holiday, zoning out the monotonous voice of the priest. She was physically here, to show her respects, but she didn't have to be present in her head, or her heart.

After the service, Celia hovered on the edge of the group, hoping to give Bob her condolences and get back to Eagle Court.

Seeing Iris approaching, her heart sank. 'Thank you for coming, Celia. Bob will have appreciated it.' They watched as their neighbour went through the motions of greeting the small number of mourners. 'He wanted bright colours. And –

141

can you believe this? – to take her body to the crematorium in that awful campervan. He said it's what Trish would have wanted. Didn't really know what he was doing, poor man,' Iris confided in an undertone.

'I can't believe it! I didn't really know them, but for this to happen so soon...' Celia just wanted to get home and get on with her life. She didn't want to think about death and all its implications. But Trish's sudden death had shaken her, much as she tried not to let it.

'She spoke all this nonsense about burial. Returning to the ground – for a natural process to take place.' Iris tucked a loose strand of hair behind her ear. 'But cremations are much tidier and more efficient. You can always have a nice rose bush planted to remember them by.'

Suddenly, Celia saw Emma's grave, left untended. Closing her eyes and shaking her head, she tried to make the picture go away.

'Is everything alright?' She felt Iris's hand on her arm. 'I know. What a terrible way to come back from your holiday.'

Celia had to get away. She took a breath and forced a smile. 'I'm fine. Just a bit tired after the flight. I think I'll head off now. Can you give Bob my condolences?'

'Of course. I'm sure he'll understand.'

On the way home, her hands shaking on the steering wheel, Celia couldn't keep thoughts of Emma at bay. She had never been able to bring herself to go and visit her baby, buried under the ground, and had no idea if any of her other children had. They just never talked about it. They had all erased Emma from their lives, like an inconvenient mishap.

There was a pot of scarlet geraniums by the front door when Celia got back. She picked it up and turned it around, wondering who had brought it, but there was no note. She returned it to the step, appreciating the splash of colour. Maybe Daisy had left it. The thought melted any lingering resentment.

Once she had finished unpacking, Celia found herself glad to be back in the silence of her bungalow after the constant noise of the holiday. She had forgotten how noisy it was to be outdoors all day, birds, dogs barking, the rolling and breaking waves, people, jets overhead, the wind, and that was before she factored in the more immediate sounds of her family. Sensing some tension between Daisy and Mark, she had kept her distance when they were together without the children and had spent time reading on her e-reader. But, one evening, she had not escaped in time to avoid overhearing a conversation carried out in angry whispers.

'Why haven't you asked her yet?'

'For God's sake, Mark. You saw the state she was in before we left. We need to get the timing right. We can't rush it.'

'If we're going to get Seb in for this academic year, we need to be moving now to confirm the place they've saved for him.'

'I know, I know! I'll sort it.'

Celia had gone to her room, all thoughts of her book abandoned. She hadn't forgotten Daisy's request a month or so ago, hoping, as nothing had been said since, that they had explored other options such as Mark's family. But now she needed to make a decision. The question would almost certainly arise tomorrow before they flew back the following day.

She decided to get ahead of the curve the following morning, once the children were busy with activities laid on by the holiday company. 'Look, Daisy, about the school fees you mentioned.'

Daisy looked up from her book.

'I'm happy to pay for my grandchildren's education and it's what your father would have wanted. Just let me know the details.'

'Really?' Daisy gave a sigh which Celia sensed contained an element of relief. She turned, and in an uncharacteristic gesture, took Celia's hand. 'Thank you, Mum. That means so much.'

A warmth had flowed through Celia at this gratitude from her daughter. Even though she had brought her children up to be as no-nonsense as she was, at times she regretted it when she realised, that, like her, they were unable to show affection. So although she knew she was paying for it, she revelled in the gesture.

That evening was the happiest of the whole holiday, as, in the local taverna, Daisy and Mark seemed happy, making a fuss of Celia. So unlike the previous weeks where Mark had been patronising and made unkind comments about her, even in front of the children. That night it had been, 'You kids are so lucky to have such a lovely Granny.' Mark had even been slightly flirty, which Celia had found very unsettling. Maybe it was worth spending thousands to get affection and respect from your family.

Relieved the issue had been resolved, Celia felt good about helping her grandchildren get on in the world. She wouldn't think about how she had been pressurised to comply with

144

Daisy and Mark's wishes. Now she could get on with her life as she had planned. The disturbing events that had happened before the holiday seemed so distant that she could persuade herself that she had imagined them.

Celia thought she might resume her morning coffees with Iris. While on holiday, thinking back over the last few weeks, she had been ashamed of her snobbishness. Iris had meant well and had given up a lot of time to help her, and kindness to Bob went well beyond what might be expected of any good neighbour. So around half an hour later, when there was a knock on the door, she was pleased to see Iris on the doorstep, holding the pot of flowers.

'Didn't you see these? I left them for you.' She tapped her finger on the door frame. 'To say welcome home.'

Celia opened her mouth to speak, but Iris rushed on. 'Bob's not coping, so I'm going to have to help him sort things out – you know.'

'That's so good of you, Iris.' Celia took a breath. 'I've missed our coffees.'

A smile appeared.

Although a wave of disappointment had washed over Celia that it wasn't Daisy who had left the plant, impulsively, she invited Iris in.

'Oh sorry, Celia. Now's not a good time. I've got to get Bob's shopping.' Iris turned to go, and then, seemingly as an afterthought, said, 'Maybe tomorrow?'

Celia felt strangely put-out. Iris had never refused an invitation to coffee before.

Over the next few days, Celia noticed that Iris did indeed seem to be spending a lot of time at Bob's and suppressed a twinge of jealousy, as the promised visit the following day did not materialise. She spoke sternly to herself. The poor man had just lost his wife, and it was just like Iris to want to help him. The offers of shopping had also stopped – which was fair enough now that she was perfectly able to get her own pinot grigio. Although In a strange way Celia found she missed the company. It was like when she used to always have a coffee with her cleaner, Olive. It wasn't that they were friends exactly, but she could talk to her, and Olive had been with her for years. Even babysitting the children when they were small.

Olive had been there when... Sometimes it was impossible to drive the memory away, and Trish's funeral seemed to have sparked a flame that Celia couldn't extinguish.

Even now, after thirty years, she felt a chill creep over her when she remembered going into Emma's room to find her lifeless little body in the cot. Olive had rung the ambulance and gently led Celia away. It was Olive who had held her when weeks later she cried out her broken heart. Celia hadn't been able to articulate any grief in front of Alan. She knew that if she did, she wouldn't be able to stop crying, that she would shatter into tiny pieces. She needed to be strong for him and for the family. She and Alan were never the same after that. Some part of Celia knew she'd been wrong to shut down any conversation about Emma. But it had been the only way to cope. For all of them. And now no one ever mentioned their absent little sister or daughter.

◈—⁙—————⁙—◈

Iris smiled as she made her way around the supermarket. Celia could wait; she would braise nicely in the oven for a week or two. She consulted Bob's sparse list and frowned. He was hardly eating. Following the habit she'd got into over the last few days, she added a few treats. A custard tart and a trifle, knowing he was partial to those having confided one day that his first wife, Ann, used to make them. Iris thought that she would have got on well with Ann even though cooking was not one of her strengths. They would have seen eye-to-eye. She would have been a perfect resident for Eagle Court.

Looking at her watch, she headed for the till, anxious to catch up with Zed before delivering Bob his shopping and getting started on the cleaning. There was nothing like being a cleaner for finding out about people and nosing around in their private possessions. Iris wondered why she'd never thought of it before.

Humming to herself as she drove, Iris went over the things she needed Zed to do. He was demanding quite a bit of money and she had a suspicion she was being fleeced. But Iris didn't care. For once, she had plenty of money and was enjoying herself. The voice in her head had retreated –which made Iris feel even better.

She entered the fast-food restaurant and noticed that, for once, Zed wasn't crouched over his laptop. He was staring into space, a half-eaten donut in his hand dripping jam onto the table.

'Zed.' She waved a hand in front of his face. He jumped, almost as if he had been caught doing something he shouldn't, and stuffed the rest of the donut into his mouth, chewing rapidly.

'Everything alright?' Iris said as she took a seat and a sip of her coffee. Why they made these in such huge cups, Iris could never fathom. After four or five sips, she'd usually had enough.

Zed swallowed the donut and cleared his throat. 'Yup, good to go.'

'What about Daisy Sinclair?'

'Here, see for yourself. Seems to have the perfect family and the perfect life,' Zed sneered as he turned the laptop. Iris saw that her predictions had been right as she scrolled through the smiling family pictures, framed by beaches and boats surrounded by a perfect blue sea, complete with candlelit evenings in tavernas. She studied Celia and noticed the fixed smile for the camera. Family Woman had not had a good time, she would put money on it on it.

'Anything else?'

'If you scroll further...'

Iris gingerly coordinated her fingers to scroll down, imagining that the page would go blank at any minute. 'Oh my! So who's paying for that, then?' She turned the screen back to Zed along with the post of Seb, scowling in his Milford College uniform, above the caption:

So proud of our boy getting into Milford. Growing up so fast (crying emoji) We're sure he'll go on to do great things.

'Are they trying to pretend he's got a scholarship? I'll bet Celia is paying for this.' Iris looked up. She had got into the grammar school on a scholarship, but even if Facebook had been around in those days, she doubted her success would have warranted a mention from her parents. 'That boy couldn't get a scholarship into a dustbin!'

Zed leaned back in the chair, looking at her in a way that made Iris slightly uncomfortable. He had hardly glanced at her before.

'Celia's back.' Iris wanted to get back to Bob and was anxious to move the conversation on.

'Oh great. What do you think? More texts?'

'Whatever you think, Zed. Be creative.'

'Mmm. I'm thinking she might have other Wi-fi appliances.' He started tapping the table. 'Most people do.'

'I think there's some kind of heating system that you control from your phone.'

'That'll do for starters. I'm going to enjoy this!'

Iris experienced a shiver of doubt about unleashing Zed and his tech know-how, but quickly suppressed it. After all, he couldn't do any serious harm.

'Everything alright, Zed?' she said casually as she stood to leave.

'Yeah, great thanks.' He was already buried in the next task. Iris slipped a bundle of notes into his pocket as she left.

Zed raised his hand in thanks.

Chapter 23

As soon as Iris appeared in the kitchen, Wendy was at her side giving her a hug. Iris stiffened at the unwelcome physical contact. She couldn't stand these huggy types. Most of them were hypocrites. But she returned a smile.

'It's not been the same without you. Lots of the regulars have missed you. Every week I've had to deal with a chorus of, "Where's Iris?"'

Iris's smile grew warmer. 'I've missed them, too.' Looking around, she saw no evidence of Tina. 'Where's the boss?'

'Off looking after her mother. Final stages of cancer,' Wendy muttered conspiratorially. 'Talking of which, how is your neighbour?'

'She passed, I'm afraid.' Iris put her apron on. 'It was a relief in the end,' she said with a half sob, half sigh.

'Well, she was lucky to have a neighbour like you, that's all I can say.'

'I couldn't let Bob, her husband, manage all that on his own, so I did what I could. I'm not one to speak ill of the dead, but she was a difficult woman. Refused any medical help until it was too late.'

Wendy shook her head. 'Poor man.'

Iris smoothed her apron. 'Right! Where do you want me?'.

'We need to get cracking cooking the mince and doing the potatoes for the cottage pie. Mince or potatoes?'

'Potatoes,' said Iris. She knew her limitations where cooking for the masses was concerned.

Iris felt a warm glow as a chorus of 'Iris is back!' and 'Woo-hoo!' and 'Hello bigger portions!' greeted her when the doors were opened by a frowning Stan. 'Hold on, you lot. Wait until I've secured the door properly. Health and safety. We don't want any accidents.' Ignored by the tide of hungry people, he was left standing, arms folded, a disapproving frown on his face.

'You're a saint. We heard you were off looking after a sick neighbour, so we can forgive you this once,' said Maurice guiding his tray along with shaking hands.

'I'm back now, so no need to worry.' Iris pointed to his hands. Make sure you see the medic while you're here today. You need sorting.'

'Yes, nurse,' Maurice replied with mock humility, to cheers and cat-calls from the others in the queue.

Once they had all filed through, Iris noticed there was no Mabel.

'Where's Mabel?' she asked Wendy.

'In hospital having her legs seen to. Covered in ulcers, apparently. Poor woman.' Wendy threw up her hands in a gesture of hopelessness. 'She'll be back soon enough and then the whole cycle will begin again.' She sighed. 'Sometimes it seems as if we're getting nowhere. Nothing's really being done to help them, just sticking plasters. Nothing to sort out underlying issues. Sometimes it seems so depressing.'

'But they're getting a good meal once a week, which has got to be something. Prepared by an expert cook who knows what they like,' added Iris with a smile.

'I suppose so,' acknowledged Wendy as she took the pans back into the kitchen and fetched the dessert. 'Sponge and custard today with a bit of extra jam.'

However much she pretended not to see him, there was no escaping George's piercing gaze. Iris avoided any eye contact as he passed with his tray. But now, something about him drew her over, something like a magnet that she couldn't control. He was the only person she could talk to about revenge and getting your own back, even though she knew she wouldn't like what he had to say.

She sat in silence as George finished the last of the sponge and custard. Pushing the dish to one side, he sat back and patted his stomach in satisfaction.

'I love Saturdays.' He looked at Iris. 'How've you been, Iris?'

'Fine. Not that it's any of your business.' Iris took a sudden breath and fought hard to compose herself. 'Anyway, it's not about me. How have *you* been, George?'

'Nothing to report. Same old, same old.' He turned. 'But it *is* about you, Iris, whether you like it or not.'

Iris sat in silence. She felt strangely defenceless and didn't want to hear what he had to say.

'You still bent on getting revenge?'

'What else is there? Somebody has to do something about all those bastards out there who don't appreciate what they have and think they're better than everyone else.' Iris closed her mouth firmly before more of her resentment could escape. What was it about George?

'But are they your battles to fight, Iris? Haven't you fought enough battles in your life? Aren't you tired of it?'

'No, I'm not, George. It's what gives me energy and purpose. That's what gets me up in the morning.'

'It'll destroy you. You know that, don't you?'

'Well, that's me. Take me as you find me.' Iris gave a thin smile.

'It's never too late to step into the unknown. To become a different person.'

'Why should I? I'm perfectly happy as I am. Nobody's going to get the better of me!' Iris stood abruptly and cleared George's plates. As she turned towards the kitchen, George said, 'You know, I'll be thinking positive thoughts and hoping you can find the strength and courage to change.'

Iris exhaled an angry breath and strode towards the kitchen, dropping the dishes into the washing-up bowl so that water and suds splashed everywhere.

'Whoa!' Wendy stood with hands in the air, palms facing Iris. 'That's not like you, Iris.'

'Sorry, they just slipped out of my hands.' Iris found a grin from somewhere and turned to Wendy. 'Butterfingers!' As my mother would have said.

Chapter 24

B ob sat, head in his hands. His world was falling apart. He felt a sudden flash of anger towards Ann. Why had she left him? If she'd been here, none of this would have happened and he would still have a safe, vague fantasy of living a wild life, a fantasy that would never be realised. Ann would have kept him safe with her no-nonsense attitude to life and would have laughed at his adventurous dreams.

'Really, Bob! At your age? Come on. What shall we watch tonight? There's a new drama starting that everyone's talking about.'

If only he could be back with Ann, safe in their ordered home where the only drama had been on TV.

But Ann was gone. She had left him. And what a mess he had made of things. It wasn't that he hadn't been fond of Trish – he always admired her get-up-and-go courage and how she was fearless about the unknown. He knew now that he could never have been like that. It just wasn't him. And now, Trish had unwittingly left him a poisonous legacy.

He reached again for the solicitor's letter and re-read it carefully, making sure he hadn't misunderstood. There was no doubt. Ocean and Thor were contesting Trish's hastily made will. Iris had purchased a DIY pack from WH Smith and had witnessed the will as Trish had left what little she had to Bob. He imagined there would be debts. According to his solicitor, it wouldn't stand any scrutiny and now her children wanted what they saw as their inheritance, which was half of everything Bob owned, even though Trish had brought no money into the marriage. That, it seemed, was irrelevant as far as the courts were concerned. He could lose the bungalow, Dusty Roads, everything.

Bob could see no way out.

As he stared at the washing flapping on the line outside, he heard Iris coming in with the shopping. Solid, sensible, dependable, Iris. Bob hadn't even noticed her hanging it out.

'Only me.' He heard her put the bags down in the kitchen and she was already putting things away when he made himself get up and help her.

'I got us some of those lovely egg custards. We'll have them with our—'

Iris turned as she closed the cupboard door. 'Goodness, Bob. Whatever's the matter? You look as if you've seen a ghost. Here, sit down.' She pulled out a chair and led him to it. 'What is it?'

A shuddering sigh was the only sound Bob seemed able to make. He handed Iris the letter.

As her eyes travelled down the page Iris's mouth tightened into a thin line, and as she threw the paper onto the table her eyes flashed with an anger that Bob hadn't known she was capable of. An anger that was slightly frightening.

She sat and took Bob's hand. 'They're not going to get a penny of your money. We'll see to that!' she hissed. 'I'm here, Bob, and we'll fight them together.'

Although the relief of sharing his problem made Bob feel better, he was doubtful that, even with Iris's optimism, it was a battle that could be won.

After their customary mug of tea, he listened to Iris vacuuming in the other room and wondered what Ann would be saying. He knew all too well. She'd be telling him to stop worrying about things he couldn't change and to do something to take his mind off the problem.

But what? He glanced over at Dusty Roads sitting, forlorn, on the drive. There was nothing to stop him going on a few road trips of his own. He had the time, and for the time being, the money. Maybe he could make some of his dreams of freedom come true. Once the idea had taken hold in his mind, he felt a sudden surge of energy and reached for the road maps. Maybe now was the time to keep his promise to Sam and visit his old neighbours. But somehow, he couldn't face it so soon after Trish's death. He wasn't ready to go back to that world yet. There was plenty of time for that, he thought with a twinge of guilt. Another thought had started niggling at the back of his mind. He wanted to do something to help others, to give something back to society. Bob had no idea where this had come from, maybe from Iris. She always seemed to be there whenever anyone was in trouble. She was always giving.

Later, as he gazed out of the window, a half-eaten sandwich in his hand, the solution came to him. It was obvious. Why hadn't he thought of it before? He would ask Iris about going along to those lunches for the homeless she went to every week. It would only be one day out of the week and he was sure Iris would introduce him to whoever ran them. Yes, that was the thing to do. He turned back to the maps with renewed energy.

Iris couldn't concentrate on *The Chase*, even though it was The Beast today – her favourite chaser. She paced up and down, unable to keep still, driven by a mixture of adrenaline, and anger on Bob's behalf. She thought back to Ocean eyeing things up on her visit to Number 3. Maybe that had been the whole reason for going – not to see her mother at all. Even so, Iris was determined not to feel sorry for Trish.

Wills were tricky things, and sometimes you had to take matters into your own hands, just as she had done with her mother's. Looking through her papers and personal effects before the house clearance people came, Iris had found bank statements telling her that there was around £30,000 sitting in an account which, it seemed, her mother had saved into over the last thirty or forty years. Iris had ground her teeth and hissed. Then, in the bed-side cabinet she had discovered a handbag full of cash. When she counted it, around £1500. She, Iris, had never been allowed to keep her carer's allowance, her mother giving her a measly £10.00 a week 'spending money'.

But when she had come across a will, witnessed by their neighbour, Iris had cried out and thrown the things on her mother's dressing table at the mirror. The hairbrush, still containing strands of wiry, grey hair, was closely followed by a pot of E45 cream, a jar of cough medicine, several bottles of pills. Iris had stood, motionless, watching the dark, sticky liquid travel down over the cracked looking glass, pooling on the table before it dripped onto the carpet, leaving a brown stain over the garish pattern. This was the final insult. Her mother had left everything to the local cats' shelter.

Downstairs, hands clenched, Iris strode up and down the room where she and her mother had spent countless, toxic hours together. It was a good ten minutes before it occurred to her that this was likely the only copy of the will. The information had been entered on a basic form, with no mention of a solicitor.

This would be her revenge for her mother's final and brutal humiliation. This time she could do something. She burnt the will in the garden, watching the charred ashes fly away in the breeze. But even that didn't take away the anger, humiliation and pain ingrained deep inside her.

Remembering all this, Iris understood exactly what Bob was going through. Someone was trying to take away what was rightfully his. Her mind raced with all sorts of plans to put things right for Bob, but the one she like most was good, old-fashioned stalking. She knew where Ocean and Thor lived as their addresses had been on the solicitor's letter. She would start with Ocean first, imagining a big house on a new-build housing estate, maybe gated – which would be a problem – and a duplicate, perfect family, just like Daisy. They were two of a kind, these women, in spite of their different backgrounds; both were self-serving, greedy and complacent about the lives they had. She didn't know about Ocean's children, as none had been at the funeral. But Daisy was different, Iris needed to keep her on side. She had to be an accomplice in taking Celia down for once and for all. There would be plenty of time for Daisy later.

An irritated sigh escaped Iris as she remembered that she had promised to have coffee with Family Woman. She'd already put it off a few times and couldn't leave Celia to her own devices for too long. Iris reminded herself that she had the rest of the day to hunt down Ocean's house. It might be better to go later, anyway, and catch her coming home from work.

Something else was niggling at her. It wasn't just thoughts of Ocean, or Family Woman. As much as she tried to push him to the back of her mind, George and his blue eyes were constantly demanding her attention.

She remembered once more what George had said, and his warning. Was this getting back at people giving her a false sense of energy and purpose? Had it really become a monster inside her that was never satisfied? In some ways, maybe he was right. This anger and need for revenge was never resolved, no matter what she did. Maybe that was because she hadn't done enough yet. Maybe George had given up too soon.

Iris turned the TV off. Was she becoming a monster? But she did so many good things, unsavoury things that others would turn their noses up at. People thought she was wonderful, even Celia and Bob. So surely she wasn't all bad. And she had to do something for herself. She'd seen conversations on morning TV – 'Remember to do something for yourself,' they always said. So this was it – she was doing something for herself. It was who she was – and she did a lot of good along the way – like helping Bob keep his money. She deserved the life she had now.

And what else could she do? Iris knew no other way of scratching the permanent itch for revenge. Once someone had humiliated her, there was no going back. She just couldn't leave it. She'd tried at first when she moved into Eagle Court. Trying to turn over a new leaf. And where had that got her? People looked down their noses at her and laughed at her. Well, she was showing them. There was no alternative. She would go mad if she let people get away with things. And what meaning would her life have without this way of living that she was so good at? A way of life that gave her some sense of self-worth.

No, it was all very well for George to preach, but he hadn't walked in her shoes. This was her life, and she would live it how she pleased.

Chapter 25

I ris noticed with consternation that Family Woman seemed much like her old self, confident and bossy.

'Have a seat while I make the coffee,' she commanded.

Iris watched her moving confidently around the kitchen with narrowed eyes.

'I've got all sorts of plans for the garden. It'll be a challenge with such poor soil, but I'm sure I'll make something of it.'

Iris took a sip of coffee and bit into a Bourbon.

'I was thinking of getting someone in to dig the garden over and I thought it might be a good idea if I asked them to cut your...grass while they're at it.'

Iris nearly choked on her second bite of biscuit. 'No, thank you. I can sort that out myself.' It took a monumental effort to force this reply out. Iris congratulated herself on her self-control and took a third bite of her biscuit before any other words could escape. She reflected on her own green rectangle, now overgrown and neglected. She had kept the front looking nice though, and as Sean from the garden centre had promised, the bedding plants had done their thing. Every time Iris came into the close, she enjoyed the splash of colour on her doorstep, and Bob had been as good as his word; the post was good as new.

'Alright, but if you don't get it cut, the weeds will come through to my side and start causing problems. They are pesky things you know,' Celia added as an afterthought, as though softening the criticism.

Iris had to dig deep once more to keep a smile on her face. 'Don't you worry, Celia. I'll take care of it.'

She had taken her eye off the ball and things were getting out of hand with Family Woman. Iris could only hope that Zed would keep his word about dealing with her. Any reservations about what he might do evaporated.

'How was the holiday?' Iris was anxious to change the subject.

'Oh, it was wonderful.' Celia smiled. 'A far cry from this.' She nodded towards the September rain pattering against the window. 'There's nothing like a bit of sun, sea and family to perk you up. Just what I needed.' She smiled complacently as she took a sip of coffee.

'What about you, Iris? Don't you enjoy a bit of sun from time to time?'

Iris wanted to hit her. Instead, she gripped the edges of the chair with both hands.

'I've not had much time for holidays. I was too busy looking after my parents.'

'Oh, you've sacrificed so much over the years, haven't you, Iris? Aren't you ever sad about missing out on...' Celia swept her arm around as if gesturing her life. 'You know, family, marriage and children, career?'

Iris's fingers were cramping as she clung on to the chair. Celia looked at her, head on one side, with a patronising smile. Iris recognised that pose all too well, as it was mirrored back to her.

'It was a sacrifice I had to make. You should always look after your parents.' Iris struggled to keep her voice even as she stood. 'It's been nice to see you, Celia, but I need to get on now. Maybe we'll catch up again soon.'

The door closed with a firm click almost before Celia realised that her neighbour had gone. Maybe she'd offended Iris. Had she been a bit too direct? She remembered how the patronising comments from the women at the book club had made her feel and wondered if Iris had felt the same way. But that was different, she reminded herself. She'd known them for years and had even gone to school with Eleanor. Smiling, she remembered that Eleanor had been bossy even then, revelling in her post as head girl. Celia thought back to Iris. She hadn't meant to upset her. She had spoken with sincerity. Maybe Iris didn't respond well to sympathy, especially coming from someone who'd had everything she hadn't. Celia admonished herself for being insensitive and vowed to avoid any careless comments to Iris in the future, however well-meant.

She looked at her watch; just time to get to the bank before lunch. Celia felt good about paying for her grandchildren's education. After all, what else was she going to spend the money on? Even so, as she got into the car, still revelling in the novelty of being able to drive again, a sense of unease niggled somewhere deep inside her. A memory that she'd been railroaded into paying the school fees. That somehow she'd been manipulated, especially after what she'd overheard on holiday. She pushed the thoughts away and drove to the bank, humming along with the radio. After all, if she was honest, it meant that Daisy would be in her debt and Mark, especially, would be forced to treat her with more respect.

Once the standing order had been set up, Celia messaged Daisy:

All sorted. Seb's education secure.

She added a smiley face emoji and her finger hovered over the red heart and decided against it. They weren't a red-heart emoji family.

◆ ─────── ◆

By 5 o'clock, Iris was approaching Ocean's house having consulted the A–Z beforehand. You could never beat a good, old-fashioned map; not like these new-fangled sat-nav things that led you down narrow lanes leading to dead ends. Only today there had been something on the news about a lorry getting stuck in a small lane and completely blocking it.

Iris scanned the road names until she reached Beech Road. She turned in and parked under some trees – beeches, presumably. Iris knew nothing about trees. She also knew nothing about this area but could tell from the size of the mock-Tudor houses that it was nothing like the council estate she'd grown up on – an estate of pre-fabs thrown up after the war and improved over the years with council investment. Most of their neighbours had been people like her parents, hardworking, employed in the local car works, or the nearby soup factory. When Iris had been a child, everyone had taken pride in keeping their houses and gardens neat. Front lawns edged with interchanged blue and white flowers in the summer. Not inhabited by gardeners, Iris's house had made do with a patch of scruffy lawn. As Iris got older, those who had bought their houses moved out to posher areas, but her mother refused to move and so Iris watched as surrounding properties were snapped up by greedy landlords and rented out to all and sundry. Everything went downhill and front gardens were left to their own devices. Graffiti and drug use was commonplace, and it became unsafe to go out after dark. It was on one such rare occasion that Iris had met Zed.

Starting the car, she crawled along the road until she reached her target. Having driven past, Iris turned and came back, stopping the car just before Number 15. Fortunately, there was a bend in the road and she could watch without attracting attention.

Iris enjoyed the early autumn evening as she settled down to enjoy her sandwiches and opened her flask of tea. There was no action at Number 15 or any of the other houses, come to that. Maybe they all worked late.

Hearing a squealing of brakes as the driver took the corner too fast, Iris carefully laid her half-eaten sandwich down on the passenger seat. A BMW, the same one Iris had seen Ocean drive to Eagle Court, came into sight at the end of the road. Approaching rapidly, it turned angrily into the drive of Number 15 and juddered to a stop.

Iris watched, sandwich and tea forgotten, as Ocean got out of the car, and wrenching the passenger door open, shouted at the occupant. The same tall, pimply youth she had seen at Trish's funeral got out of the car, and ignoring his mother, headed for the house.

'Don't you turn your back on me! This is the last time I'm going to bail you out, Mitchell. Understand?'

165

Iris was sure that all the neighbours must have heard the commotion but saw no signs of activity. There were no twitching curtains these days, as most people had blinds.

The boy turned. 'Oh, and you're so perfect, mother dear, aren't you?' Iris admired the boy's pluck. She wished she could have talked to her mother like that.

Ocean walked past her son and strode into the house, slamming the door behind her.

The boy leaned against the garden wall and rolled a spliff. With the window open, Iris could smell it quite clearly. She resumed her sandwich and took a sip of tea. 'Bail you out.' What had Ocean meant? The boy looked too old to be at school, so maybe work, or trouble with the police? *Mitchell Brown.* She made a note of the name.

After Mitchell had disappeared indoors, Iris was just about to head for home when a black Mercedes glided up to the house. A dark-suited man emerged and knocked briskly on the door of Number 15. Iris noted that his driver remained in the car. This was exciting. She knew from the crime dramas on TV that dark-suited men in chauffeur-driven black cars always meant trouble. A tingle of excitement travelled through her body. What she would have given for a listening device! The door opened and the mysterious stranger disappeared inside.

After around twenty minutes, Ocean reappeared with the man.

Iris kept the window open a crack. 'Don't worry, Mr Knowles, you'll get the money, just as soon as my mother's estate is sorted.' This Ocean didn't sound as arrogant, more...cowed.

Iris licked her lips in anticipation. She had never expected a gift like this to fall into her lap so easily. Ocean was somehow in debt to this shady character. Not a good look for a banker.

Zed would have more work to do, and so would she.

Chapter 26

Celia had enjoyed the U3A gardening group. Although she hadn't been for a while, everyone had welcomed her back, and she enjoyed a couple of hours immersed in the finer points of shade-loving plants.

Now she was relaxing in front of the TV, watching a rerun of *Inspector Morse*. She was enjoying a trip down memory lane, recalling her Oxford days and recognising familiar places where she had first got to know Alan. Taking a sip of wine, she sighed, revelling in the peace and comfort of her new home. The crippling sense of loss was fading now, and she was strong enough to face the future – although there was still the occasional twinge of regret at leaving the old house.

Celia stretched her legs on the stool and wiggled her toes. It was good to feel more like herself. Contented again and in control of things. That time before she'd gone on holiday had been scary, but now all that was behind her and everything was back to normal.

Suddenly, Morse disappeared to be replaced with some dreadful sales channel, promising everlasting youthful skin. Celia tutted in exasperation, and, picking up the remote, tried to change back to the channel she had been watching. Instead, she found herself confronted with some kind of horror film, the screams echoing around in her head. In haste, Celia tried to turn the TV off. When it didn't respond, she pulled the plug out of the wall.

In the morning, she would have to get hold of the place where she'd bought it. Maybe it was a fault with the remote. She'd try changing the batteries first. But not now. Suddenly, she was tired. Taking a last sip of wine, she took the glass into the kitchen and placed it in the sink, checking on her phone that the heating had gone off as programmed. Then she took a sleeping tablet.

Celia looked at her bedside clock. It was 2 am. She threw the covers off and sat up. It was so hot, far too hot for a late September night. She opened the window and breathed in the fresh breeze.

Sweat trickled down her back as she touched the radiator, drawing her hand away quickly. It was too hot. Damn this automatic heating system. Daisy had shown her how to use it, but Celia hadn't taken much notice. She opened the app on her phone and saw that the temperature was showing 28 degrees. Celia huffed in irritation and turned the dial back to 7 degrees. She didn't know how to turn it off.

The house was unbearable, so Celia put on a dressing gown and sat outside on the patio, listening to the radiator ticking in the kitchen as the house cooled down.

There was something soothing about sitting outside in the middle of the night and Celia smiled as she heard a barn owl hooting in the distance. She closed her eyes and enjoyed the cool, remembering Cornish camping trips she and Alan had taken with the children when they were younger. Times were different then, and the children had gone off on their own, armed only with jam sandwiches and lemonade. Sometimes, Alan would take them on midnight walks, scaring them with ghost stories, which they all loved. Celia wondered if they still remembered those times. Probably not.

Bringing herself back to the present, Celia noted that she would have to check on the heating before she went to bed tomorrow night – or tonight, as it was now. It was a long time before it was cool enough to return to bed and Celia awoke the next morning groggy and out of sorts.

When she met her friends at the book club, she made the whole thing into a joke and they all had a good laugh about it.

'Did you ever read that book...Oh I forget what it was now, but this girl was driving in a Tesla and a man was controlling it by tapping into the Wi-fi. He made it stop, or go too fast, opening and closing the window. In the end, she was locked in. It was creepy,' said Wanda.

'Well, let's hope no one is tapping into my Wi-fi,' Celia laughed. It all sounded a bit far-fetched.

'Seriously though, maybe you should get on to the provider and check it's not malfunctioning,' said Joanne, taking another sip of wine and shaking her head as Wanda passed the home-made sponge around.

'Mmm. This is amazing!' mumbled Anna her hand over her mouth as she chewed. 'How do you do this, Wanda?'

'Years of practice and lots of hungry children and grandchildren.' There was a hint of one-upmanship in Wanda's comment.

As if reading her thoughts, she turned to Celia. 'How are you getting on in the bungalow, darling? It must be a little more bearable now you've got your arm back again.' She gestured towards Celia's arm.

'Yes, I'm much better. It was lovely to be on holiday with Daisy and the children. Did me the world of good. It's the first proper holiday she's had in years, since Covid. The first time the surgery could spare her.' Two could play at that game, Celia thought.

'Of course. Where would we be without the good old NHS?' added Anna. 'They do come into their own in an emergency, as *you* know, Celia.' She gave a small laugh. 'We none of us know when we're going to have a fall, do we?'

Celia felt her face reddening.

'Let's get back to the book, shall we? I think it was *Still Life* by Sarah Winman. I'll kick off.' And before anyone could side track her, Celia carried on determinedly. 'I thought it had a real depth, and I loved the way the characters developed throughout the book.'

There was silence as the others munched on cake and took sips of wine.

In spite of the humiliation Celia felt, in a group where once she had been the organiser, she was glad of it to break up the evening and stop her overthinking things and having to turn the TV on. She'd not mentioned the channel-hopping to anyone. When Celia got home, pleasantly tired and relaxed after several glasses of wine, she remembered to check that the heating had obediently turned itself off before she went to bed. She decided not to say anything to Daisy. Things were just like the old days now, and she didn't want to rock the boat.

She did, however, mention the TV incident and the heating to Iris when she visited. Somehow, the more she talked about it and laughed, the less of a deal it seemed.

Iris frowned. 'I don't trust any of these Wi-fi things. I wouldn't have any of it in my house.' She sniffed disapprovingly.

'We have to keep up with the times, Iris. I wouldn't be able to keep in touch with anyone if I wasn't on Facebook or WhatsApp. Not that I ever post anything,' she added hastily. 'But I can see what everyone else is doing and I can talk to my son in Australia.'

'You don't talk about your sons much.' Iris swivelled her head and pinned Celia down with a grey, questioning gaze.

Celia shifted in her seat, and after a moment said, 'I'm hoping to go out to Australia to visit Luke soon. They've just had a new baby. He's done so well, becoming a professor in his twenties,' she added.

Iris smiled and said nothing, gazing around the room. Celia saw her notice the box of tablets on the dresser. Before she could think of any response, Iris was on her feet, studying the packet.

'Goodness, is everything alright, Celia?'

'Oh those. They're just some sleeping pills. I hardly ever need them. Just in case, you know. What with everything that's happened, sometimes it's hard to sleep.'

Iris finished her biscuit and brushed the crumbs from the table into her hand. 'And what about your other son, Fred, is it? And didn't I see another baby in some of your photos? Maybe she wasn't yours...' Celia put her mug down so abruptly on the table that some of the coffee sloshed over the side.

Under Iris's hawk-like gaze, Celia struggled to keep herself together. After a brief silence, she reverted to the subject of Wi-fi, ignoring Iris's question. 'And if you had broadband and Freeview, you'd be able watch loads more programmes. I know you like your TV, Iris.'

'How do you know about what I watch on TV?'

Celia was taken aback at the sudden hostility. She assumed that women like Olive, and Iris who lived on their own, watched lots of TV. What else would they be doing for most of the day and in the evenings?

'Sorry, I just thought...'

'You just thought that's what women like me do!' Iris stood to go. 'I'll be off now. I'll see myself out.'

Celia let out a deep breath. She'd been completely blind-sided by Iris's casual mention of Fred and Emma. On reflection, she guessed that Iris had simply been making conversation. Celia was not going to have that conversation, not with Iris. She wasn't sure why, she just knew she would never share her grief with Iris. And then apparently *she'd* offended *her*! Just by talking about TV. Maybe she shouldn't have made such a generalisation, although she knew she was probably right. It seemed that Iris was easily offended these days. Perhaps looking after Bob was wearing her out. Whatever, she hadn't seemed herself. Celia thought she would give the morning coffees a break for a while.

Iris strode into Burgers for U, head held high. The power of having all these stuck-up people under her control was intoxicating. Wrong-footing Celia and flouncing out had given her a real buzz. It was something she would never have done before. But somehow, now, she didn't care. Zed would make sure Celia had what was coming to her.

She tapped Zed on the shoulder.

'Oh, it's you,' he said without looking up.

'Yes, it's me.'

'Just a sec.'

Iris surveyed the restaurant. Several lone figures were munching their way through a variety of burgers, engrossed in their phones. She noticed a couple by the window having a whispered row that was growing in volume until the girl threw back her chair and marched out, throwing a 'Fuck you!' over her shoulder. Her erstwhile partner simply continued chewing on his burger, apparently unconcerned.

'Right. What you want, Iris?'

There was a coldness in Zed's tone that set Iris's nerves on edge. Had she done something to upset him? She decided to ignore it for now. There were more important things to deal with.

'How are you getting on with Celia?'

Iris relaxed a little as Zed grinned, now more like his usual self. 'I'm experimenting with the heating. And I've got a few other things up my sleeve.' He tapped the side of his nose in a secretive gesture.

'Good. I need you to find out about a certain Mitchell Brown. I think he might be a drug dealer working for someone... Hang on a minute.' Iris rifled through her bag and produced a crumpled piece of paper, '...called Mr Knowles.'

Zed looked up, his fingers hovering over the keyboard. 'Mr Knowles?' He ran his fingers through his long, unkempt hair. 'That's some serious shit, Iris. I'm not touching that.'

'I think Trish's daughter, Ocean, owes him money.'

'Then she is in bi-ig trouble.' He drew out the word before lowering his voice and leaning in towards Iris. 'He controls all the sales in this town. It's his patch, you know what I mean?'

Iris nodded. She thought she knew what he meant.

After glancing around, Zed continued. 'If this Mitchell is selling for him – which he will be – you need to keep well clear.'

A plan was forming in Iris's head and this time she wouldn't need Zed's help. 'Okay, I get the message.'

Reassured, Zed continued typing. Realising that Iris hadn't moved and was still watching, he looked up. 'What?' There was an unmistakeable tone of irritation in his voice.

'I need you to disable some cameras for me.'

'Not if it's going anywhere near Mr K and his gang.'

'No, they're domestic cameras, on Ocean's house.' Iris gave him the address. 'For a couple of hours between 2 and 4 the day after tomorrow. Can you do that?'

Zed scowled. 'It'll cost you.'

'Is this enough?' Iris slid several fifty-pound notes across the table.

Zed grunted. Iris took that as a yes and stood to go. Reaching the door, she looked back, relieved to see Zed typing at speed.

Chapter 27

The holiday seemed to have done everyone good, and even Seb was in a better mood when Daisy and the children popped in later that afternoon.

'Everything alright, Mum?' Daisy turned as she poured the tea.

'Absolutely fine, darling. I'm making plans for the garden. Having a small space is a challenge, but you should see what some of the gardeners manage to create at Chelsea.'

'That's great. Maybe you could do with a little helper.' Daisy nodded in Lucy's direction.

'Yes please! Can I help you, Grandma? I'm in the gardening club at school,' she said importantly.

'Actually, yes. Now I come to think of it, I do need an assistant.'

'Cool! When can we start?' Lucy leapt out of her chair and jumped up and down.

'If you've got a bit of time, Mum, could she help you now for an hour or two? Seb and I need to go shopping for a few extra bits and pieces for school.'

'Please! Please! Say yes, Grandma.'

Celia smiled and said, 'I don't see why we shouldn't make a start.'

Lucy was a willing helper, and soon they had all the paths measured out, and mapped with string and pegs. Celia imagined something less formal than her old garden and had thought of winding paths that gave an impression of size.

Celia explained about the arrangement of trees and shrubs hiding the grim, brown fence that currently held the garden prisoner.

'It's going to be a secret garden, Grandma,' Lucy said as they admired their handiwork, each with a cold drink in hand. 'This'll go towards my Brownie's gardening badge.'

Hearing her mother coming through the front door, Lucy leaned over and whispered, 'Can I come again and help you make your secret garden? Can we do it together?'

Celia smiled. She was so much like Daisy had been at that age. 'I don't see why not. Let's talk to Mummy.'

Later, even though she was tired, Celia took two tablets. Checking the heating, she went to bed, her head full of what she and Lucy could achieve in the garden.

Celia had no memory of falling asleep, but she did remember waking up. Waking up and being unable to move. The heat in the room was ferocious and it seemed that she was pinned to the bed, pains shooting up and down her legs. She tried to control her breathing and think rationally, but she couldn't control the waves of panic rolling over her, drenching the bed in sweat.

Raising herself up to see the time seemed an impossible feat, like climbing Everest. Giving up, she fell back to the pillows as a sob caught in her throat. What was happening? Was this the end? Was this how she was destined to die? No. she would not let this happen! 'Come on, Celia,' she muttered to herself.

Summoning up the little strength she had, Celia forced herself to take deep breaths until she could turn on to her side. After more deep breaths produced by iron-strong will power, she summoned up enough strength to reach for her phone and dial Iris. She couldn't even think about getting into the app to turn the heating down. It occurred to her that Iris didn't have a key, and more panic paralysed her. She just wanted to sleep and forget all of this.

Iris woke with a start. It took her a while to locate the source of the noise back to the phone, where she saw a missed call from Celia. The time had been 3.15 and it was now 3.20. What was Family Woman doing up at this time? Something must be wrong. So, pulling on some trousers and a top, she went and banged on Celia's door. When there was no response, Iris hovered on the steps, chewing her nail. What should she do? *For God's sake, Iris. Just do something! Don't stand there like a drip.*

Iris went back indoors and called 999. She waited, striding up and down the Court. When the police arrived, they brushed her aside. 'Don't you worry now, madam. We'll take care of this.'

Iris stood, her heart beating in her mouth as, having got no response, the police battered down the door. She noticed the initial response as they stood a few steps backwards.

'It's like a bloody oven in here!'

Iris's blood ran cold.

After a minute or two, they emerged carrying an unconscious Celia. Iris leapt forwards. 'Is she...is she alright? I mean, is she alive?'

'Stand back, please.' The policeman beckoned another officer over. 'Could you see to this lady?'

'Come on, love. Let's give them space to do their job.'

Iris felt herself being firmly steered away from Number 2.

At that point, the ambulance arrived and Eagle Court was full of blue lights and efficient people in uniforms. At any other time, Iris would have been thrilled to be at the centre of the action, but this all felt too real.

She noticed Bob, in his dressing gown, standing in the doorway of Number 3 and went over to him. 'What on earth's going on? What's happened to Celia?'

'I don't know. She tried to call me. I couldn't get in, so I called the police.'

'Thank goodness she had your number.'

Iris and Bob looked on as the medics were in the back of the ambulance with Celia for a long time. Eventually, they reappeared and conferred with one of the policemen.

A policeman approached her. 'Was it you who made the call?'

Yes. Is she okay?'

'We won't know until she gets to the hospital, but you may have saved her life, Mrs...'

'Miss,' said Iris, stiffly. 'Miss Walker. You said it was hot in there. I know she's got one of these new heating systems that you control with your phone. Maybe she turned it up too high

179

by mistake. She told me she had woken up a few nights ago because the house was too hot.'

'Any idea of next-of-kin?' asked the policeman as he wrote.

'There's her daughter, Daisy Sinclair. You'll be able to find her number in Celia's phone.'

'Thank you, Miss Walker. You've been very helpful. We need you to make a statement to this officer.' He indicated a young man, standing a few feet away.

Iris was beginning to enjoy herself and told the young man about being woken by the call. She handed over her phone. 'I know you'll want to see my call history.' She continued talking as the officer checked her phone. 'I couldn't do anything as I don't have a key. So I called 999.' She waited as he recorded the information.

Iris was relieved that Family Woman had survived, although there was a thrill at being in the centre of all the drama and potential for death.

'Thank you Miss Walker. You've been very helpful.' The young officer closed his notebook.

Bob and Iris watched as Eagle Court emptied of blue lights and activity until it was just the two of them in the cool night air.

'Come on, Iris. I think we could both do with a coffee,' said Bob.

Iris found that she was shaking and felt that a coffee might be just the thing. Maybe with a nip of brandy for the shock.

When she eventually got home it was 5 am, but she was too wired to sleep. She sat looking at the blank TV, her head in a whirl.

Things were going too fast. Zed had taken things too far.

The thought that anyone's life would be in danger had never occurred to her. She had only thought as far as making people suffer. But now that it had almost happened, Iris's thoughts were in turmoil. One thing was for certain; there was no getting away from the fact that she had saved Celia's life. She had done a good thing.

However, anger towards Zed fizzled in her thoughts. He had no right to take things that far. He hadn't consulted her, and she was the one who made the decisions. She was in charge. She had an uneasy feeling that he was becoming difficult to control. However, she had learnt that here was something thrilling about taking someone to the edge, and then being the one who saved them. Iris would stay with that thought for now.

Chapter 28

Wasting no time the next morning, Iris was at Burgers for U by 9 o'clock, only to find that Zed wasn't there. By 9.30 she'd tried all the other fast-food places without success and returned to the branch on the ring-road where she'd met him last. Still no Zed.

Exasperated, she approached one of the staff behind the counter.

'What can I get you today?'

'Nothing, thank you. I'm looking for a young man who comes in here a lot. Tall, long hair?'

The girl wrinkled her face in thought. Then her face cleared. 'Oh you mean Zed. The guy with the laptop! Here's never here before ten, sometimes later.' She smiled. 'Are you sure I can't get you anything?'

'A coffee,' said Iris grudgingly. She was here now and so might as well wait. It was annoying. She had things to do. But she needed to rein Zed in now that the police were involved.

While she waited, Iris composed a letter in her head, smiling here and there when she came up with a particularly good phrase. Having jotted everything down in the notebook she always carried with her these days, Iris drummed her fingers on the table. It was already 10.15.

At last. Just as she was thinking of giving up, half the morning wasted, Zed appeared. He seemed not to notice her and sat at a table on the far side of the restaurant with a burger and milkshake. It occurred to Iris that he might be deliberately avoiding her and her patience was wearing thin as she strode over to him. 'What did you do last night?'

'Last night?' He looked up at her through bleary eyes.

'Last night, when you turned Celia's heating up!' Now it was Iris who looked furtively around as she hissed the words.

'Oh yeah! I turned it up good and proper. Thirty-five degrees I think.' He grinned.

'You nearly killed her, you...' Iris's fury wouldn't let her finish the sentence.

'What, thirty-five degrees? No hotter than, say, Turkey.' Zed seemed unconcerned.

'Maybe not in Turkey, but inside someone's home, when they are asleep, it can be lethal. She rang me in the night and I didn't get a response, so I had to call the police. She's lucky to be alive.'

'Cool!'

A chill travelled down Iris's spine.

Zed's grin morphed into a frown. 'Wait! You called the police?'

'Of course! I saved her life. What else was I going to do.' Now that she thought of it this way, Iris could see that Zed might actually have done her a good turn. He had put Family Woman in danger and as a result. she, Iris Walker, was now the hero of the day.

Zed's frown had deepened. 'What did you tell them?'

'Who?'

'The police, Iris! What did you tell them?' Zed spoke in a half-whisper, keeping his voice low.

'I just said that Celia was going a bit batty and most likely didn't know how to work the heating app.'

Zed nodded, thinking for a few moments. 'And they accepted that?'

'As far as I know.' Zed was beginning to get on Iris's nerves.
All he thought about was himself. 'What are you worried
about? Surely an expert like you knows how to cover their
tracks.' She leant back in the chair and smiled. 'After all, that's
what I pay you for.'

'You know I'm the best Iris. I just don't like the idea of the
police sniffing around. It might compromise my work.'

Iris stifled a laugh. 'Your work?'

Zed closed his laptop with a snap and picked his bag up
from the floor.

'Okay, okay. I'm sorry.' She still needed Zed. 'I'm not in the
business of murder, that's all.'

'Maybe not. But you've got to admit, it's pretty cool having
that kind of power. Especially for people like us.'

'What do you mean, people like us?' Iris wasn't aware of
having anything in common with Zed, especially not now.

'We're the same. People who've always been ignored,
abandoned, people who everyone thought would never
amount to much.'

Iris sat back in the chair, all the breath leaving her body.
How could Zed have known all this about her?

'Wondering how I recognised a fellow conspirator?' Zed
grinned. 'I knew from the first time you asked me to teach
you about graffiti. Here's someone who wants to get their own
back, I thought.'

'You and I have nothing in common at all!' she hissed,
getting up and putting her coat on. 'Don't forget the cameras
for tomorrow.'

Zed ignored her, tapping away on the keyboard until she
was about to move away. 'Oh, and by the way, whatever you

say, we have more in common than you think.' There was a hint of acid in his tone.

Iris hurried back to her car, where she sat for a few minutes, thinking about Zed. Up to this point, he had always been compliant, willing to carry out orders as long as she paid him well. But now there was something different. Maybe something she could no longer control. However, there was no time to think about that – the morning was almost gone and Iris needed to visit the hospital and then get home. She had a lot to do before tomorrow afternoon.

Chapter 29

C elia opened her eyes and looked at the white walls. She swivelled her head to see a window with a view of the grey sky, framed by white blinds. She heard the beeping of machines. Sounds she recognised all too well from the time Alan had spent in hospital.

She tried to sit up, thinking that she must be in some kind of nightmare. A hand on her arm restrained her. 'Take it easy, Mum. Don't rush.'

Celia gingerly eased herself into a sitting position as Daisy rearranged the pillows.

'Thank God, Mum. You've had us all so worried.'

'Daisy. What am—'

'You're in hospital, Mum. Do you remember anything about last night?'

'Last night?' Celia racked her brains. She remembered watching Morse, and yes, the TV had changed channels on its own. But that wouldn't have landed her in hospital. Then she had another thought. Had that been last night or some other night?

'The television...' she croaked. 'It kept changing channels.' Suddenly she became aware of a raging thirst. 'Could you get me some water?'

'Here you go, Mum.' Celia went to take the glass, but some-how her arms wouldn't work. Instead, she saw Daisy holding out a glass with a paper straw. She tipped her head forward and enjoyed the moisture of the water in her parched mouth.

'What's the matter with me?' Panic was setting in now. She could feel pins and needles in her legs.

'It's okay, Mum. The heat stroke has made you feel poorly. You'll be alright in a day or two.'

'Heat stroke?'

'You had the heating on too high, Mum. If it wasn't for Iris calling the police you could have died.'

Alarmed, Celia tried to gather her thoughts and summoned up a vague memory of waking up in the night, reaching for her phone and calling Iris. It was all too much. She closed her eyes.

'You sleep now, Mum. You need to rest.'

The sound of someone coming into the room awoke Celia for a second time.

'How're you doing, Celia?' She heard a familiar voice and felt a rush of gratitude for Iris. She tried to sit up, but every movement seemed like climbing a mountain. Iris stepped forward to help her into a sitting position.

'Much better thanks to you, Iris. I hear you saved my life.'

'Goodness, you gave us all a fright.' Iris smiled. 'What a good job I had your number. I told you it might come in handy.'

'You were right.' Celia smiled, thankful now for Iris's pushy behaviour.

Iris was silent, reflecting the smile with an understanding tilt of the head.

'I just want to get home.' Celia was shocked at the plaintive, almost childish voice that came from her own mouth.

'Tell you what? Why don't you give me your key and I can get everything ready for you – get some pinot grigio in.' Iris was businesslike. 'I'm sure they won't be keeping you in much longer.'

Celia hesitated. Somewhere in the back of her mind, a voice was still telling her not to trust Iris. But she had saved her life, so how could she not be trusted?

'You don't want to be coming back to an empty fridge, and I doubt Daisy will have time.'

She knew Iris was right. 'Pass me my bag. It would be nice to come home to a well-stocked fridge. Thank you, Iris.' She rooted around in her bag. 'There you go.'

'Shall I get another key cut? After what happened, it might be useful.' Celia felt powerless under the penetrating gaze of the blank, grey eyes.

'I suppose so. But I'm sure you won't need it.'

'Well, you never know. Better safe than sorry.'

Iris met Daisy, returning, as she came out of the ward.

'How is she?'

'She's going to be okay. Thanks to you, Iris.'

'Can I tell you something?' Iris led Daisy to a row of chairs and, and as they sat, turned towards her. 'I didn't want to say, because your mother has seemed so much better in herself since she came back from that lovely holiday.' She smiled. 'It's so lovely to see you looking after your mum and including her. Many wouldn't, you know.'

Iris sensed that Daisy was getting impatient, undoing the belt on her coat as if she was in a hurry to go.

'What I wanted to say was...this isn't the first time.'

'What do you mean?' She had Daisy's attention now.

'A few nights ago your mother left the heating turned up too high. Luckily she discovered it in time to turn it down. She ended up sitting in the garden for most of the night until the house was cool enough.'

'How do you know all this?' Daisy's eyes narrowed.

'She told me. Tried to make it into a joke, but I could tell it had shaken her up.'

There was a sharp intake of breath from Daisy. 'Do you know anything about problems with the TV? Mum was saying something about channels changing.'

'She did mention that and I have to say, I'm not surprised. She'd probably forgotten how to work the remote. And she has certainly been forgetting things, just like before the holiday. Just small things like forgetting where she puts her keys.' Iris paused. 'And I've had to remind her several times about meetings she's arranged with friends.'

She could see Daisy processing this information.

After a few minutes, Iris tip-toed into uncharted territory. 'Do you think she's safe to be living in Eagle Court on her own? I mean, I'm always happy to look out for her as I did before, but I can't be there all the time...'

Again, Daisy didn't respond, her attention fixed on a poster about home-care services on the wall opposite.

189

Iris thought she had said enough and anyway she had to get home. She had a lot to do before tomorrow afternoon.

As she stood and picked up her bag, Daisy came back to life. 'It's a difficult thing to come to terms with – such a rapid decline. You always think your parents are going to be there for you, don't you?'

Iris responded with a sympathetic smile.

'She seemed so well when we were away.'

'If you think about it, everything was done *for* her, wasn't it? She didn't have to cook meals, or deal with heating, or anything. Just like in some kind of managed accommodation.'

Iris wondered if she'd gone too far.

Daisy reverted to her usual, business-like self. 'I'll get in touch with my brothers and we'll decide what to do. Thank you again, Iris. I don't know what we'd have done without you.'

'I know it's none of my business, but have you thought about power of attorney? I know from looking after my own mother, the problems that happen if you leave it too late.'

Iris couldn't resist that last question and could practically see the pound signs in Daisy's eyes as she thought about it. Although she didn't particularly want Daisy having control of all Family Woman's money, Iris reminded herself that her main goal was to get her own back on Celia and this way, she would lose any vestige of control over her own life.

Chapter 30

I ris put her bag and the shopping on the counter with a sigh of relief. A quick lunch and then she could get on. So when there was a knock at the front door, she tutted and rolled her eyes.

From the window she could see Bob on the doorstep. All this managing of people was turning into a full-time job. Hiding her irritation behind a smile, Iris opened the door.

'Hello Bob. Everything okay?'

'Fine thanks. I just wanted to know how Celia is. Is she...?'

'She'll be fine.' Iris answered more curtly than she'd meant to. 'She's had a bit of a shock, but she's okay and hopefully she'll be home tomorrow.' She paused. 'Although if I know anything about Celia, she'll make as much fuss as she can about it all. She loves a drama, you know.' This last comment was uttered in a conspiratorial whisper.

'Really?' Bob seemed surprised at this revelation. 'Well, I'm glad she's alright.'

'Between you and me,' Iris leant forward, towering over Bob, 'she's beginning to lose the plot. I was just talking to her daughter, Daisy, about it.'

'Goodness!' Bob shifted on the doorstep. Iris tried to hide her impatience. She had things to do, and time was getting on if she was going to be ready by tomorrow afternoon. Even so, she couldn't resist saying, 'I'm not sure how much longer she'll be with us in Eagle Court.' Before he could reply, Iris said, 'I've got a lot to do this afternoon, but I'll be over to make us some tea later. Macaroni cheese okay for you?'

'Thanks, Iris. Actually, I've decided to take Dusty Roads out for a little trip to the coast. She needs a bit of a run after standing all this time. I'll get myself some fish and chips.'

Iris remained silent. She'd bought all the ingredients. And now, just on a whim, Bob was saying he didn't need her? She should have known. You put yourself out for people and then they discard you like an old rag.

Bob went to go and then turned back. 'The other thing is, I've decided I need to get out and about more, so I'd like to come along to your homeless lunch. I've checked on the website and it says that any volunteers can just turn up. Do you think it would be alright if I pop along on Saturday?'

Iris's world tilted on its axis.

She could think of nothing to say. After all she'd done for Bob, this was all the thanks she got! Just a casual question, as if it wasn't important. Summoning up a weak smile, she nodded and closed the door.

Iris staggered to the chair and sat down. The Homeless Dinner was her place. That world and Eagle Court were separate. She hit the arms of the chair several times with her flat hands. How dare Bob do this to her? Come to her place. How dare he? But what could she do about it? She chewed the corner of her thumbnail, thinking about the letter she was about to create. Why should she to go to all that trouble to help Bob now? An idea formed in her mind. She would make Bob pay – and that Ocean – both at the same time. She felt her energy returning.

It was almost 2 o'clock and she still hadn't had her lunch. Iris liked things to happen at their allotted times, and today was proving to be more than challenging. But maybe this could turn out to be one of her best things yet. Making two people pay at once.

First things first. After a quick sandwich, Iris wrote her message out on a piece of paper, rewriting sections until she was happy with it. As she got the magazines out, she was buzzing with excitement.

Putting on gloves that she had bought on her last shopping trip, Iris flexed her fingers. She needed to take more care this time, pretty sure that Ocean would not let this pass without calling the police. Iris scanned various pages. The letters had to be just the right height and colour.

◈—◈

When she looked up at the clock, Iris couldn't believe the time. The work had been so absorbing she'd forgotten all about her afternoon programmes. Standing back, she surveyed her handiwork. Just as good as last time, maybe even better. Iris treated herself to a mug of tea, a fondant fancy, and *The Chase*. It was Jenny today. The Vixen. She settled down to enjoy the way Jenny put people down when they overstepped the mark by suggesting her offers were insulting.

By the time she went to bed, Iris had recovered her equilibrium and was looking forward to delivering the letter tomorrow afternoon. She had briefly considered getting one of the Homeless to do it for her, but they were unreliable and had no sense of time except when it came to Saturday dinner times. No, it was something she needed to do herself. She'd wear a

193

hood, so if Zed had got stroppy and not turned the cameras off, she'd be okay.

Iris wondered if there was some way to get Bob to handle the letter, so his prints would be on it. She dismissed the idea – too complicated. And thinking about it, Ocean was likely to confront Bob with the letter and give it to him to read, so his prints would be on it, anyway. As her thoughts turned to Bob, Iris ground her teeth at the thought of him coming to the Homeless Dinner. She needed to put that thought out of her head for now and concentrate on the task in hand.

Iris took one more look at her handiwork. Who knew that cutting and sticking could be so much fun?

Hello Ocean (She had managed to find letters with a nautical background for this.)

What kind of bitch visits her mother on her deathbed just to scout out what she can get?

Drop your claim to Bob Randall's property, otherwise some very unpleasant things will start happening to you and your family. And that includes your brother, Thor. (Black granite background for this.) Bob can be very unpleasant if he doesn't get his way.

P.S. I know all about you and your drug-pushing son, Mitchell. How would owing money to a drug baron look at work? Not good, I'm guessing.

Chapter 31

As she had nothing in particular to do the next morning Iris consulted her A-Z to find out where Thor lived. She knew nothing about him but had studied him from a distance at his mother's funeral. Iris had thought that he could do with a good, square meal – he was so thin, encased in a black suit that hung off him, obviously borrowed for the occasion. Thor, it seemed, hadn't been as successful as his sister, and Iris doubted whether the contesting of the will had been his idea. Even so, it wouldn't do any harm to see where he lived. From the address, it sounded like a flat.

After about forty minutes, Iris located the building on the busy high street of a neighbouring town. She parked the car and approached the door. The discoloured, white PVC was marked and scratched where an attempt had been made to kick it open.

'I wouldn't be knocking on there if I was you.'

A short, wiry man had appeared at her side. Iris, noticing his branded shirt, identified him as the grocer from the shop next door.

'I was looking for someone called Thor.'

The grocer made a sound halfway between a sniff and a tut. 'He's the worst of them. Coming and going at all hours. We've complained, but the police never do anything.'

'Is it drugs?'

'That's a bit of an understatement. They're all off their heads most of the time.'

'Thanks for warning me.' Iris smiled at the grocer. 'I think I'll leave well alone.' She knew enough.

There was just time to hurry to the shops and get another key cut. Iris felt a fizz of excitement in her stomach at the thought of letting herself into Family Woman's bungalow and sitting in her chair, boiling her kettle and making a drink, and generally poking around. Even though she had already seen many of Celia's things when she had helped unpack, Iris was pretty sure there had been other items that had been hidden from her.

After a successful shopping trip, pleased with herself, Iris drove to her usual garden centre and bought a pot of tea along with a scone with jam and cream. To have the power to control these people's lives was intoxicating. As she munched, she thought about Ocean and Thor. How dare they think they deserved Bob's money? A good, hardworking man like Bob, who'd saved and valued everything he had. Iris sniffed at the thought that if Ocean or Thor got the money, it would all be spent on drugs and fancy living. No. It just wouldn't be fair. Even so, she'd changed her mind about Bob. Maybe he didn't deserve the money either.

Iris's fingers closed around the key in her pocket, and a warmth washed over her. Maybe she could prepare things for Celia's return tomorrow morning before she went to the Homeless Dinner. Was a little crossword tampering in order? Her heart fluttered at the thought. For now, though, she had to focus on delivering Ocean's letter.

Heart thumping, Iris drove to Beech Road and, as before, parked several doors away from Ocean's house. She sat for a while, making sure that all was quiet, listening to the tick of the engine as it cooled. And then, adrenaline pumping, she got out of the car and put on the hooded coat. Fortunately it didn't look out of place in the autumn weather. Just as she was about to set off, a delivery van drew up to the house next door to Number 15. Iris busied herself rummaging in her bag. The driver didn't notice her, intent on getting rid of his parcel and hurrying on to the next delivery. He rang the bell and shuffled impatiently. When there was no answer, he put the parcel on the doorstep and, turning his van with practised ease, drove off.

Iris's confidence grew now she knew Ocean's neighbour was out, and she set off, walking with long strides towards the house. As she came close, she put the hood up, pulling it well over her face. She couldn't be sure that Zed had kept his word. Best to be careful.

Walking up the path, she slipped the envelope through the letter box, but as she turned, a sudden gust of wind blew her hood back. Iris hurriedly pulled it back up and walked nonchalantly back to her car. She wouldn't worry. Zed had probably kept his word, and it didn't look as if any of the neighbours were in.

197

Iris wrinkled her brow in confusion. Just like last time, these clues were a load of mumbo-jumbo. They were nothing like the crossword magazines she used to get for her mother. Sometimes they did them in the afternoon if there was nothing on TV, and the whole thing had bored Iris silly, but her mother insisted on them doing them together.

'What are you doing now, Iris?'

'I just thought I'd pop down to the shop and get us a nice cake to have with our tea.'

'I need you to do this with me. You know I can't read the clues. And anyway, you shouldn't be eating cakes, you're chubby enough as it is. You'd think it wouldn't show on someone your height, but there you go.'

Another attempted escaped foiled. And Iris would read out the clues through gritted teeth.

In the end, as she didn't have much time, she just wrote in any old thing, only partially completing some of the answers. If the writing wasn't exact, she could always blame it on the shock Celia had had had. Fortunately, the delivery had been early this morning.

Iris was standing on Family Woman's porch, key in hand, newspaper under her arm, carrier bag at her feet when she heard Bob's voice.

'Morning Iris.' He waved as she turned. 'Looking forward to the homeless lunch later.'

Iris stiffened, realising that she maybe she needed to provide an explanation for entering Number 2. 'Just getting a few essentials in for Celia,' she called. 'She gave me her key.' Iris jiggled it in the air.

Bob nodded and waved. 'See you later.'

Iris tutted at the sound of Dusty Roads starting up as she put the key in the door.

Once inside, she stood for a moment, revelling in being in Family Woman's space. Having put the food in the fridge, she wandered around the bungalow, picking up items here and there, opening cupboards and drawers. Iris made a coffee and sat at Celia's kitchen table. In the garden, work was already underway and someone had dug the soil over.

She wondered what Celia thought about as she sat at this table. Regretting the loss of her posh, middle-class lifestyle, no doubt. Iris had no idea what kind of man Alan had been, but Family Woman obviously missed him, and they'd looked happy in the photos she'd seen.

The thought of photos gave Iris an idea, and she headed into Celia's bedroom, where she guessed other personal stuff might be kept. Sure enough, after a thorough search through cupboards and drawers, at the back of the wardrobe, she struck gold.

Her hands closed around a wooden box. Grunting as she lifted it out, Iris placed it on the bed. The name, Emma, was stencilled on the lid. Opening it, she discovered a baby blanket, a few Babygros, various outfits for an older baby, along with a yellow teddy bear and a few toys, a lock of blonde hair, carefully wrapped in a piece of tissue, and finally, a hospital tag.

Emma Morris, born 6th January 1990

Iris sat back on her heels, a hand over her mouth. So Emma had been the baby Family Woman wouldn't talk about. A baby who had died. Iris would put money on it that Celia and her family never talked about Emma. They were just that kind of family who buttoned up their feelings. Iris held the blanket to her cheek, and genuine tears came into her eyes. The silence thickened as the presence of Celia's dead daughter filled the room. Iris could sense Emma. Could feel her anger.

'I'll get pay-back for you, Emma,' she whispered. 'Trust me.'

As she was taking care to replace the box exactly as she'd found it, an unbidden thought wormed its way into Iris's head. What about *her* child? The son she had pushed to the back of her mind, only thinking of her offspring as 'it'. But it was different for her, Iris reasoned to herself. She had only known her child for a few minutes, and she assumed he was still alive. He was someone else's son, not hers. Celia's daughter must have been at least 9 months old when she'd died if the clothes and toys in the box were anything to go by. A completely different thing. Iris sniffed as she gathered her things and locked Celia's front door.

A completely different thing.

Chapter 32

For once Iris was late arriving at the church hall.

'Everything alright, Iris?' asked Wendy, elbow deep in flour. 'Not like you to be late.'

Glancing through the half-raised serving hatch, Iris saw that Bob had been set to work laying the tables and putting out chairs. He was deep in conversation with Stan, who was uncharacteristically animated. At least he wasn't in the kitchen.

Wendy cocked her head in Bob's direction. 'Says's he's your neighbour.'

Iris put on an apron and got ready to tackle the potatoes.

'Thinks very highly of you. Apparently, it was his wife you were looking after. He seems a nice man.' Wendy carried on kneading the pastry. 'What a shame to lose his wife like that.'

'Yes, well, that's all well and good.' Iris couldn't stop the anger from showing.

'Has something happened?' Wendy looked over at Iris. Her hands still.

'Something and nothing,' Iris muttered. 'So what's on the menu for today?'

'Steak and kidney pie. Staffords, the butchers on the High Street, you know them?' Iris nodded. 'They've donated the steak and kidney for today's meal. Said they had a lot of kidney over and threw in some steak as well. So everyone will be eating a good meal today.'

'That's wonderful.' Iris forced herself to sound cheerful. 'I doubt there'll be any left for us, though.'

'You doubt right,' Wendy laughed. 'When you've done the spuds, can you make a start on the carrots?'

'Will do. Where's Tina? Still off?'

Wendy nodded. 'I'm afraid so. I do feel sorry for her. It must be awful watching your mother die a slow death like that.'

Iris grunted, rapidly peeling the potatoes.

'Oh! I'm so sorry, Iris. I'm such a big-mouth sometimes! Of course, you would know.'

Iris made a humming sound and carried on with her work. She wasn't going to let Wendy off that easily.

As they placed the hot food on the counter, the moment Iris had been dreading arrived. Bob saw her and came over. 'I had no idea this was such a big enterprise. You've kept that well-hidden, Iris.'

Iris busied herself fluffing up the mashed potato.

'I've been chatting to Stan over there. Turns out he knows a fair bit about old RVs and is happy to give Dusty Roads the once over. I'll take her round to his garage next week sometime. She's running smoothly enough, but—'

Bob was cut off by the sound of the doors opening and many bodies elbowing their way to the counter. The vicar, as usual, tried to keep some semblance of order.

'Come on, guys. You don't need to push, there's plenty for everybody.'

'He don't know nothing with his posh house!' someone muttered.

'He needs to spend a week on the streets with us,' said another, not bothering to lower his voice.

Bob looked taken aback at the sudden influx of unwashed, ungraceful humanity that flooded towards the food.

Iris grinned. 'Right, lads. Steak and kidney today.'

'Come on, Iris, you beauty, dish up!'

'None of your cheek, Maurice.'

'Alright Tinker?'

'I'll be better if you give us an extra-large spoonful.'

'Come on, Tink. Stop chatting Iris up. Some of us have places to be.'

This was followed by a thin smattering of cynical laughter. 'Speak for yourself, man.'

Iris gave a covert glance at Bob as she played to the audience more than usual, enjoying his obvious disquiet as he hovered by the tables, unsure what to do.

Once the hall was quiet except for the sound of chewing and the occasional burp, Iris made her way over to Mabel. She noticed Bob sitting at a table with George and some of the others, all awkwardness apparently gone as they laughed and joked.

She turned towards Mabel. 'How's the legs, Mabel?'

Mabel huffed, spraying breadcrumbs across the table. 'Patched me up. Gave me a few pain killers and cheerio.'

'At least you'll feel better for a bit though, hey?'

'Don't know how I'm gonna manage with winter coming on and everything.'

'You must have some family somewhere, surely.'

'Only that bitch of a daughter-in-law.' Mabel wiped the plate clean with the last of the pie crust. 'Turned my lad against me, she did. They just took and took. Look where I've ended up. That's where kindness gets you!'

Iris couldn't help thinking that Mabel had a point.

The journey of collecting plates eventually led Iris to George's table, where Tinker announced, 'You'll never guess what, Iris. This Bob's a good'un. He's only gone and promised to take us all to the seaside tomorrow!'

Iris did her best to concentrate on piling plates and cutlery onto the trolley.

'What d'you think of that, Iris?' said Tinker.

'I hope Bob knows what he's taking on with you lot.' Iris did her best to mask her horror behind a gibe.

George appeared at her side as Iris wheeled the trolley towards the kitchen.

'You must be furious, Iris. After all you've done for him.' He passed her some plates. 'Fancy him invading your space like this and getting all the attention.'

Iris couldn't trust herself to speak. It was as if George could see right inside her head, a place that had always been hidden from the outside world – up until now.

'Anyone with a pair of eyes in their head can see your anger.'

Iris turned, thrusting a plate deep into George's stomach, making him stumble. 'Just leave me alone!' she hissed. 'Who do you think you are? It's none of your business.'

George stood his ground. 'It's getting to you. It's eating away at you, just as I said it would, Iris. You can't hide it anymore.'

Iris pushed the trolley roughly to the next table.

George followed her. 'This is your last chance to change, to confront this rage and anger inside. I'm getting a feeling that things are getting out of control with Bob and the others. You can't control them for ever, Iris, and some people you can't destroy. They're too strong for you, and I think Bob,' he indicated Bob with a nod of his head, 'is one of those.'

'I don't know what you're talking about.'

'You do! You can stop this. Go to any support group, AA, or anything. They're happy to hear from those with any kind of addiction. Do it, Iris, before it's too late. Face the ones you've been inflicting your own torment on.'

204

'That's ridiculous!' hissed Iris. 'Those groups are for these kind of people.' She swept her arm around the room. 'Not people like me! I never heard such a load of rubbish.' Iris glared at George, astonished that he could think such things. Maybe he was going a bit bonkers.

'Well then, you'll be the architect of your own downfall.' George turned back to Bob's table, where plans for the next day's trip were at an advanced stage.

Iris clung on to the trolley, certain in the knowledge that she was doing the right thing. Maybe George was right about fighting constant battles, but that was what she, Iris Walker, did. No one was going to get the better of her, never again. Who did George think he was, telling her what to do?

Iris stood tall and marched the trolley into the kitchen.

Chapter 33

Bob and Dusty Roads were waiting outside the church hall by 9.30 the next morning. He looked at his phone. Twenty minutes had passed. Maybe they weren't coming. He should have thought – maybe they didn't have any sense of time. It wasn't as if they had phones and watches.

'She sounds like she's running pretty smoothly,' announced Stan, running his hand across the dashboard. He leant back in the passenger seat. 'You don't know these homeless like I do. They'll never turn up. No sense of time. The only thing they know is Saturday lunchtimes. It's great having an extra pair of hands to tidy up after them. Much appreciated.' He nodded at Bob.

At 10 o'clock, Bob said, 'Come on Dusty. Looks like it's just you and me and Stan for the seaside today.' Just as he was reversing to turn, a motley group came into sight. He could make out George and Maurice, along with a few others, and his heart sank as he noted Mabel trailing along at the back with numerous carrier bags in a supermarket trolley.

Maurice wrenched the door open. 'Watcha mate!' He beamed at Bob. 'Stan.' He acknowledged him with a nod. 'Shall we all pile in?'

Before Bob could answer, the rear door was open and George was loading Mabel's bags into the dining area.

Mabel wailed in protest.

'If you want to come, we'll have to leave the trolley behind, Mab.'

'Will they be alright?' There was still a tremor in Mabel's voice.

'Don't you worry, girl. You can sit in the back and keep an eye on them all the way. Up you go!' George and Tinker hefted her up into the van. Maurice and George ensconced themselves behind the front seat.

Bob tried to hold his breath to protect himself from the overwhelming smell of body odour, unwashed clothes, and something else even more unpleasant. Under the pretext of blowing his nose, he got a handkerchief out of his pocket. Never had he been more thankful to Ann for insisting that a gentleman must always carry a proper handkerchief.

'Alright if we open all the windows?' Maurice asked, already unwinding the rear passenger window and gesturing to George to open as many windows as possible in the back. Stan grimaced and shifted in his seat.

'No, go ahead,' answered Bob, gratefully, wishing he had brought a pair of gloves.

'See, we don't like being cooped up, we like to be in touch with the outdoors.' The others muttered agreement with Tink.

Once the windows had been wound down and the initial shock subsided, Bob found he was able to function. Dusty Roads, creaking under the unaccustomed weight, settled, and soon they were gently cruising along the road to the sea. Glancing in the rear-view mirror, Bob was relieved to see nothing behind them, desperate to get past. He relaxed and tuned in to the conversation going on around him.

'My father used to bring me along this very road,' Mabel was saying. 'We used to go fishing of a Sunday. He was a great one for fishing off the pier.' She was quiet for a few minutes. The others waited, as if they knew she was forming more sentences in her head. 'And then we always had fish and chips...rain or shine.'

In the mirror, Bob saw a tear track its way down Mabel's weathered cheek.

'What did he do, your dad?' prompted George.

'Oh, he was an architect. Loved buildings and was always pointing them out to me. I wanted to be one too. He taught me mechanical drawing and everything.' Mabel was more animated now.

'So why didn't you? Become an architect?' Bob's curiosity was getting the better of him.

'Oh, that...'

Eventually Mabel continued. 'He died and I couldn't do it anymore. There were other things to do then.' Mabel's fingers picked at her woollen skirt as she glanced back at the bags.

'My dad never did anything with me,' said Tink, simply stating the fact. 'Except call me "you little tinker" before he fell asleep of a night. I guess the name stuck.'

'So what's your real name?' Bob was glad the question had come from one of the others.

Tink wrinkled his brow in thought. 'I think it was Elvis.'

Laughter erupted around the van. 'My dad was an Elvis fan,' Tink shouted defensively, before joining in the laughter.

'Well, we shan't be forgetting that – Elvis!' chortled Maurice.

'What about you, Bob? How come you've got a cool van like this? Must have cost a pretty penny.'

'It's a long story.' Bob gave them a short account of his brief time with Trish.

'She sounds like a real goer,' called Mabel from the back. 'I'd have got on with her.'

'The problem is that her children are contesting her will and want to take half of everything I've got.' Bob closed his mouth abruptly. Where had that come from?

'Shit,' muttered Stan under his breath.

'Is that so bad? You'll still have half?' said Tinker.

Bob stared at the road, annoyed with himself, at how tactless he'd been.

'Sometimes the less you have, the less you have to worry about. Isn't that right, Mab?' Maurice turned and winked at Mabel, who gave him the finger.

'Right, let's see who'll be the first to see the sea,' George exclaimed.

Everyone leaned out of the open windows, scanning the horizon.

Bob knew exactly when the sea would come into view and slowed Dusty Roads as they crawled to the top of a hill.

'I think there's a bit of a rattle when you change down to second, Bob. I'll take a look when we get here.' But the clamour as the coast came into view drowned out anything Stan had to say. There were gasps at the sea, sparkling in the autumn sun.

'There. There!'

'Oh my God!'

'Oh, would you look at that!!'

Dusty Roads creaked as excited passengers threw themselves around in the van.

Bob was relieved to find a space on the seafront. Now that it was autumn, the beach was mostly populated by dog walkers.

Pulling the handbrake on, he rubbed his hands together and blew on his fingers to warm them up. A cup of tea was in order. Before he could suggest it, his passengers had piled out of the van and were already walking up and down the prom. All except Mabel.

'I'll stay here and see if I can locate that rattle,' said Stan.

'You sure?'

'Absolutely. I'll be as happy as a pig in muck.'

'I'm not leaving my stuff here. I'll wait until you all come back.'

'But what about the pier, Mabel?' Stan asked, a note of panic in his voice. Mabel hesitated. 'Come on, you can't miss that.'

'Only if I can bring my stuff.' She settled herself in the seat with a determined look.

Bob searched for the others who had wandered a hundred yards or so up the prom towards the pier. He jogged towards them, calling. Just as he was leaning, hands on his knees to catch his breath. Tink turned.

'Mabel,' Bob shouted in a whisper, gesturing towards the van.

Tink nudged the others, and they hurried towards him with concerned faces. 'Wassup, mate?' asked Maurice patting him on the back.

'It's Mabel. She won't get out of the van unless we bring her bags.'

There was a collective sigh.

'So we'll carry them for her,' said George decisively. 'Come on.'

After the fuss about who would carry what, they set off in the general direction of the pier. Bob smiled as passers-by turned to stare at several unkempt men struggling under the weight of numerous, battered, carrier bags.

'Bloody hell, Mabel. What you got in here?' Tink exaggerated his movements, staggering under the weight of the bags.

'None of your business.' Mabel stretched her arms up and sighed. Unencumbered for the first time in years, Bob imagined.

When, at last, they at last reached the pier cafe, Bob was glad to see there was still outside seating, and the party arranged themselves around two of the tables while he went in to order.

'We don't serve vagrants here,' said the stern woman behind the counter.

'They're with me,' replied Bob, wondering how long that would be true. 'They're on an escorted outing. I'll have five teas and five donuts, please.' He summoned up the authoritative voice he had used in his driving instructor days.

The stern woman tutted and turned to put the order together. As he waited, Bob saw a Mabel-like figure flit past him with surprising agility, heading for the toilets. Thankful that the patron hadn't noticed, he made a great fuss about arranging things on trays and paying until Mabel reappeared.

The woman reluctantly brought one of the trays out, not hiding her disdain. As soon as she'd turned her back, Mabel couldn't contain her excitement. 'You must see those toilets! Proper clean and even with hand cream.' She was still rubbing the excess cream into her hands.

Bob shuddered. She must have emptied half the tub.

'Wow! Isn't this something?' Maurice grinned, leaning back and lacing his fingers behind his head.

'I'll say!' Tinker sighed as he swallowed a large bite of donut, jam running down his chin.

Bob tried to imagine what it must be like to savour such a simple thing as a cup of tea and a donut, and realised how much he took for granted. Here he was, worrying about losing only half of his money and expecting this group to understand. A fresh wave of shame washed over him at his insensitivity.

Fortified by tea and donuts, they headed along the pier, Mabel striding ahead in excitement. The group drew many side-long looks from other visitors as they moved to the far

211

side, putting distance between themselves and the woman dressed in a strange collection of coats, skirts and trousers, followed by three unkempt men toiling under the weight of numerous carrier bags. Bob couldn't help smiling at how the group carried on regardless until Mabel reached the rails at the end of the pier.

'It was here! This was where I came with my father!'

They stood looking out to sea as a large oil tanker glided along, moving so slowly its progress was imperceptible. After a while, Bob, ready to move, realised that the others were happy to stay, sitting on benches and gazing at the view.

'Don't you want to do something else?'

'It's what we do,' explained George. 'We sit all day and watch. We don't need to do anything else.'

Bob felt suitably rebuked.

Time flowed by without meaning until an officious man came along, jingling a set of keys. 'Pier's closing now,' he said. 'No rough sleepers here.'

Before Bob could object to the man's offensive tone, George cut across him. 'Right, that's us, then,' he said calmly. 'Time to get going.'

There were groans and huffing as the group struggled to get themselves into a standing position. The security guard followed them all the way down the pier and made a big show of locking the gates as they passed.

'Bastard!' muttered Mabel.

Sprits were raised, however, by Bob's suggestion of fish and chips. 'You can't come to the sea and not have fish and chips.'

When they piled into the van, all supplied with fish and chips, Bob hoped the fried food would mask the less pleasant odours.

There were many appreciative sounds as the meal was devoured.

'Thanks for this, mate.' Stan tucked into the meal along with everyone else. 'I think I've sorted the problem. She should run as smooth as anything now.'

'Thanks Stan, I'll bring her in for a proper service next week.'

Placing all the papers in the bin, Bob started Dusty Roads. Ready for home.

Maurice started on a long story about Moby Dick which he had spent many hours studying in the library, and before long, as Dusty Roads sped along, most of the passengers were asleep. Bob was glad of the open windows, otherwise he might have joined them.

'Thanks, Stan. You've worked wonders.'

'She's purring like a kitten now,' said Stan pleased with his work.

It was beginning to get dark as they pulled into the church hall carpark in silence. Even Maurice had been lulled to sleep by his own story.

Bob turned and said, 'We're back.'

He crescendoed to a shout 'We're back!!'

Everyone stirred.

'What a day. That was great, mate. Let's do it again some-time.'

'Thanks, you're a real diamond, Bob.'

'Come on, Mab. Let's get you sorted.'

Bob watched as the group organised themselves and dis-appeared into the gloom, fading away like sprites, only to reappear again next Saturday. He wondered where they were going.

He dropped Stan off and drove home, looking forward to a hot chocolate and getting warm for the first time all day. As he turned into Eagle Court, he wondered, not really caring, how long the smell would linger in Dusty Roads. A BMW was

213

parked in Dusty's usual spot so, sighing, he manoeuvred and parked Dusty next to it as best he could.

As Bob climbed down and locked the door, Ocean emerged from the car and strode towards him, anger spitting from every stride. Thor trailed after her.

'How dare you!' She waved a sheet of paper in his face. 'This is a bit low, even for you, Bob.'

Ocean stood back, hands on hips, as Bob read the letter. 'What? Oh come on, Ocean, you can't think—'

'That you had something to do with this? It seems pretty obvious to me.' Ocean shifted on her feet. 'I can imagine it came as a shock that we would actually want our mother's inheritance, but this?' She spat the words. 'Blackmail and threats? I would have thought a solicitor would have been more your style.'

Bob couldn't think of anything to say. He had been lulled into a welcome sense of calm after a day with his friends in the sea air, and now reality was slapping him awake.

'We're within our rights! Thor?' She turned and gave him a shove.

Thor shifted on his feet. 'Yeah. Right.'

Ocean huffed.

As Bob re-read the letter, several things began to click into place in his mind. There was only one person who could have done this. Only one other person he'd shown the solicitor's letter to. A tremor passed through his body as he realised that sturdy, dependable, saintly, Iris, was someone else entirely.

'Well?'

Bob's gaze returned to the angry woman in front of him, her brother looking at the ground. 'I didn't do this.' As Ocean made a disbelieving sound, Bob continued, 'But I know who did.'

Thor looked up.

'I know who delivered it! We caught Iris on our security cameras. We looked back to check when Mitchell, my son, showed it to me earlier. Apparently, he found it on Friday and then forgot to mention it!' Bob felt a tinge of pity for Mitchell. 'So, yes, I know you didn't actually *deliver* it.' The acid sarcasm didn't disturb the strange calm that had, once more, enveloped Bob.

'You can believe it or not. I had no knowledge of this, and I'm horrified that Iris took it upon herself to do such a thing.' Bob took a step back, resting his hand on Dusty's warm bonnet. 'You can have the money. I don't care. All I ask is that you leave me my RV and a few personal items.'

Ocean's mouth dropped open. 'You're not going to challenge?'

'Nope, you take it. But I'll be glad if you could move off my drive – while it's still mine – so that I can park Dusty here in her usual place.'

Thor gave a small smile and something of a half-wave. Ocean elbowed him roughly. 'Come on. Fat use you've been!'

The acceptance was ungracious and abrupt. Bob no longer cared. He was already thinking about the repercussions of the discovery he'd just made.

Chapter 34

B ob listened to the whine of the vacuum cleaner. He peered through the doorway, noticing the rough pushes and pulls as the machine was manoeuvred around the room. Iris had her back to him, but he could imagine her mouth set in a tight line. Something had happened. Maybe she knew that he was on to her. Part of him wished he could confront her there and then, but he needed more evidence.

Once he was satisfied that Iris was occupied, and ignoring her bad mood, Bob went to her bag. Listening to check that she was still busy, he took a deep breath and undid the zip. Rooting around, around, Bob felt like a criminal in his own house as he searched through Iris's belongings. His hands clumsy in thick gardening gloves, Bob was amazed at the contents of Iris's cavernous bag. He laid an old-fashioned mobile phone, a comb, a bunch of keys, a large notebook with a pen slotted in along the spine, a camera, and a canister of spray paint on the table, as well as a purse bulging with banknotes. Finally, he came across a collection of shopping lists, carefully secured with a paper clip, inside a cardboard folder.

Picking up the cannister, he examined the label – neon pink. Putting the spray paint to one side, he flicked through the notebook and was astonished to see a cutting of a crossword and attempts to imitate the handwriting, improving as they went along. Bob, open-mouthed, gasped horror as he turned the pages. Iris was trying to imitate someone's handwriting. Someone who apparently did crosswords. He was frozen for a few moments as he tried to think what it all meant.

He remembered that Celia next door always had a paper delivered, and imagined she would be the type to do crosswords. And then he remembered Celia's accident. The notebook slipped from his hands and hit the table with a slap. Had Iris been targeting Celia as well?

Hearing the vacuum cleaner come to a stop, he hurriedly replaced all the objects back in the bag, except the notebook. If Iris noticed it was missing, he hoped she would think she'd left it somewhere. Bob wasn't ready to show his hand yet.

'Coffee?' The tone was curt and business-like.

'I'll make it, Iris, you sit down.' Bob hoped he was disguising his dismay behind a kind voice.

Iris frowned at him. 'But I always make the coffee.'

'Well, it's your day for a treat, after all you do. You just sit there and rest, Iris.' Bob smiled what he hoped was a grateful smile. He would never eat or drink anything Iris had made again. Thinking of her rooting around all his possessions made him shudder.

As he returned with the coffee, he produced a plate of chocolate biscuits. 'What's all this then?' Iris asked, taking off her overall.

'Like I said, you deserve a treat, Iris. After all, when does anybody ever treat you?'

Bingo! Tears appeared like magic in Iris's eyes. '

'I do my best, even if I don't get any thanks. Thanks Bob.' She softened towards him.

Once Iris had finished her drink, she put on her coat and gave him a curt nod before departing without a word. The chilly Iris had returned.

217

As the door clicked shut behind her, Bob leaned against it and let out a long sigh. How on earth did Iris keep up all this pretence of being kind? It was exhausting!

Having waited until Iris disappeared in her car after lunch, Bob tapped gingerly on the door of Number 2. He waited several minutes, and was just about to knock again, when Celia eventually appeared.

'Bob?'

Bob recognised the dark circles of a non-sleeper under her eyes. He had been there many times himself.

'Sorry to bother you, Celia. Could I come in? It's important.'

Celia's eyes widened and there was a brief hesitation before she answered. 'Of course.'

Bob followed her into the kitchen, knowing exactly where it was. The layout was identical to his own bungalow.

'Can I get you a cup of tea?' There was a quaver in her voice. 'That's if I can. Sometimes I forget where things are.'

'Let me come and help.' Bob followed her into the kitchen and was shocked to see post-it notes dotted around, labelling everything from tea and coffee to what was in the fridge. There was even a note on the fridge saying *No coffee in here!* followed by a smiley face.

Celia made them some tea with no issues and sat with Bob at the table.

'What is it?'

Now that he was here and could see the extent of Iris's activities, Bob couldn't think where to begin.

'It's' Iris, he said. All this...you, it's Iris.'

'What on earth are you talking about?' Celia placed her mug carefully on the table.

'Has something strange been happening with your crosswords?'

Celia looked at him. And after a shaky breath, she replied, 'Sometimes the clues are filled in all wrong.' She shook her head. 'And I know that I've done it earlier and can't remember anything about it.' A tear fell on to the table, and Celia wiped her eye with an abrupt gesture, using the back of her hand.

'But how do you know *you* did it?' Bob leaned towards her.

'Because it was my handwriting.'

'No, it wasn't.' Bob produced the notebook from his pocket and slid it across the table to Celia.

'What's this?'

'It's Iris's.' Bob sipped his tea and watched as Celia flicked through the pages, her eyes widening. She became very still for a few moments, before roughly pushing the notebook away.

'But...that's impossible!' She was silent for a few seconds, before saying abruptly, 'How do you know this is Iris's?' Her tone was angry, but Bob could sense fear and panic in her voice.

'I took it from her bag while she was cleaning this morning.'

'What? You went through Iris's things?' Celia glared at him.

'Look, it doesn't matter about that now, Celia. The main thing is that Iris has been tampering with your crosswords.'

'I don't know.' Celia shook her head as she stood and paced around the kitchen. 'I don't know what to think. How do I know this isn't *your* notebook?' She turned and pointed a finger at Bob. 'And that you're not telling a pack of lies!'

'Remember the graffiti on the RV?' Bob kept his calm. 'I found the can of spray paint in her bag as well.'

Who put all these post-it notes up?' He gestured around the room, breaking the silence.

'Iris.' Celia paused. 'But she did it to help me.'

She sat down. 'How did you find all this out? What were you doing going through Iris's bag?'

'I had a visit from Trish's daughter, Ocean, yesterday. You may have heard some...disturbance.' When Celia didn't answer, Bob continued, 'She came to accuse me of sending her an anonymous letter and putting Iris up to delivering it. I did no such thing.' He leaned towards Celia. 'You have to believe me. But Ocean caught Iris on her security cameras, so there was no doubt about who delivered it.' Bob rubbed his eyes underneath his glasses, causing them to perch uncertainly on the end of his nose. 'So that set me thinking about everything else that's happened – to me and to you.'

Celia was pale. 'Why would Iris be sending Trish's daughter an anonymous letter?'

Bob placed his head in his hands. 'It's a long story.' He looked up. 'I think Iris thought she was doing me a good turn. But it's back-fired on me – big time.'

'I don't know what to think.' Celia muttered after a pause.

'Tell you what we'll do.' Bob had a firm plan in his head now. 'I have a mate who installs security cameras. How about I get him to install some in your place and mine, and we'll see what Iris gets up to when we're not around. She's got a key to yours. Hasn't she?'

Celia nodded uncertainly.

'Then we'll know one way or another.' Bob stood to go, anxious to put his plan into action? 'You up for it, Celia? If not, we'll just do mine. But I think she gets up to plenty in your house.'

Celia nodded, suddenly calm. 'Yes, let's do it. Then we'll know one way or another.'

Chapter 35

I ris emptied her bag out onto the table. The notebook was definitely missing. She thought back over the last few days, trying to remember when she last used it. Most likely when she'd worked on Celia's crossword a few days ago, but a thorough search of Number 1 produced nothing.

This was the reason Iris kept everything in her bag; she liked to have tools near her at all times – you never knew when an opportunity might arise. Also, it meant that there was no evidence lying around for prying eyes to find.

Sighing, she sat down and leaned her head back against the chair. The only other thing she could think of was that she might have left it with Zed. Although it was a long shot, as she hadn't seen him for a few days.

Before checking in with Zed, however, there was work to do. She'd seen the confrontation between Ocean and Bob the other night, smiling in grim satisfaction at Bob's distraught face. Iris hadn't been able to hear what was said, as Celia had chosen that moment to cut her lawn, but she would put money on the fact that Ocean thought Bob had written the letter and hadn't accepted Bob's denial.

Thinking of Celia, there was more to be done. She needed to make a trip to the shops.

The following afternoon, after returning from the shops, Iris was standing motionless behind the curtain, as Family Woman left for her book group. She couldn't see the point of books, herself, when you could watch everything on the TV with much less effort. She watched the clock, letting ten minutes elapse. There was always the possibility that Celia might make an unexpected return.

Closing her own front door quietly, Iris walked the few steps over to Number 2. Although the distance was short, it seemed like stepping from one world to another, and her heart was thundering with excitement as she let herself in.

She stood in the silent hallway, savouring the moment. Iris had never got over the novelty of being alone in Celia's house, but this time was even more special. She had dressed for the occasion. Straightening the striped top which had been brought out of her wardrobe for the occasion, Iris wondered whether she might be too hot in the green, quilted body warmer that had been purchased especially. But it had been expensive, and it was important to keep it on to complete the look. After checking her freshly styled hair in the hall mirror, and smoothing the expensive chinos over her hips, Iris was ready for action.

Something drew her to Celia's bedroom and the box at the back of the wardrobe. Somehow, Iris couldn't resist revisiting the evidence of Celia's grief. Grief that she'd kept locked away all these years. She felt a dark satisfaction knowing that Celia's life wasn't so perfect after all. What a hypocrite she was, in her expensive clothes, thinking she was better than the likes of Iris. Having examined all the contents once more, Iris went to put them away, but her hand hovered over the teddy bear. Maybe it was time for Celia to be confronted by Emma. Maybe it was time that Emma came out of the box. Putting the rest of the items carefully away, and placing the box back in the wardrobe, Iris laid the teddy on the bed, propping it up against the pillows, carefully straightening the frayed ribbon around its neck.

It was time to move on before Celia got back. She went into the kitchen and put the shopping away, including three bottles of pinot grigio that Celia hadn't asked for. She hadn't done Celia's shopping for quite a while, so it would be a nice surprise for her to come home to. Sitting at the table, Iris carefully doctored a previous list, changing the 1 to a 3. After taking a final look around, stretching out the last few minutes, Iris returned to Number 1, where she carefully replaced the clothes in the wardrobe and settled down with a hot chocolate.

Two doors away, Celia watched, eyes wide in horror. A breath caught in her throat when she saw Iris on the screen. 'I can't... I can't believe it,' she whispered.

'Is that...? But she looks like you!' Bob stammered.

She watched in silence, unable to utter a word as Iris-dressed-as-Celia headed for Emma's box. An icy sensation travelled down Celia's spine as Iris entered the bedroom. She knew where her neighbour was going before she even opened the wardrobe door. From a distance Celia heard herself give a muffled sob as good, kind, Iris, rifled through the most private part of her life.

And then realisation dawned on her that this wasn't the first time. Iris already knew where the box was. How many times had she visited her house, pretending to be Celia? The thought was unthinkable.

She felt Bob's hand, solid in hers, and was grateful that he asked no questions. When Iris laid Emma's teddy on the bed it was almost too much and Bob went to close the laptop.

'No.' Celia reached out and put her hand on his arm. 'No. I want to see everything.'

They watched as Iris put away the shopping and altered the list, leaving three bottles of wine on the table. The smile on Iris's face as she admired her handiwork sent such a chill through Celia's body that she actually shivered.

'You were right, Bob,' she said, closing the laptop. 'I just didn't want to believe it. How could I not have seen it? How could I have been so gullible?'

'She had me fooled as well, don't forget. She's very convincing.' Bob cleared his throat. 'She's due to come to mine tomorrow, and I'll take a look myself after she's gone.'

Celia was grateful for Bob's thoughtfulness and squeezed his hand in response. Suddenly overwhelmed with fatigue, she leant her elbows on the table, her head in her hands before another thought occured to her. She looked up at Bob. 'But what about the heating? The texts from Alan? Switching the TV channels? Iris wouldn't have the know-how to do any of that, surely.'

'She must have an accomplice. Someone who's tech savvy.' Bob stood up and paced around the kitchen. 'I don't think we've got to the bottom of this, yet.'

'But why? Why is she doing this? Why is she tormenting us like this? Is she after money?'

'I don't think so. Iris has plenty of money. I think it's more about anger. Maybe about the life she's had…or rather hasn't had. And…maybe she just hates us because we're not her. Who knows.'

They sat in silence for a few minutes before Celia stood up. 'I think we should go round and confront her. She won't be able to wriggle out of this one, no matter how clever her patter is. The proof is all here.' Celia was quivering with rage as she jabbed the laptop with her index finger. 'And first thing tomorrow, I'm going to get my locks changed. That's the last time Iris comes into my home.'

'Hold on, Celia. Let's think this through. I agree, we've got to do something. But it's too soon to confront her now, though. I think that's a job for the police. Iris is quite capable of distorting anything we might say to her – we shouldn't underestimate her. We need to go through the right channels.'

Celia sat back down. She would have given anything to be able to confront her tormentor, there and then. The woman who had so very nearly destroyed her. No, the woman who had almost killed her. And for what? Bob was right. She must have been working with someone else. Celia cast her mind back to the conversation about Wi-fi and the limited use Iris made of her phone. She knew for a fact that someone else was involved, probably someone younger. Celia shuddered at the thought that another person wished her ill – someone she had never even met.

'Why would someone who doesn't even know us do these things?'

'My guess is that she made it worth their while.' Bob paused. 'As I said, I don't think she's short of money.'

'What kind of person would do things like that for money?'

'Oh, I think there are plenty of people out there who would do almost anything for money – especially if it means doing things remotely. To them, it would almost seem as if they weren't involved. I think we should follow her over the next few days and see what she's up to, and who she meets. The more evidence we can get, the better.'

'I know you're right, Bob. But I just...' Celia spoke through clenched teeth, banging the table in frustration.

'Let's meet in the morning. Unplug your Wi-fi at the wall. You need a good night's sleep, Celia.'

Celia took several deep breaths. 'Right. We'll keep an eye out and if either of us sees Iris getting ready to go out, we'll text. She takes ages locking up, looking around the Court and getting in the car, so we can be ready the minute she goes.'

Chapter 36

Celia and Bob were ready when, after lunch, Iris set off in her car, turning left out of the Court.

'We'll take my car,' Celia said. 'Your RV doesn't exactly blend in.'

'Dusty Roads. That's what she's called.' Bob patted her bonnet fondly as they passed.

As they followed Iris, Celia said, 'We used to go on lots of camping trips when the children were small. Under canvas, not in an RV like yours, though.'

'I'll show you around when we have a chance. Especially as it might be my home in a few months.'

Celia looked at him. 'What? Are you serious?'

''Fraid so. As I mentioned before, Trish, my wife—' Celia was taken aback that Bob lived next door and still felt the need to clarify who Trish was, as if Celia didn't know. She had been to her funeral, for God's sake! She was glad that she held back the terse comment that had had hovered on her tongue. '–has two children who are contesting the will. They want half of everything.'

'That's outrageous!' spluttered Celia.

'Heads up, she's turning into Burgers for U.' Bob leaned forward.

'What? So she is!'

Celia indicated left and pulled into a space at the far end of the car park.

'What should we do? She'll notice us if we go in.' Celia drummed her fingers on the steering wheel in frustration as she peered into the rear-view mirror. 'She's getting out of the car and going in. Seems in a hurry.' Celia undid the seatbelt. 'Right. Let's go.'

'I think you should stay here. I'll go and take a look in from outside. Good job I brought this,' said Bob grinning as he put on a baseball cap.

Celia watched, frowning, as Bob strolled along outside the restaurant, pausing every so often to glance in.

'Well?' She was impatient when he got back in the car.

'She's talking to some geeky young chap. I think we've found our accomplice.'

'So what are we waiting for? Let's go in and confront both of them!'

'I've got a better plan.' Bob ignored Celia's bossiness. 'We wait until Iris has gone, and then we go in and tackle this guy on his own. He pulled a wallet out of his pocket and counted out some notes.'

'Got any cash on you?'

'Well yes, but I'm not giving that lout any.'

Bob put his hand on Celia's arm. 'I'm sure he'll be happy to tell all if we offer him enough cash. As I said last night, people like that will do almost anything if they're offered enough money. More evidence, see?'

'Were you a detective in a previous life?'

'No, just a plain old driving instructor.'

Celia laughed, sensing herself relaxing in Bob's company. 'I'll be very self-conscious about my driving now.' Reluctantly, she had to acknowledge that he was right. They had to be cautious until they had enough evidence. She glanced into the rear-view mirror once more. 'Goodness! She's leaving, already.'

They turned in their seats and watched as Iris strode across the car park, anger evident in her rigid gait and the way she flung open the door of the car.

'Doesn't look as if the meeting went well,' muttered Bob.

Iris drove home, not wanting to think about what Zed had said. But when she sat down to watch *Deal or no Deal,* anger and humiliation overwhelmed her as she recalled their conversation. Not so much a conversation as a battle, barbed arrows flying between them. She felt wounded.

She'd confronted Zed as soon as she reached the table. 'I want my money back. You didn't turn those cameras off, you little bastard!' she hissed over his shoulder.

When she sat down he'd simply stared at her, unmoving. His fingers still for once.

'I need you to step up things with Celia now. Do whatever,' she said, no longer caring about Family Woman's safety. She was past that now. But Zed was still unresponsive, gazing at her with a strange intensity that Iris found unnerving.

'Zed!' she'd hissed impatiently. 'Oh I get it,' she said and hoisted her bag off the floor. 'You want more money? How much?'

'I don't want your money.'

'What, then? What's going on?' Iris couldn't be bothered to control her anger.

'Want to know? Right then, I'll tell you, *Iris*.' At the emphasis on her name, a tickle of unease curled in her stomach.

'You know I was adopted...'

'Yes, I know all about that.' Iris made a dismissive movement.

'So, I've been doing a bit of digging, and you know what? I found out that you're my grandmother.'

Iris felt the blood drain from her face and then her body. Zed turned his attention back to the laptop and started typing before turning once more to Iris. 'It was when you said you'd pretended to be my aunt. It got me thinking.'

She clutched the edge of the table to steady herself as Zed continued pounding the keyboard, unable to process what he'd just said.

She took a deep breath and swallowed.

'I'm...'

'Yeah, bad news, *Iris*!'

Iris felt her world fragmenting as it started to spin out of control. 'I'm not. Don't be ridiculous. There must be some mistake.'

'Nope. No mistake.' Zed stopped typing and looked up at Iris. 'And know what? I hate the thought that you're my grandmother. You're a nasty, bitter, conniving old woman and I can quite believe that you could give my father away without a second thought.'

The silence lengthened.

'He might as well not have been born, really. You know how I ended up in care?'

Iris couldn't speak.

'He and my mother were both dopeheads. They died together, of an overdose of bad stuff when I was a few weeks old. A neighbour found me, and that was that. So that was what you did to your precious son!'

Iris vaguely registered the acid, febrile glint in Zed's eyes.

'But... I had no choice.'

Suddenly anger flowed, propelling Iris back to life. Anger at the thought of Zed, of all people, rummaging around in her past. Anger at this monster her son had produced.

As if reading her thoughts, Zed said, 'Bet I'm a real disappointment as a grandson, aren't I?' Iris didn't answer. She couldn't think of the words fast enough to describe how much she despised him in that moment.

For humiliating her.

For digging around in her past and disturbing things that should have been left as they were.

For blaming her for something that wasn't even her fault.

For making her have to even think about all that.

His smirk was too much. Iris released her grip on the table as anger – more visceral than anything she'd ever felt before – filled the vacuum, as shock receded.

Without answering, she stood and hurled herself out of the restaurant, only pausing to take a few gasps of air before letting anger and fear carry her to the car.

Bob indicated Iris's accomplice sitting near the back of the restaurant. He seemed lost in another world, staring into space.

Bob was ready and determined to get this young man to speak as his hand closed around the wallet in his pocket. He strode to the table and sat opposite him, vaguely aware of Celia at his side. But before he could open his mouth with the opening speech he had prepared in his head, Celia cut in.

'What is your connection with Iris?'

Zed looked up, closed his laptop and put it in his backpack.

'We just want to talk to you. You're not in any trouble,' Bob added in what he hoped was a more conciliatory tone as Zed, his coat on, was ready for flight.

'We can pay you.' Celia's intervention clinched it, and the young man sat down, wary, ready for flight at any moment.

'You the cops?'

His eyes widened as Bob put a wad of notes on the table.

'We just want to ask you a few things.'

Bob was aware of Zed's leg jiggling under the table. They were going to have to tread carefully.

'How do you know Iris?' he asked.

'I do a few jobs for her from time to time. But I'm sick of her now – it's like she owns me or something.'

Bob squeezed Celia's hand under the table as he could see from her face that she had put two and two together and realised that this individual had almost killed her.

Bob pushed the money towards him. 'What kind of jobs?'

'Why should I tell you?' He picked up the cash and stuffed it in his pocket. 'Who are you anyway?'

'Just tell us,' Celia intervened, her voice trembling.

'Just hacking, sending messages, fiddling with Wi-fi devices, stuff like that. And I was the one who taught her how to use spray paint.' There was a hint of pride in this last confession.

Bob noticed Celia's mouth was clamped shut. He could almost see the gritted teeth through her taut skin.

Zed broke the silence. 'And I fucking hate that she's my grandmother!'

'Your *grandmother*?' Celia spoke in a breathy voice, as if she'd been sprinting.

'Yeah. Imagine having *her* for a grandmother. She acts like she owns me. Do this. Do that. Now I see her for the conniving, manipulative bitch she is. She doesn't care about anybody but herself. And she had the nerve to be disappointed in me!' Zed sat back, as though exhausted after such a long speech.

'Who are you anyway?' His eyes narrowed in suspicion.

'We're Iris's next-door neighbours.' Bob stated the fact calmly.

'You mean...?' Zed closed his eyes. 'Look, I was just doing a job. I don't want any trouble.' He spoke rapidly, once more making ready to go. 'It wasn't personal,' he added.

Bob heard Celia's cynical laugh, followed by an acid comment. '*Not personal?*'

'Look. All we want is to take Iris down. Make her pay for what's she's been doing.' He saw a gleam appear in Zed's eye.

'How? How are you going to make her pay?'

'We're going to the police.' Celia's voice was cold. 'And you're coming with us. We've got all the evidence we need now, with what you've told us.'

'Not fucking likely! Are you mad? I could go down for this!'

'Not necessarily. Not if you turn yourself in and explain that Iris paid you to do these things.' Bob sensed that Iris's accomplice wasn't going to be persuaded.

'No way! I shouldn't have spoken to you in the first place!'

Zed gathered his belongings and was gone before Celia or Bob could say anything else.

Bob released a sigh. 'Well, that's one witness gone. I suppose it was always a long shot. But at least we have some answers now.'

234

'We don't even know his name!' Celia banged the table with her fist in frustration. A sharp pain travelled up her arm, and she was unable to suppress a grimace.

'Are you alright?'

'I'm fine! I just forgot that I broke this arm a month or so back, and it's still a bit tender.' Celia smiled. 'Serves me right for being so impatient.'

'I know it's frustrating not to get him onside. However, something tells me that Iris will be more than happy to throw him under the bus when her back is to the wall, grandson or not.' Bob felt some grim satisfaction at the thought. They deserved each other.

'Surely not. What kind of...monster would do that?'

'Do you really need me to answer that question?' He turned to Celia. 'Fancy a burger?'

Eventually, once she realised he was joking, this forced a smile from Celia, and then a laugh.

'I think we can do better than that. Let's have a drink in the Red Lion. We've both earned it.'

Chapter 37

It wasn't until after a second glass of wine that Celia was ready to talk about what had happened. She was grateful for Bob's understanding small talk and silence. She had to remind herself that it was just as bad for him – that he had lost his wife and might even lose his home.

'I trusted her,' she said at last. 'How could I have been so stupid?'

'Me too.' Bob took a sip of beer. 'She was very convincing. You don't expect this from a neighbour. I suppose you're already thinking the best of them when you move in.'

'But why? Why us? What did we do?' This was the question that was constantly whirling around in Celia's head. Why them? What had she and Bob ever done to Iris? She would feel better if there were answers that would enable her to rationalise or understand Iris's behaviour.

Bob sighed as he looked out of the window. 'Who knows? I suspect we'll never really know.'

'Maybe you were right the other day. Maybe it's more about Iris herself than anything we've done.'

'Hmm.' Bob sipped his beer. 'Who knows what goes on in Iris's mind.'

'Daisy, my daughter...' Celia swallowed. 'She was all ready to ship me off to a care home. Iris persuaded her that I wasn't coping. How could my own daughter have been taken in? Was it that easy?' Her voice trembled as tears filled her eyes.

Bob patted her hand. 'Don't torment yourself, Celia. All these questions are for another time.'

As the food was delivered, he said, 'The question now is, what do we do next?'

'We go to the police – in the morning,' Celia said firmly. 'Tonight we go home and organise all our evidence, including the material from the camera in your place.'

Celia saw Bob's face pale.

'I'm so sorry, Bob.'

He took a deep breath. 'Look at it like this. It's all more evidence.'

'I'll sneak over to yours when Iris is safely indoors watching TV.'

Bob laughed. 'Very clandestine.'

Celia couldn't help smiling.

'You know she's tried to prevent us getting to know each other, planting little seeds of doubt, for months.'

'I know. She told me you were a bit of an attention seeker, making a drama out of nothing when you were in hospital.'

Celia raised her eyebrows. 'And did you believe her?'

'To be honest, I had too much going on in my own life to take much notice. We didn't really know each other at all, did we?'

'We'll keep up the pretence until tomorrow,' said Celia, 'and then, after that, we can get to know each other better. Maybe you could even take me for a spin in that campervan of yours.'

'Dusty Roads,' corrected Bob swallowing a mouthful of chips. 'And she's an RV. You're on! Although I might need to fumigate her first since I took some homeless people on a trip to the seaside last weekend.'

Celia, wishing she hadn't made the request, recoiled in horror.

'Don't worry, it's not too bad,' he said, nudging her arm and laughing. 'Eat up. We've got work to do.'

Celia couldn't bring herself to eat very much, as the horror of Iris whirled around in her head. She wouldn't rest until Iris was arrested. And Daisy...? As Bob had said, maybe that was an issue for another time. But try as she might, Celia couldn't get her daughter out of her head.

Later that evening, she was still struggling to make sense of it all. Surely the betrayal of a daughter was something more than the betrayal of a neighbour. She remembered the whispered conversation between Daisy and Iris. The one she'd interrupted that day on the drive. How solicitous Daisy had been when they went indoors. She could imagine now what Iris had been saying, the sympathetic tone she would have used, the commiserating tilt of the head. A wave of shame washed over Celia as she remembered the post-it notes. How had she allowed Iris to do this to her? How had she allowed her mind to be manipulated so easily? She thought back to the crosswords, the shopping lists, the mislaid items. It had never occurred to her for one moment that Iris had been behind any of it. She'd only allowed herself one explanation – that she was going mad. That she was no longer capable.

The humiliation was almost too much to bear. And not just humiliation. A sense of being violated – her innermost secrets being rummaged through by Iris's long, probing fingers. Celia watched the CCTV again and again – Iris touching Emma's things. Holding them to her cheek. She thought that if she watched enough times, the trauma would diminish with familiarity – instead, it grew larger and larger in her head. Even after she had closed the laptop, her eyes closed, Celia could still see Iris coldly intruding upon her grief, briefly taking ownership of her home and her very self. Panicking at not being able to control her thoughts, she downed two sleeping pills to numb her mind.

Iris was still reeling from her conversation with Zed, and although it was past eleven o'clock the next morning, she was still sitting in her kitchen, a mug of cold tea on the table in front of her. Unusually, the TV was silent.

How dare Zed intrude on her past? She couldn't stand the thought that he, of all people, knew her secret. But deep down, beyond the anger, was the thought gnawing away deep inside that Zed was her grandson and that he hated her. Was she equally as disappointed in him? Iris had no opinion either way beyond the worry that he was quite capable of using it against her. And her son was dead. She persuaded herself that she had no thoughts about that either. He had never been a person to her, anyway.

A sharp knock on the door made her jump. Iris stayed where she was. Celia or Bob could wait. It had to be or other of them.

The knock came again, more insistent this time, followed by a voice she didn't recognise.

'Iris Walker? Could you come to the door, please?'

Iris huffed and strode to the door, flinging it open. She took a step back at the sight of two police officers on her doorstep.

'Iris Walker?'

'Yes. What is it?' Iris put on her best grammar-school voice, glancing across the Court to make sure neither Celia nor Bob was about.

'We'd like you to come with us, please.'

'What? What on earth for?'

'We can talk more down at the station.'

Iris looked at the police car and glanced around the Court. No one was about. At least if she went with them, it would get the police car away from her bungalow. It wasn't a good look for Eagle Court. Not good at all.

'Well whatever it is that's so urgent, can we make it quick? I have lunch to make down at the church hall. For the homeless, you know. Poor things.'

Iris coiled herself into the back seat and sat back straight and arms folded, holding herself in, until they reached the police station.

She took in the grey, functional room lit by the unforgiving glare of two strip lights. The table was bolted to the floor. She had watched many scenes play out in rooms just like this in the crime dramas she watched. Surely they could have found somewhere a bit less formal to hear her evidence. It wasn't as she was a criminal.

She looked up as a male police officer entered the room. Without speaking, he sat opposite her and opened a file, leafing through some pages.

Iris felt that he was very rude. 'What can I do for you? I don't have a lot of time. I told your colleague that.'

He looked up and steepled his fingers, elbows resting on the table. 'Iris, we've had some very serious allegations made about you from your neighbours.'

Iris was stunned. This was unexpected, and she hated anything that wasn't planned. She'd always feared surprises – not that she'd had many. Looking at the police officer, she realised he was waiting for her to say something.

She marshalled her thoughts. 'For a start, you don't want to take any notice of Celia next door, she's as batty as they come. Doesn't know what day it is most of the time.' Iris leaned forward. 'Between you and me, her daughter is looking for a place in a care home for her. She's a GP, you know. And as for Bob, after all I've done for him, he's just cast me aside. Out and about in that campervan thing. Not a bit of gratitude.'

Iris sat back, pleased with how calm she'd been. How she'd covered her outrage that Celia and Bob could have done this. And Zed? Was he part of this? She'd make them all pay. They'd regret this.

The detective handed her a photo. 'Iris, is this you delivering a letter to Sarah Brown's house last Friday?'

Iris took a breath. Damn Zed. 'Yes. What of it? I can deliver a letter can't I? In fact I was doing Bob a good turn.'

The officer passed a sheet of paper across the table and Iris saw a copy of her art work. 'Is this what you were delivering?'

Iris clenched her hands under the table. She would not be bullied by this man. 'Yes, I was rather proud of this, actually. See how I've used pictures of the sea for Ocean's name? That is her real name, you know. As I said, I was doing Bob a good turn. They're trying to fleece him out of all his money.'

She folded her arms, more confident now. She had his attention. He was listening to her. Soon they would all understand. 'But I don't know why I bothered. Ungrateful man! And you need to look into her and her son, Mitchell. They're thick as thieves with Mr Knowles, who I believe is a local gangster. You must know about him. Not a good look for a banker, is it?'

'Can you take a look at this, Iris, and tell me what you see?'

A laptop was pushed across the table and Iris was filled with rage.

241

'Is this you in Mrs Morris's house, dressed as her?'

'How dare she film me! That's illegal isn't it? Filming someone without their consent.'

'What were you doing alone in Mrs Morris's house?'

'Tidying, cleaning, delivering shopping. She gave me a key so that I could do that. Ungrateful—' Iris stopped herself just in time. 'I can wear what I like. Surely there's no law against that.'

'Mrs Morris alleges that you and an accomplice, a young man – he referred to a sheet of paper in the folder – Zed, adjusted various devices in her home which resulted in a serious incident involving a hospital stay.'

Iris's wrath with Zed spilled over. 'Nothing to do with me. I didn't do any of those things,' she spat.

'But you paid him to do things for you, dangerous things.'

'Who told you that?'

'Let's just say we know.' The detective's voice was expressionless.

Iris's breath caught in her throat. That bastard, Zed. He'd actually shopped her to the police! She couldn't believe it. Well, she would sort him for good.

Putting her elbows on the table, she leaned towards the detective. 'Zed – that's what he calls himself – put me up to it. All that Wi-fi stuff, that was all his idea, nothing to do with me. You need to speak to him. You can find him in any Burgers for U restaurant.' Iris thought of something else. 'He even sprayed graffiti on my neighbour's campervan, even though I pleaded with him not to.' Iris forced a tear into her eye.

'We have reason to believe that you were the graffiti artist on that occasion.' The detective fixed her with a gaze.

'You're joking! What would an older, respectable woman like me know about graffiti?'

242

'I think you were unwise enough to keep the spray can in your bag, where it was discovered by Mr Randall.'

Iris clenched her hands together, digging the nails into her skin. This was all going wrong. Everyone was out to get her. Nothing had changed. She looked at the floor, pressing her feet down as hard as she could. Tears came easily and when she looked up, they were running down her cheeks.

She sobbed. 'You have to understand. I'm the victim here. They all hate me. Celia, Bob, and Zed. I don't know why, but they do. They've framed me. Forced me to do things. I didn't want to do any of it.'

Unmoved, the detective said, 'Iris Walker, I am arresting you for recklessly endangering life, trespass, and criminal damage. You do not have to say anything. But it may harm your defence if you do not mention when questioned something which you later rely on in court. Anything you do say may be given in evidence.'

Iris gasped. 'But it's not my fault! It's them. They made me do it.'

Chapter 38

Wendy tackled Bob as soon as he arrived. 'Is it true what they're saying about Iris? I can't believe it!'

Bob, not wanting to get into conversation about Iris, simply replied, 'It seems so.'

'I always sensed something toxic about her,' Tina said. 'But I could never put my finger on it. I never imagined that Iris, of all people, would send such vile anonymous letters.' Tears welled in her eyes.

'She sent you anonymous letters?' Wendy stopped kneading the pastry and looked at Tina.

'Only one. Vile stuff about me and my...girlfriend.'

'That's ridiculous in this day and age!' Wendy's scoff blew flour into the air. 'Wiping her forehead with her arm, she turned to Tina. 'So what's your girlfriend called?'

'Monica.' A half-smile appeared on Tina's face.

'You'll have to bring her in to meet us all sometime.' Wendy turned back to the pastry, but Bob didn't miss Tina's smile and the drop of her shoulders, as if a weight had been lifted.

'Will do. You'd get on with Monica, Wendy. She's a chef.'

'Well, fancy that!' Wendy laughed.

'Thank you for coming forward, Tina. That took guts.' Bob turned from washing his hands. 'The more of us that give evidence, the better.'

'I didn't keep the letter. We couldn't bear to have it in the house.' Tina shuddered. 'But I did take pictures on my phone. And the fact that they're dated means they are useful as evidence, apparently.'

The sound of Stan huffing and shoving furniture around in the hall galvanised them into action. 'Bob, you give Stan a hand before he implodes, and Wendy and I will crack on here. Carol should be here soon.'

Wendy raised an eyebrow. 'Carol?'

'I didn't I mention? She's a new volunteer, starting today.'

There was a pause, so brief it was hardly noticeable.

'Right-ho. I could certainly use some help. Can you give me a hand, Bob, when Stan is sorted?'

'Will do.' Bob gave her a wave as he left the kitchen.

He had never expected Saturday lunchtimes to become the focus of his week. Yes, he had enjoyed taking Dusty out on a few road trips, but somehow he felt that on Saturdays he was doing something useful, something to give back to society. But not in the patronising way Iris had, using the lunches to boost her own ego. He just wanted to do something useful. And as he'd got to know this group of friends over the weeks – and yes, they were friends – Bob had realised the fragility of the things he took for granted.

A few weeks ago, Bob, noticing the tremor in Maurice's hands – some weeks worse than others – had asked, 'What did you do before...'

Maurice finished the question for him. '...this?'

Bob flushed. He hadn't meant to be so direct.

'It's okay, Bob. We like to call a spade a spade here. Any time for pussyfooting around went out the window long ago.' He took a breath and laid his hands on the table as if to still them.

'I used to be in the army. I had a purpose, a routine, and all I had to do was follow orders. But eventually the time came when they didn't need me anymore and so I was discharged. Somehow, I couldn't cope. My life fell apart. I started drinking. My wife thew me out and I haven't seen the kids in years.' He clenched his hands together. 'I still can't get my life together. As you can see, I'm still drinking. I guess this is it until one day someone finds me in a doorway.'

Bob tried to hide his shock at the brutal words and had opened his mouth to speak. 'Don't suggest I do this that or the other, Bob, I just don't want to. This is me now.' He turned to George. 'Your turn, George.'

George closed his eyes for a few moments. 'I used to be one of them.' He glanced over at the vicar, gliding from table to table.

Tinker gasped. 'No way! A vicar? You're kidding me!'

The others chuckled. 'A regular pillar of society,' said Maurice. 'He can marry you if you want. How about it, Mabel?'

Mabel made a tutting sound that turned into a hiss.

Bob couldn't imagine how George had made the transition from such an elevated position to living on the streets.

George answered Bob's unspoken question. 'It's quite simple, really. I betrayed the trust of my parishioners and my family. We lived in a well-off area, but we didn't have the money that the people around us had. I couldn't stand to see my children missing out on all the things the other kids took for granted. I stole from church funds. Just a little bit at first, and when nothing was flagged up, a bit more. The diocese accepted all the accounts I returned, and so it went on. In the end, I had stolen thousands. Although it was worth it to see the kids have everything their friends had, the weight of guilt was dragging me down. I couldn't stand in the pulpit every week, facing the people who put their trust in me. I was a hypocrite.'

'What did you do?' Tinker asked, mouth open.

'My wife insisted on me telling her where the money was coming from. I confessed. I told my family. They were horrified. My children were ashamed of me and said they would rather have gone without. That was the worst thing, really. That I'd done it all for nothing. That I'd been the worst role model possible.' George paused. 'Anyway. I confessed to the archdeacon, and to cut a long story short, it was all in the papers. My wife threw me out and my family had to move to another area because of the scandal.' Bob took a jagged breath. 'Prison was too good. I wasn't being punished enough, so when I got out, I chose this life and I've still not been punished enough...for other things, too.'

At that point the conversation had been interrupted by the vicar. 'Come on, guys. Time to go.' All eyes had turned to George, who shook his head. A small gesture that made it clear he didn't want them to say anything.

Bob had replayed that conversation in his head many times, realising that he himself was only a few steps away from that life. It just took fate to throw the dice against you a few times, a few wrong decisions and suddenly you were grateful for a free cooked meal once a week.

Bob stood beside Carol as she dished out the chicken casserole to familiar faces, receiving a smile or a nod in response, along with the occasional, 'Thanks mate.' He was thankful that no one asked about Iris, although he knew that the homeless grapevine had been buzzing with news of her arrest. Maybe there was an unspoken knowledge that a queue of hungry people was not the place for in-depth conversation. He also sensed an unease about saying anything in front of Carol, who didn't smile or attempt any conversation. Bob put it down to nerves, remembering how overwhelmed he had been on his first visit.

Once the meal had been served, Bob left Carol to gather the dishes and headed to his usual table, where Maurice, Tinker, and George were tucking in, all thoughts of Iris pushed to one side until their hunger was salved. A loud burp from Mabel attracted their attention.

'Come on, Mab. If you're going to sit at the posh table, show some manners!' Tinker nudged her gently.

Over the last few weeks, Mabel had gradually moved closer and closer to the group to eat her meal. George said, 'Come and sit with us, Mabel. Shove up, you lot. Make some space.'

Bob had observed this and was glad he had bitten back the urge to step in earlier. These men knew Mabel, and the invitation had to be timed just right. Too soon, and she would have retreated like a frightened animal. Now, it seemed, that Mabel was part of the group.

The seaside trip had bound them together and they often talked about it. Bob felt that a second visit would be due soon, now that the summer crowds had gone.

Inevitably, now that stomachs were full, the conversation turned to Iris.

'I can't believe she did all that to you, and the poor lady next door – Celia is it?'

Bob's eyes widened at the extent of their knowledge. 'How did you...'

Maurice tapped the side of his nose. 'We have our ways.'

'But...'

'Don't worry.' George winked. 'Nothing we say is going to jeopardise any court case. Who would listen to a group of outcasts like us?'

This was followed by agreement and some degree of cynical laughter from the group.

'It just goes to show. Never trust anyone. I was stupid enough to be taken in by her. I actually thought she cared about me!' Mabel took a shaky breath. 'But it was all so she could feel better.'

There was silence.

'It just confirms what I've always thought. Never trust anybody.'

George laid a hand on her arm. 'Don't let one person make you feel like that. What about us? You've got us.'

'I dunno.' Mabel stood and shambled over to the supermarket trolley. 'I'm better off on my own.'

Bob went to follow, but George laid a hand on his arm. 'Not now. She's got to work her own way round this.'

'I reckon we've all been bloody well taken for a ride. Who's to say she – he nodded in the direction of Carol – the newest volunteer, isn't the same? I'm not going to be taken in twice!' Tinker shook his head. 'Anyway, we've got more important things to worry about than her!'

'Iris was sick. She was too sick to change.' George muttered.

'Oh yeah. That's what they say now when someone's committed a crime – even murder. They're ill. And they just get carted off to hospital where they get three good meals a day and everything else they want. What's wrong with just calling people evil?' Tinker raised his voice as he got into his stride. And voices of agreement echoed around the hall.

'Yeah. They get a better life than us, and what have we ever done? Except a bit of theft here and there,' he added hastily.

Sensing the wave of unrest, the vicar began ushering people out. 'Okay. Show's over, time to go, folks.'

'You – all of you – are a drain on society. People like me, we work and pay our taxes while you lot just sit around expecting charity like this.' Carol, standing behind the tables, gestured, waving her arm around at them, her eyes glinting with anger.

Bob felt a wave of panic in the moment of icy silence that followed.

'You are all a blight on society. People don't come into town because of you and your filthy habits!'

The silence was broken by a man on the other side of the room. 'Why, you stuck-up bitch! I bet you've never had to do a day's work in your life.'

There were rumblings around the room and chairs scraped on the floor as their occupants stood as one. Bob noticed the vicar's face turn a deathly shade of bluish pale.

'Carol, a word!' A hush fell as Tina strode up to the newest volunteer and ushered her firmly into the kitchen.

Everyone craned to hear what was being said. 'I don't think we'll be needing your services again. Please take your things and leave. This is not what we are.'

'I'm off, don't you worry. I just wanted to have my say.'

The slam of kitchen door was followed by spontaneous cheers. 'Go Tina!' became a chant echoing around the room.

'Wow! I haven't had this much fun in years,' said Tinker.

'Shut up!' Bob had never heard George speak with such anger. 'Come on, let's go.'

As they cleared up, Bob heard the vicar, whose complexion had regained its colour, talking to Tina. 'I think maybe we need to interview potential volunteers after this.'

Chapter 39

'I can't believe it.' Daisy stirred her coffee. 'How could I have been so stupid? Why didn't I see what she was doing?'

'Maybe you didn't want to see,' Celia murmured.

'What do you mean by that?'

For once, Celia wasn't intimidated by Daisy's short fuse.

'I meant that you didn't have to worry about me, because Iris was doing everything.' Celia pressed on before Daisy could interrupt. 'The ironic thing is that you didn't need to do anything for me, anyway. I was quite capable – until she came along.'

'But your arm...'

'I could have managed, Daisy.'

Celia gave her daughter a level gaze. 'Losing your father was hard, but I was still me. Nothing changed just because I was living in a bungalow. You made me feel, somehow...old.'

'Me?' Daisy gave a cynical laugh. 'So one minute you're blaming me for relying on Iris and the next you're saying that you didn't need me.' She looked out of the window. 'Great. Just great.'

'And I can't help thinking that you were more than happy to have me deposited in a care home – at Iris's suggestion.' Celia held her breath. There, she'd said it.

'But I thought you were ill, Mum. I was scared when I saw you in the hospital like that. I—I just believed Iris when she said those things.' There was a pause. 'I'm so sorry, Mum. I just panicked.'

Celia couldn't help enjoying this rare apology from her daughter. 'Okay, but we'll have no more talk of nursing homes and the like,' she said sternly.

Daisy was silent for a few minutes and Celia wondered what she was thinking. Instead of bustling on to talk about some other trivia, she waited until her daughter was ready.

'But did it ever occur to you, Mum, that I needed something from you when Dad died? I needed to be able to talk about him. I lost him too, you know.'

Daisy leaned forward on her elbows. 'You're so buttoned up. You never show any emotion. Do you know how stifling that is?'

Celia was stunned. 'But...'

'Yes, I know. It's what we do in this family. Put a positive slant on things and carry on as if nothing's happened. But somehow...' Daisy stifled a sob. 'Somehow, I just can't do it anymore.'

'Oh darling.' Celia reached across and held Daisy in an awkward hug. 'I thought I was doing the right thing, being strong for everyone.'

'It was only when you were in that hospital bed that I saw a glimpse of the real you. Someone who wasn't invincible.'

'But *you* were the one that wanted me to move, sell the house. Move here. You and your brothers.'

'I know.' Daisy intertwined her fingers and rested her head on them. 'But I wanted you to say no. I wanted you to show how much you missed Dad, and to say so. But you gave in so easily. It was almost as if none of it mattered.'

Celia looked at her daughter. 'But of course it mattered and I've missed our home so much. I've... I've sat here remembering every room, every Christmas we had there, everything.'

Daisy turned to her mother. 'But you never said so.'

'I miss your father dreadfully, and sometimes,' Celia swallowed, 'he seems to appear, here, in this room, and talk to me.'

'I miss him all the time. It's like a gap.' Daisy reached for a tissue and wiped her eyes. She looked at Celia. 'What does he say?'

'Oh, Dad things, about cheering up and making the best of it, that things will get better. Keep moving forwards. Things like that.'

'Yup. That was Dad,' muttered Daisy. 'He never listened, never tried to understand any problem. There were just these bland phrases he trotted out. That everlasting cheerfulness – it was hard sometimes.'

After a pause, Celia took Daisy's hand and held it to her cheek. 'You're right. And sometimes it was hard.'

There was silence for a few minutes and Celia listened to the sparrows bickering amongst themselves in the ceanothus she had planted in the garden.

'Mum.' Daisy kept hold of Celia's hand. Celia tightened her grip, knowing what was coming, and knowing that she had to face it, head-on.

'Emma,' she said, softly. 'I know.'

'We've never talked about her.'

'I know, and I'm sorry. I thought it was the right thing. Your father wouldn't talk about her either.' Celia felt tears fall as she openly mourned her dead daughter for the first time.

'Do you know how that silence stifled us all? We were children – we couldn't even talk about it to each other. We didn't know how. Because you never showed us.'

253

Celia looked at Daisy. How could she have let her children down so badly?

'It drove Luke and Fred away. They needed to be free of the unspoken – thing – Emma.' She swallowed. 'Luke and me, we're more resilient and we've found a way to live and move forward, But Fred...he just couldn't.'

Celia's world was imploding. All the carefully constructed defences and carefully argued reasons, crumbling to dust.

Hiding her face behind her hands, she was still for a few moments.

'Mum? I'm sorry, but it's the truth.'

She had to do things differently. Celia took a breath, and dropping her hands to the table, turned to Daisy.

'Emma was...is part of this family, and we're going to start acknowledging that,' she said. 'In a few weeks it will be her birthday. She would have been 25.' Celia paused before taking a deep breath, 'And we're going to get together as a family and celebrate that.'

Daisy smiled. 'That would be great, Mum. We'll make Luke come over and you can meet your fourth grandchild for the first time. I know that nothing will stop him coming.'

'What about Fred?'

'I think it's about time we made him feel welcome in this family.'

'You've been in touch with him?' Celia's heart fluttered in her chest.

'I've always been in touch – off and on. I've tried to help him, Mum, referring him to rehab programmes and other support services, but these things never get to the root of the problem.'

Daisy took her mother's hand. 'He needs to feel accepted, not judged, by his family. He...we all need to be able to talk about things.'

Celia hung her head, nodding, before giving her daughter a long hug. 'Things will be different now. *I'm* going to be different. I know sometimes I'll slide back into old ways – it's a hard habit to break. You just have to tell me. Remind me. Say something like, "Get real, Mum!"'

'Really?' Daisy laughed. 'That sounds like something Seb would say.'

'How is Seb doing? Is he enjoying Milford College?'

Daisy looked away. 'I think so, although he doesn't say much. He hasn't been in trouble yet, so that's something.'

'About that. While we're putting everything out there.' Celia took Daisy's hands and looked her in the eye. 'I felt railroaded into paying his school fees.'

Daisy pulled her hands back abruptly. 'For God's sake, Mum. That's ridiculous. You could have said no.'

'Hear me out. The way you mentioned it just before you were leaving that day. It felt, I don't know, somehow contrived. As if you meant to wrong-foot me.'

Seeing Daisy's brows form into an ominous frown, Celia ploughed on. 'I overheard you and Mark while we were away. Him asking when I'd make up my mind.'

Daisy shifted uncomfortably on the chair. Suddenly she was seven years old and Celia had to hide a smile. She kept her voice steady.

'Does Seb know I'm paying his school fees? Do your brothers know?'

The question hit home as a tell-tail blush crept up Daisy's neck.

'I thought not.'

'I'm sorry, Mum.' Daisy was close to tears.

'So this is what's going to happen.' Celia took Daisy's hand. 'When we all meet to celebrate Emma's birthday, I'm going to

255

give each of you 30,000 pounds. I know I've already given you all something after the sale of the house, but this is it.'

Daisy looked down, wiping tears with the back of her hand.

'That's it. No more requests for money, Nothing.' Celia was amazed at the authority in her voice.

Daisy looked up. 'Thanks, Mum.' She sniffed and Celia passed her a tissue. 'I'm so sorry...for everything.' Celia squeezed her daughter's hand.

'I hope the children grow up to realise what an amazing woman their grandmother is,' said Daisy.

'Come on, before we completely lose our old, buttoned-up ways, let's have a glass of wine and you can admire my attempts at garden design.'

As they sat on the newly installed bench, Celia felt as if a weight had lifted from the core of her being. She couldn't describe it, but it felt good.

'Wow! This is amazing, Mum,' said Daisy looking at the beds and shrubs. 'It looks as if it's been here for years.'

'I have to thank Wanda for that. She sourced all the shrubs and the apple trees for me. And of course, I had my other little helper.'

'Lucy has loved helping you with the garden. Granny's secret garden is all she talks about when she comes home.'

'I've loved having her and getting to know her. I think you might have a future garden designer on your hands there.'

Well, she certainly doesn't get that from her parents.' Daisy laughed. 'Has she told you about the little patch we've given her in the garden at home?'

Celia nodded, raising her hands. 'I have to confess to encouraging a little plant smuggling.'

'We wondered where those geranium seedlings had come from. She was so secretive.'

'Enjoying her amazement and wonder, when each time she comes, something has grown or produced a flower or a seed, has... It's made me very happy.'

'What about next door?' Daisy nodded in the direction of Iris's garden.

'I asked if I could arrange for some basic maintenance to be done while she's in prison. Just to keep all this hard work from being overrun with weeds.'

'But she'll come back though, won't she?'

Celia shook her head. 'I don't think she'd ever want to live here again, and in any case, she will have a permanent restraining order preventing her from entering the Court. The police have assured us about that.'

'Thank God,' said Daisy. 'Cheers!' She clinked her glass with Celia. 'And here's to the future.'

'Absolutely.' And for the first time, Celia could see a future. A life in Eagle Court.

Chapter 40

Bob manoeuvred Dusty into a parking space on the seafront. This was what he loved about the seaside in autumn and winter – only hardy souls visited and there was always somewhere to park.

Resting his hands on the steering wheel, he leaned his head back and released a long sigh. Events of the last few weeks had unfolded so rapidly that he'd been swept along on a wave with no time to think.

Iris was in custody, awaiting trial. Bail had not been granted as there were fears that her rage and anger might have led to more assaults on Celia, Bob, and Zed.

He wondered if Zed, whose real name was revealed to be Kyle Brown, aged 21, regretted not going to the police with him and Celia when he'd had the chance. Things might have been better for him then. But as it was, he was facing a long stretch for recklessly endangering life and hacking into private Wi-fi networks. The fact that Iris had paid him to do these things had not been seen as mitigating circumstances in the end, as it soon became apparent that he'd been a more than willing accomplice. And that was before his other crimes of drug possession and vandalism had been taken into account.

'Do you really think Iris could have had a child?'

Bob turned to Celia. 'Who knows? Maybe Zed, Kyle, got the whole thing wrong and there's another Iris Walker out there.'

'God forbid!' Celia exclaimed. 'But I was wondering about her fascination with…Emma's things.' Celia swallowed, still getting used to saying her daughter's name aloud. 'Maybe it was something that connected with her own past.'

'Maybe. Who knows?' Bob said, opening the RV door. 'Come on, time for fish and chips.'

'My goodness, Bob, you are leading me into bad ways.' Celia linked her arm through his in a way that felt completely natural. The horror they had both experienced and the way they had come together to defeat Iris had led to a valued friendship.

'No worse than a couple of glasses of wine of a night.'

'No, I guess not. But I think I'll keep the wine for book club nights.'

'So what happens at these…book club nights, then?'

'The idea is that we all read the same book and then talk about it when we meet. But really, it's just an excuse for gossip and, yes, wine.' Celia chuckled. 'Although Eleanor tries to keep us on track, bless her.'

'So I thought you were going to give up going. Something about them all looking down their noses at you.'

'How did you know that?'

Bob felt a moment of panic at Celia's abrupt tone. 'I'm sorry. I guess it was something Iris said.' He held his breath and was relieved that her arm remained linked through his after an initial flinch.

'I think that was more in my head than anything real. I think I was sort of looking down my nose at myself, if you know what I mean,' Celia said after a pause.

Bob squeezed her arm. 'Cod or haddock?'

'I'm happy with either. It's been a long time since I had fish and chips at the seaside.' Celia gave a sudden laugh. 'It seems a long time since I did a lot of things.'

'So what's happened about Ocean's claim?' Celia asked once they had made their purchase.

Bob was enjoying eating fish and chips, perched on the wall. The sunset was glorious and he found that maybe he was happy.

'Bob?' Celia nudged him.

'Oh, it seems she's dropped it.'

'What? Just like that?' Celia turned to look at him.

'It's a long story, but basically Iris told the police that Ocean's son, Mitchell, was selling drugs for some gangster known locally as Mr K. She also told them that Ocean was in debt to this Mr K. Hence her need for my money. Ocean eventually confessed all this, after some resistance. I can't blame her for being scared. Apparently this Mr K is a nasty piece of work. Anyway, eventually, after reassurance that her and Mitchell's evidence would be enough to arrest him, she spilled the beans. So now she's no longer in debt. She doesn't need my money, but I've given her enough to send Mitchell to college. Apparently, he's pretty good with wood.'

'You've given her money? After the way she treated you? I thought she was a rich banker.'

'Turns out she's quite low down the food chain. More of a call-centre worker. The BMW, the posh house, was all a front. Hence the debt to Mr K. She wanted everyone to believe she was more than she was. And in a funny kind of way, I think she was trying to impress Trish.' Bob gave a wry laugh, 'Shows how little she knew her.'

'You are a soft touch, Bob.' She leant over and nudged him.

Bob shrugged. 'I know. But that's me, and I guess there are worse faults to have.'

'So was Iris blackmailing her?'

Bob nodded as he swallowed his food. 'She was threatening to go to the big bank Ocean works for and tell them she was in debt to a local gangster.'

'But why?'

'Because she hated Ocean for trying to take my money. That was when she still thought I was dependent on her. But when I showed I didn't need her help, that's when I fell from grace. So she tried to insinuate in the anonymous letter that it was from me.'

Celia sighed. 'How can one person cause so much misery?'

'I suppose anyone can – if they put their mind to it.' He stood, taking Celia's arm once more. 'Come on, let's have a walk before it gets dark.'

They walked in silence for a few minutes before Bob spoke. 'You know, Trish saw through Iris right from the start. I didn't believe her. Trish could be very dramatic sometimes.'

Celia squeezed his arm as Bob reflected that, in some ways, Trish had been wiser than he realised.

'Isn't this wonderful?' Celia sighed and closed her eyes. 'Sometimes it's good to get away from everything and forget about all the bad things. You realise that in spite of all the dramas we go though, the tide still comes in and out, just as it's done for centuries.'

Epilogue

Iris clutched the prison cutlery as tightly as she could without breaking it. She didn't belong here. This was all wrong. She kept saying it, but nobody listened. She wondered if she was in some kind of nightmare. Maybe soon she would wake up, safe and sound in Eagle Court, where she belonged. In the meantime, she would have to make the best of things. Keeping her head down and avoiding eye-contact, she ate what she could. The rage that had consumed her over the first few weeks had worn itself out, to be replaced by a kind of numbness. In some ways, she had returned to the rigid routine she'd had with her mother. This was just another kind of prison, but more dangerous.

She risked a glance around the canteen and recoiled at the women around her. Hardened criminals, all of them, she imagined. She avoided any interaction, and so far they had taken no notice of her.

Her solicitor said it would be months before the trial. The last time they had met, she'd been angry. She had a feeling that he was not defending her as he should. Maybe she could try and get a better one. She could afford it.

'What you in for?'

The hand on her shoulder was firm and demanded an answer.

'I'm... I haven't done anything. I shouldn't be here. It's all a mistake.'

The laughter that ricocheted around the hall made Iris look up in surprise.

'She really believes it, don't she? Oh my God!' This was followed by cackles and whistles.

Iris made to stand but the firm hand kept her in place. 'This your first time?'

'Yes, and last. I'll be out of here soon enough.'

As the hand tightened its grip Iris felt all the breath leave her body and she leant against the table.

'We not good enough for you, Iris Walker. That it?'

Iris turned to face her captor. A surprisingly small woman with spiky ginger hair grinned back at her.

'Maybe we'll have some fun while you're here, then.'

'Good idea, Irene,' someone shouted.

'So what did you *not* do?' The voice came from the next table.

It came to Iris. Maybe some of these women had been framed like her? Maybe some of them knew they were innocent.

'It was my neighbours. They framed me when all I was doing was trying to help them. And not just them. My grandson too. They're all in on it.'

Iris widened her eyes at the catcalls, noticing one woman doing a wrong-in-the-head gesture with her forefinger.

'Surely some of *you* think you're innocent!' Iris was determined to stand her ground.

'Maybe, but we're not mental!' the woman behind her hissed. 'And who rats on their own grandson?'

Iris couldn't believe the jeers and hostile glares that greeted this last statement. How did they know about Zed?

'He...' any further words were drowned out by a chorus of disapproval.

'Come on, ladies, time to go.' Iris was relieved to hear the warder's voice, as everyone made their way out of the canteen and headed back to their respective cells.

Iris curled up on the bottom bunk and squeezed her eyes shut. This could not be happening to her. Yes, it was still just a bad dream. She would wake up and it would all go away. Iris willed herself to wake up.

'You take the top. I always have the bottom.'

Iris jolted at the voice and opened her eyes to see to a large, heavily tattooed woman looming in the doorway.

'This is your new cellmate, Iris. Say hello to Sonia.'

Also by Sheena Billett

The Woman Who Wrote In Green Ink

A voice from the past causes Amber's world to spiral out of
control

From Manchester To The Arctic

Nurse Sanders embarks on an adventure that will change her
life

Shifting Horizons

Short stories of lives lived and journeys taken

About Sheena's writing

Sheena has long been fascinated by the everyday and the knowledge that everyone has a story, no matter how unremarkable they might seem. The theme that connects all of her writing is that of journeying through life. This might be a literal journey, as in From Manchester To The Arctic, or an emotional journey where characters are sometimes pushed out of their comfort zones through having to deal with a crisis or unforeseen event. Sometimes the journey results in growth and exciting new horizons, but in other cases, there are those who refuse to take any steps along the journey, and consequently remain stunted, often damaging the people around them as a result.

Sheena lives with her wife in Nottinghamshire.

All of Sheena's books are available at https://sheenaiswriting .com and on Amazon

If you enjoyed Eagle Court, please leave a review or even a quick rating on Amazon and/or Goodreads.
You can also email sheenaiswriting@vanstonepublishing.com with your review. We would love to hear from you.

Printed in Great Britain
by Amazon

46525998R00158